MW00467292

BIRD IN HAND

A Sam Tate Mystery

by
Nikki Stern

Ruthenia
Press

445 Sayre Drive
Princeton, NJ 08540
rutheniapress@gmail.com

ISBN: 978-0-9995487-4-5 (print book)
        978-0-9995487-5-2 (ebook)
LCCN: 2020911716

Library of Congress Cataloging-in-Publication Data is on file with the Library of Congress.

This is a work of fiction. Names, characters, businesses, places, events and incidents are either the products of the author's imagination or used in a fictitious manner. Any resemblance to actual persons, living or dead, or actual events is purely coincidental.

Acknowledgements

My appreciation goes out first and foremost to the ever-helpful Sheriff Joe Gamble, Talbot County (MD) Sheriff's Office. His input allowed me to sort through the procedural, political, and even personal challenges of working a homicide investigation involving multiple agencies.

Thanks to my editor Naomi Williams, who was a pleasure to work with. Thanks also to proofreaders Sarah Scanga, Jennifer Guy, and the truly eagle-eyed Jeanette DeMain.

Once again, the incomparable Diana Ani Stokely provided creative design, including the evocative cover.

My beloved muse, friend, and younger sister Deborah died just before I finished this novel. She was an early reader/editor in the writing process and offered both insight and encouragement in equal measure. I miss her more than all the words at my disposal can convey. I trust I have done her proud.

"Better one byrd in hand than ten in the wood."

~ English proverb circa 1530

"Ah, but a man's reach should exceed his grasp. Or what's a heaven for?"

~ *Men and Women and Other Poems*, Robert Browning

Prologue

The weak light of the moon glinted off the padlock on Arley Fitchett's customized outbuilding. He saw no one, felt no presence, yet he hesitated. Years of habit informed his caution, along with the conviction he had something to protect. Satisfied no one lingered, he unlocked the door with a key he'd hidden in the small garden and made his way to the back of the structure.

Some physical effort was required to clear a path through the clutter. Arley had deliberately overloaded the place with boxes and old furniture, tools and cumbersome machinery, some of it outdated. He wanted the space to seem unused, a place where excess or unnecessary items were stored away and forgotten. A space not worth searching.

Though not a large man, Arley's lean frame was hardened by years of outdoor work. He moved according to plan and practice. He located a small passageway and threaded himself through the makeshift piles until he arrived at the back wall. With a soft grunt, he slid it sideways, revealing a second space, little larger than a closet. He tugged on a string attached to a tin lamp overhead, and the area lit up.

Arley stood with his elbows out, his hands shoved in the rear pockets of his well-worn jeans. He was a weathered forty-three, with deep lines around his mouth and eyes. A weak chin was offset by an engaging smile and eyes like an ocean before a storm. Women liked him well enough. He liked them back, always without entanglement.

Now he reviewed the display before him. He reached up, made an adjustment, stepped back, nodded with satisfaction. Then he removed several items from carefully labeled boxes he'd stored beneath the display.

The exhibit suggested a presentation that might accompany a history lecture, or the project of a slightly deranged mind. Arley wasn't crazy, though. He was methodical and focused. He had to be in his line of work. Especially now, especially given the stakes.

The world held undiscovered riches; that was a fact without dispute. Arley's purpose and his profession were to find those riches and bring them into the light. He didn't care about natural resources. He respected those who tunneled for precious stones or mined for metals or drilled for oil and gas, but he had little interest in what the earth might willingly offer. Nor did he scavenge, not like the amateurs. He didn't walk along the beaches looking for loose pocket change or shiny objects.

Arley Fitchett hunted treasure. He described himself as a mix of Indiana Jones and Sherlock Holmes with a lot of truffle-sniffing pig thrown in. He was good at ferreting out the missing, the disappeared, the presumed lost. Such work was unpredictable and unreliable. Fortunately, Arley was both knowledgeable and personable. He knew his way around a range of rigs and understood the vagaries of the ocean tides. His expertise had gotten him invited onto several large-scale dives, some of them led by noted explorers.

Wealthy hobbyists often employed him to look for artifacts at flea markets or estate sales. Arley had traveled around the world in search of a particular relic coveted by a rich investor. On several occasions, he succeeded in locating a piece only to be thwarted by bureaucracy. True, a palm could be greased, an inspector paid to look the other way. Arley tried to avoid those situations. The laws governing antiques in most countries were understandably strict. Smuggling was a multi-billion-dollar business that local authorities believed drained their coffers and robbed them of their culture. He had no intention of ending up in a foreign prison.

Since coming to the Eastern Shore, Arley had carved out a living taking visitors on so-called "pirate" tours. He was popular and as successful as he needed to be. He was always careful to let his customers know that stories about eighteenth-century pirates on the Chesapeake Bay were just that, stories no one really believed.

Arley did, though. He had proof.

Ahead of him lay a future in which he might conceivably be able to retire. Arley doubted he ever would. He thirsted for the chase, lived to hunt what the rest of the world refused to acknowledge. His latest discovery would upend history and rattle the art world. So said one of his contacts, a would-be partner with the requisite scholarly credentials and an appetite for fame within certain rarified circles. Arley's name might find its way into the public record, the man intimated.

The notion pleased Arley, he had to admit. More than that, though, he looked forward to proving the self-satisfied naysayers wrong, those know-it-all academics with their unimaginative approach to human nature. Arley had never lacked for imagination.

His phone dinged. Just a single note, nothing fancy. A text requesting a meeting, though it was clearly a demand. Fifteen minutes from now, which put it close to midnight. The location came next. Nothing else.

He could ask why so late and why in person, but what was the point? He would comply. For all his exploits on and off the water over the course of his life, Arley rarely took chances. He'd made a single exception in order to finance this particular venture. In doing so, he risked quite a bit. If the legitimate relationships he'd carefully cultivated ever learned the source of his initial credit, he might well frighten them away. The people to whom he owed money were not known for their patience.

On the other hand, he viewed this particular cash advance as more of an investment. He suspected the financial backers found his project amusing and fascinating, what little they knew of it. Perhaps his discovery might add to their legitimacy as well as their cash reserves. Surely everyone had an interest in an enhanced reputation, even those whose business normally occurred in the shadows.

Arley shook himself like a wet dog. He yanked the string that shut off the single light and pulled the door to seal his handiwork from prying eyes. Then he jumped into his 2008 Honda Civic Hatchback and headed to the boat launch at Claiborne Landing.

He made good time and twenty minutes later, he parked the car in the small launch area. The site was technically closed from 11pm to 4am. Such mundane regulations didn't seem to affect the people he was meeting.

At least it was easy to spot the black Escalade. Just the one car and a single boat moored haphazardly, as if its owners weren't planning to stay.

Are we going for a boat ride? he wondered. His stomach clenched.

The peremptory call, the isolated location, the late hour, even the car, all fit with what he'd heard about his lenders. As did the cadaverous-looking driver and the burly guy in the leather jacket who emerged from the front seat and opened the back door as if for royalty.

He squinted in the dim light at the embarking passenger. Was that—? It couldn't be. He stared, tried to get his bearings, tried to keep the shock off his face.

"Hello, Arley. It's been awhile. You're remarkably unchanged. Worn out, but that's to be expected."

The voice was unmistakable even across the years. "You look different," Arley replied. "Better. Guess you did well for yourself."

"Necessity is the mother of invention."

Arley's brain scrambled for purchase. "What are you doing here?

"I get the impression you're not happy to see me."

"No love lost between us," Arley replied. "Let's leave it at that. What's with the entourage?"

"I find a little protection goes a long way. Given the chilly reception, I think I made the smart choice."

Arley shoved his hands in his pockets, then realized he ought to keep them visible, in case the big man was trigger-happy. He stood, legs apart, weight forward, balanced on his toes. Not that he could outrun a bullet.

"Mind?" he asked as he withdrew a pack of cigarettes and a Bic from his jacket pocket. Without waiting for an answer, he lit the smoke, working hard to steady his trembling hands. He inhaled and began to feel calm. "I'd offer you one," he said, "but I don't think it would be safe."

"I'm surprised you can joke about it." His companion indicated the bench. "Shall we sit?"

"I'll stand, thanks. Don't want the smoke to get in your eyes." Arley moved closer to study the face of someone he once thought he knew. Someone who didn't deserve his trust, let alone his affection, as he'd learned the hard way. He didn't intend to make the same mistake twice. "Let's cut to the chase," he continued. "I don't know what your angle is. I don't care. I have an important meeting. This is my deal, and I don't want any interference."

"Interesting place to discuss financing for your latest venture. Do your lenders want to renegotiate terms? Do you suppose they're going to tighten the strings, move up your deadline? That won't be good for you."

Arley stared. "What do you know about that?"

"I know you've borrowed money from some nasty people in order to pay for a group of letters that point you to a prize. Expensive proposition, isn't it? Oh, did you think you were meeting with your lenders tonight to justify your need for more money? No, that isn't what's going on here."

Arley pretended a nonchalance he didn't feel. "Wanna fill me in?"

"I'm not here about any loans you took out, although I'm in a position to buy them up or call them in."

"I don't believe you."

"You should. People with money always control the narrative. We giveth, we taketh away. Mostly the latter."

"I don't know what the hell you're talking about."

"You're not a very good liar, Arley. It's not helpful in these situations. Especially when I'm here to help you out. We have a history, which is why I'm trying to stay above-board, give you the benefit of the doubt. In fact, I have a proposal to present to you."

Despite himself, Arley was curious. "What is it?"

"I'm here in person to ask you to reconsider your latest project."

Arley's brain scrambled to find an explanation. *Stall*, he ordered himself. "Reconsider my project?"

"You're a treasure hunter with his eye on a particular treasure. I doubt you'll stop with a few letters you think prove its existence. No, you want to be the first one at the finish line. Not for money, although clearly money is a factor."

"Look, I don't know why you're—"

"I understand those feelings, Arley. Sometimes, though, you need to let sleeping dogs lie. Let buried treasure stay buried. So, here's what you need to do: Stop the hunt. Stop the research. Stop bidding on items or tracking down leads. Your debts will be paid. You'll be compensated for your time as well as any expenses. Use the money to start a new life somewhere else."

Arley was stunned. "You're kidding, right?" he said. "I expect to have the rest of the original letters in my possession next week."

"What does that prove? If they can be authenticated, they may explain what happened to one of literally hundreds of ships that sailed from Europe and fell prey to bad weather or bad people. More for the historians to chew on. If they're fake, someone might still make a movie or a mini-series on Netflix or the History Channel. Or not. I'll match whatever money you think you might make."

"But the letters provide clues to the real prize," Arley protested.

"A prize that may or may not exist. Why not cut your losses?"

Arley exploded. "Are you crazy? What am I supposed to tell my partners?"

"You don't have partners, Arley. I doubt even the criminal lenders you tied yourself to will mind if you end your search as long as they're compensated. As I said, I'll make sure that happens. I don't think they'll kill you. It's not in their best business interests to do so. Be done with it, Arley. Take the offer."

"What do you really want?"

"I thought I made myself clear. A way forward. An unobstructed path. Less attention on your current venture. You gone. All of which I'm willing to pay to get."

In that moment, Arley became convinced the treasure was not only real, it had attracted the attention of some very powerful and dangerous people. Despite his precarious position, he felt almost giddy. *Time to negotiate.*

"I'm certainly open to terminating other relationships, if that's what you're after. We can discuss terms for an exclusive arrangement."

"You're not listening. I'm not interested in an arrangement. I'm asking you to find something else to occupy your otherwise dreary life. You'll get enough money to set yourself up nicely."

Arley willed himself to look his adversary in the eye. "You're the one who isn't listening," he said. "I'm close, so close. I can't quit now. I won't. We're talking about my life."

The deep sigh conveyed regret, even sorrow. "Poor Arley. So stubborn, he won't budge an inch. So certain he can beat the odds, he doesn't make contingency plans. So self-absorbed, he can't consider anything but his own desires. Never satisfied, always with an eye to the unattainable. Your entitlement feeds your obsession. Full steam ahead and damn the consequences. That's your life, Arley."

"I have to see this through." He was pleading and he hated himself for it.

"Did you ever read *Moby Dick*, Arley? Maybe during those long days and nights at sea? No? Too bad. You'd understand that your treasure hunt has become your white whale. Sadly, as in the book, it will also become your end."

The big man moved quickly and silently. Arley barely had time to process the thin but lethal wire around his neck before it cut into his throat, cut off circulation, cut off any hopes of making the discovery of a lifetime. He bucked and stomped like a corralled pony. He tried to grab at his neck, but his hands were suddenly aflame. He tried to scream, but he had no air.

"Goodbye present, Arley. Enjoy."

Arley felt his eyes bulge and go out of focus. He saw white, then red and, just before the predictable blackness from which there was no coming back, a flash of deep blue, like the rarest of sapphires.

My dearest Teresa,

I write you from Portsmouth, where I have taken lodging overnight before we set sail for the New World. I am expected at dinner shortly to meet with the captain of our aptly named ship, Fortune's Favour, which I visited earlier today. It appears to my inexperienced eyes to be an impressive and sturdy-looking vessel, with its three masts, gleaming wood, and noble bow.

I am happy to report that our trip looks to begin under fair skies, aided by a brisk spring wind. I view this as a promising omen. If only we might sail in a direct line, we should reach the far shores in a matter of weeks. However, strong headwinds necessitate a more southerly route. We will therefore travel first to the Canary Islands, an archipelago off the coast of Spain, to refresh ourselves before setting out on a lengthier journey across the sea of fifty days or thereabouts.

My visit last night with young cousin Charles went well. I still find it difficult to reconcile his new title with the solemn young boy I remember from childhood. He is a man, though, having just passed eighteen years of age, and as politically astute as his father. The decision to leave Papist ways for the loving embrace of the Church of England means the family will once again possess the Colony. God smiles on us all, even as man makes the inevitable compromises.

Charles has no intention of living in the Colony he is set to govern. As such, the position of Provisional Governor will continue to be of great significance. I have made no secret of my interest in the appointment when John Hart resigns. My political and military experiences render me a most suitable candidate, as does our familial connection. I will soon be thirty years of age, not too young for a station demanding a vigorous presence.

My father believes I set my sights too high, that I should be content with the court position in London that is all but guaranteed me. I am by nature averse to risk. Yet I cannot help but believe the Colonies offer so much more opportunity. I hope you will concur. I can think of no more satisfying future than to begin our new lives together in the New World.

I shall miss your company even as I keep you foremost in my thoughts. Until my return, I remain,

Your loving fiancé,

William

Chapter 1

Even in the pre-dawn black, hampered by clammy fog that clung to Harris Creek's surface, Tom Packard could just make out the form marooned on the tiny spit of sand. Inexperienced eyes might mistake it for a beached animal or even a piece of flotsam routinely tossed ashore by the bay and its tributaries. Packard, a Vietnam vet and an experienced waterman, knew better.

He faced a dilemma. Harris Creek was an oyster sanctuary, off-limits to fishermen. He had no business there, especially with a basket rake and a five-gallon bucket. He risked losing his license, his boat, maybe worse. He accepted that the government was making a concerted if heavy-handed effort to clean up the polluted bay and grow the oyster population. The effect was to drive the watermen out of business. What else was he supposed to do? Forty years he'd been fishing the Chesapeake. He earned his living collecting from those murky waters.

He could leave right then and let someone else figure out who'd washed up in close proximity to the million-dollar plus vacation homes that dotted the area. But though he might be a poacher in the state's eyes, Tom Packard was no civic slacker. He'd served his country; he understood duty.

The fisherman shut off the red and green running lights of his gray fishing boat, *Pearly Gates*, and trained his 200-lumen flashlight directly onto the shadowed mass. He drew a sharp breath and called 9-1-1.

* * *

Deputy Pat McCready was near the end of what he called mobile graveyard duty. That meant night patrol, which meant long hours in his car with cold coffee. Sometimes he went into McDonald's if he was on Highway 50. Talbot County felt deserted between midnight and six. Easton, the major town, rolled up the sidewalks by 11pm. Rise Up Coffee Roasters had installed a couple of a pop-up places, but they didn't open until after his shift ended. There was a new place in St. Michaels he might have to try. Rumor was it opened at 5:15 a.m.

The radio crackled. "Sheriff's Department, calling Night Hawk," the voice said. McCready recognized the dispatcher as Annie Blout. Night Hawk was the nickname given to anyone who pulled midnight to dawn patrol. McCready had seen the Edward Hopper picture with the same name. He liked it. He wished he were sitting in a well-lit café.

"Pat, you on?"

"Go ahead, Annie."

"Some waterman called in a body washed up south of Bozman near the Point."

"Halloween prank, maybe. Was there a broomstick nearby?"

"I'm serious, Pat."

"Okay, then. Who called?"

"He wouldn't give his name—you know they're not supposed to be fishing up in Harris Creek—but I figure it's Tom Packard."

"Christ, that's his third violation. He's gonna get his ass thrown in jail."

"We have bigger fish to fry, pardon my joke. Packard, or whoever called in, hinted that maybe it wasn't an accidental drowning."

McCready sat up straight in his cruiser, fatigue forgotten. "Now, how would he know that?" He ran a hand through his tousled, sandy hair. "Annie, call over to Lieutenant Samantha Tate. Don't worry about waking her, you hear me? Tell her to meet me at the end of Indian Point Road."

* * *

Sam Tate sat in the center of her tiny living room, Her dark curls piled haphazardly on top of her head, her hands at heart center. She raised one arm straight up and reached over her head. She repeated the movement on the other side, taking care to ease her way into the stretch. She went through the cycle twice more, then stood and did it again before ending in mountain pose. She followed with sets of sun salutations, nine in all, with additional poses she inserted in the middle for variety. She remembered to accompany each effort with slow breathing.

Morning yoga afforded her a sort of serenity, at least when she could keep her mind from wandering. She liked to run, sometimes alone, sometimes with Terry, when he could get up from D.C. or she could get away from her new job. FBI Special Agent Terry Sloan, her partner on the Wedding Crasher case and now her boyfriend, was also a student pursuing an advanced degree while transitioning to a supervisory role within the Bureau. They were seventy miles apart and lucky to spend two consecutive weekends together.

Come on, Tate, be in the moment. Fat chance of that. Maybe she could take a class rather than watch a video. Somehow, though, the idea of trying to still the mind while surrounded by other people seemed counterintuitive.

She gave up and went to sit in the rocker on the porch of her rented cottage, blanket wrapped around her, coffee mug in hand. She enjoyed listening to the whispering water and waiting for the world to wake up. She frequently found herself in this chair in the wee hours of the morning, brought awake too early by bad dreams.

Rocking back and forth reminded her of another cottage outside Byrdsville, Tennessee, where for three years she had rented a room from Cora Granville, a good-hearted soul who also happened to be something of a busybody. She missed chatting with the woman. She also missed easily available, high-quality bourbon, monthly poker games with county officials, and her loyal and dedicated staff. No romance in her life back then, but she'd enjoyed being sheriff of the sleepy county.

She could have stayed there. She would have, if life hadn't interfered.

A short burst of notes pulled her out of her head. A text. 10-35, major crime alert.

It took her fifteen minutes to reach Indian Point Road, which dead-ended just shy of a small estate. In the glare of her headlights, she could make out a multi-story, many-windowed house overlooking the water, flanked by a three-car garage and a swimming pool. Across a wide green lawn, a dock extended out into the water. A weekend home for a lawyer or a lobbyist. On a late October weekday, it would probably be empty.

She killed the engine. Another patrol car pulled up just behind her and did the same. McCready.

He unfolded his lanky body from the driver's side. Like her, he'd dressed in the standard issue black jacket, gray shirt, and black pants. Unlike her, he wore the broad-brim, high crowned trooper's hat. Probably popped it on to impress her. It looked good on him, with his boyish smile and square jaw. Pat McCready was twenty-four and, from what she'd picked up around the department, something of a heart-breaker.

"Lieutenant," he called out. "Sorry to bring you out on such a soggy night." He suppressed an involuntary shiver.

"Duty calls, Deputy. You did the right thing." She looked around. "Where's the person who called it in?"

McCready cleared his throat. "I'm guessing he took off."

She understood the young deputy's discomfort. Poaching was a serious offense. On the other hand, the watermen who flouted the law were friends and neighbors to people with whom she worked.

"Never mind. Let's see what he found. Grab your flashlight."

Sam pulled a handheld marine searchlight out of the trunk of her cruiser. It was a going-away gift from her staff back in Tennessee. She realized most of them had never been out of the state. All they knew was that she was headed to a community where many residents lived and died near the water.

"You got anything specific we can use as a starting point?" she asked.

"Dispatch said the caller mentioned sand. The shoreline is mostly rocky around here, but maybe there's a sliver of open space right up at the point."

Sam pulled out her phone and pulled up Google Maps. "I see it," she said. "We've got to pass between these trees and the water to get to it."

"Careful, then," McCready said. "We'll probably run into some pretty slippery going what with the mist and all."

They headed towards a copse of trees adjacent to the manicured lawn. Dawn hadn't shown itself. Absent any other illumination, they relied on their beams as they picked their way over the uneven surface.

"This is probably about the only piece of land left undeveloped around here," McCready observed. "You wouldn't believe how much building has gone on just in the last fifteen years." He stumbled. "Shit! Sorry, Lieutenant."

"Nothing I haven't heard before, Deputy."

They came upon a slip of sand about a hundred feet long and perhaps fifteen feet wide.

There it was, a body, face up, the left arm extended over the head as if to ward off a blow. The right arm rested on the chest as if in benediction. Both hands were blackened.

She set her searchlight down and crouched by the corpse. The beam coming from McCready's flashlight wavered.

"You okay, Pat?" she asked.

She heard him swallow. The light steadied. "Yeah, it's just that, damn it, that's Arley Fitchett."

"You know him?"

"Everyone knows Arley Fitchett."

"Let's see what we have here."

Sam moved closer to the body. A quick scan suggested the cadaver was a male Caucasian, neither young nor old, medium-tall and slender. He wore a canvas jacket of the type favored by fishermen, though this one looked military. She saw evidence of light feasting by various opportunistic predators. Nothing much around the face. Fairly well preserved, all things considered.

Sam squinted at the angry red mark around the victim's throat. The thin line formed a shallow trough that ran from ear to ear. It appeared to be made by a wire, though she knew better than to voice her thoughts aloud. The burnt hands were odd. Was this an accident? Did the guy get tangled in a fishing line or a trap and fall overboard right into the motor? Hard to fathom.

Suicide? He hurt himself, then decided on something more permanent. Or murder. The victim garroted, which indicated skill and planning. A professional. The method chosen to send a message.

Don't jump to any conclusions, Tate, she reminded herself. She looked up at McCready, tried to read his face by the faint beam of the flashlight.

"So, Deputy. How does everyone know Arley Fitchett?"

"He's Talbot County's very own treasure hunter."

"Treasure hunter?"

"Not the kind of stuff you find at yard sales or pick up along the shoreline and resell. There's a lot of amateur hunters like that around here. Arley is—was—the real deal." McCready warmed to his subject. "He worked with investors on the kinds of projects you see on TV."

"You mean shipwrecks, that sort of thing." Sam glanced at the waters, opaque in the misty dawn. "Not around here, though."

"You might not realize, Lieutenant, but a lot of ships have gone missing around here, what with all the little coves and creeks and such that feed into the bay. Some of them are really old. Just last year, a professional group found an old Revolutionary War battleship in the York River. A lot of people think pirates were active in the Chesapeake way back when."

"I had no idea," Sam murmured.

"Oh, yeah. We got groups coming over all the time looking for treasure. Arley even ran his own business, sort of like a tour guide. He had business cards, a website, the whole thing. I swear he knew everything about the area, the history, the stories, all of it. Being a treasure hunter helped. He'd take people up and down the shoreline, showing them where pirates might have hidden their ships or buried their treasure. Folks got their money's worth. They loved it."

"He was an enterprising sort of guy."

"He worked hard. Always had a tall tale ready." He went quiet, as if he'd gone on too long.

"Did he have any close friends?"

"I couldn't say. He's been around for a while, but like I said, he traveled." He paused. "It's like everyone knew him, but maybe no one did."

I know that feeling, Sam thought. "Was he depressed? Moody?"

"Not so I noticed."

"How about drugs? Using or selling?"

"Drugs? I don't think so." McCready looked out across the water. "As far as I could tell, he was strictly a beer and whiskey kind of guy. Maybe he overdid it once in a while, but he seemed to know his limit." He refocused on Sam. "Why'd you ask about the drugs? Do you think this was a hit?"

"I'm just collecting information at this point, Deputy."

"Guess the sheriff told you we have a problem around here, huh?"

He had. Sinaloa, the largest of the seven Mexican cartels that controlled U.S. drug markets, blanketed the East Coast with illegal or controlled substances. Baltimore had for some time been the country's unofficial heroin capital, with one in ten residents addicted. Inevitably drugs like heroin, fentanyl, and cocaine made their way onto the bucolic Eastern Shore.

Jake Donahue, her new boss, had made drug eradication a cornerstone of his campaign. Just after he took office, he was part of a sting operation coordinated by the Maryland State Police that netted $13 million dollars in narcotics. Yet opioid deaths had increased nearly 60% over the previous year.

This won't make him happy, Sam thought.

She stood. "Let's get the county forensic investigator over here." Maryland's Office of the Chief Medical Examiner used forensic investigators for death investigations outside

Baltimore, where the OCME was located. Such investigators served as the eyes and ears of the office. The investigator made preliminary assessments, wrote up reports, interviewed witnesses, if any, and arranged for the body to get back to Baltimore for autopsy.

"Martin Lloyd," McCready offered. "I got his number right here."

"Send that to my phone, will you?" Sam hoped the weak light hid her smile. She found a lot to admire in McCready's eagerness, not to mention his attention to detail. She suspected he held aspirations beyond his present position as a patrol deputy.

A deep voice answered when she rang the investigator. "Lloyd," it announced. "How can I help?" Alert, professional, almost as if he'd been waiting for her call. She introduced herself and described the scene.

"A body? Guess you know not to touch anything, Lieutenant." Wry, not scolding. Sam guessed he knew her by reputation. The serial killer-chasing sheriff from Tennessee come home to take care of her sick mother. Did he view her new position as a demotion? Why not? Most days, she did.

"I'm not far," he added. "See you in ten."

"We're not going anywhere." She clicked off, thought a minute, then sent a short text to Detective Bruce Gordy. Gordy was the senior investigating detective in the division she commanded, one of only three people in the department with significant homicide experience. Like nearly everyone else on the force, he was a life-long Eastern Shore resident, though he'd spent some years with Baltimore PD. Like Sam, he was in his mid-thirties with several years as a city homicide detective.

If he resented being passed over in favor of the outsider from Tennessee, he never let on. In the ten weeks since she'd arrived, he'd been more than helpful to her in terms of navigating the system, not to mention the personalities. For that, she was grateful.

She squatted by the body, remembering the investigator's instructions and her own training, weighing them against her curiosity. Carefully, she picked up a stick and lifted the jacket, then used it to push open his pockets.

"See anything, Lieutenant?"

"Nothing obvious," she said. "The investigator will tell us more, though."

She stood with a small groan after staying in the squat for too long. She moved her beam around the body once more and looked up at the sky.

"Switch off your light, Deputy. Dawn is breaking; we're about to see a lot more of everything."

Chapter 2

Jake Donahue arrived a little after seven, just as the sun spread its early rays along the edge of the bay. His bulk appeared against the lightening sky like that of a superhero or the former fullback he'd been. He squared his substantial shoulders against the sharp gusts that rolled off the creek and looked down.

The sheriff's arrival was unexpected, at least by Sam's reckoning. She wondered if he still had a way to go before he could trust his criminal commander to head up a crime scene investigation.

"You've had a long night," Sam said to McCready. "Your shift ends at 6am, if I'm not mistaken."

"I can wait around a little longer. In case you need something."

Sam didn't argue. A homicide was a terrible event. It was also a learning experience for a young officer and a chance to demonstrate how well he could handle a difficult situation.

"Morning, McCready, Lieutenant," Donahue's voice rumbled. "I understand you've found a body."

"Yes, sir," Sam answered.

"Guess you know we don't get too many of those around here." He looked around. "Where's the guy who called it in?"

"Gone before we got here, Sheriff," McCready volunteered.

"Goddam poacher, more than likely. Mind if I come down and take a look?" Jake Donahue didn't wait for an answer. He clambered over the rocks, unexpectedly nimble for a big man, and stopped short.

"Goddamn it."

"You recognize him." Sam didn't make it a question.

"Yeah, that's Arley Fitchett."

McCready opened his mouth, but Sam signaled him with a hand gesture. He nodded and bit his lip. No sense in advancing any theories before a more thorough investigation, including an autopsy. Besides, the case wasn't technically his to work, as much as he might want to.

"We got the forensics guy coming?" Donahue asked.

As if on cue, a car door slammed. Martin Lloyd, the forensic investigator, appeared a minute later. Donahue waved him over.

Lloyd was at least six-and-a-half feet. Unlike many tall people, he stood straight, his shoulders back, his chin raised. His thick brown hair was lightly dusted with silver, his face bronzed. His rimless glasses lent him a scholarly look. He wore a plaid shirt, a field jacket, cargo pants with plenty of pockets, and duck boots. Over one shoulder, he carried a well-worn backpack. In the other, he carried a travel mug.

Sam suddenly felt as if a hot cup of coffee would be the greatest gift in the world.

Lloyd extended a large hand to each of the officers in turn.

"Sheriff Donahue, Deputy McCready. Lieutenant Tate, pleased to meet you." The voice was low and pleasant. "That the body?" He walked over, looked down, then back at Donahue, his brown eyes bright. "Looks like Arley Fitchett. Too bad."

Did everyone know Arley Fitchett? Sam wondered.

"I'll try to run a fingerprint match, if the water and his burns don't make that impossible," Lloyd said. "We'll use a DNA sample as well. Hopefully, it won't be degraded." He rummaged in his backpack for his tools.

Sam turned to the young deputy. "Go get some sleep. I'm going to need you to be fresh later on."

Gratitude washed across his face. "Yes, ma'am."

As soon as Pat McCready took off, presumably to a hot meal and a warm bed, Donahue waved Sam over.

"How do you want to proceed, Lieutenant?"

Did he come by just to test her, see if she knew proper protocol? She was commander of his Criminal Investigative Bureau, for God's sake, not some amateur. Or maybe something else was going on, something that involved not procedure but politics.

She took a beat before she answered. "I'm going to wait until the investigators have done their work. Mr. Lloyd should be able to give us some information. Detective Gordy and CSI Davidson are on the way to help process the scene." Her phone's rhythmic riff alerted her to an incoming text. "And here they are."

Sam stuck up her arm to signal Bruce Gordy as he emerged from the tree line just ahead of a woman who looked very much like him. Bruce Gordy and Carol Davidson were siblings, with straight chestnut hair, high foreheads, and vulpine features: thin faces, long noses, and watchful gray eyes. The two of them paused on the rocks like a pair of wary foxes.

"Damn, it is Arley Fitchett," Gordy exclaimed. He trained his flashlight on the crime scene, though the sun had lifted itself off the horizon.

"Not yet confirmed but likely, I'm sorry to say." Lloyd looked up, his attention not with Gordy but on Carol, who'd moved a little closer to the body. She held the investigator's gaze an extra second or two before dropping her head to her own bag of equipment.

"I need to take some pictures, but I'll stay out of your way," she said.

Lloyd's smile brightened his face. "You won't be in my way, I promise."

Sam could swear the CSI blushed.

"I'm going to head back to the office," Donahue announced. "You'll be staying, Lieutenant?" Perhaps he was acknowledging that the crime scene—and the case—belonged to her.

"A little longer, just to see what Mr. Lloyd comes up with. We want to track down the missing witness and anyone else who might have seen something."

"I'm not sure Fitchett had any family in the immediate area. Gordy would know better. Carry on, Lieutenant Tate." Donahue turned to walk back to his car.

Sam stayed another half hour to watch the investigative team at work, especially Martin Lloyd. His thoroughness impressed her. For one thing, he displayed admirable patience. For another thing, he knew his territory.

She allowed him a little time to work before she asked, "Anything you can tell me at this point?"

"The Chesapeake is a mix of freshwater from the north and saltwater coming up from the mouth of the bay," Lloyd began. "The bay temperature is relatively warm into October. That means the freshwater predominates, at least near the surface, and that normally means maggots and blowflies could have a field day. On the other hand, the run of inclement weather we've had, along with wind, has likely altered the water's circulation and affected the saline level. All of this would potentially mess with an accurate timeline."

"No time of death?"

Lloyd bent over the corpse. "The body shows comparatively little wear and tear. I see some light feasting by scavengers, but at least he's got his limbs and his head. In saline and even mixed waters, those separate from the body within a week or two. Moreover, he's identifiable. No bloating or putrefaction. That would suggest he's been in the water between one and three days. As for when he was killed, not too long before then. Best I can do."

"Cause of death?"

He pointed to the neck. "I would venture to say the airway was constricted and oxygen cut off. An autopsy will confirm that."

"Asphyxia due to ligature strangulation."

"That's manner of death, Lieutenant. "

Sam stifled her annoyance. "I know the difference, Mr. Lloyd."

"I apologize. I have to be careful not to cross any lines or step on any toes. I'm a field forensic investigator, not a doctor, as I'm often reminded."

"Believe me, I know what it feels like to be a victim of bureaucracy," Sam told him. "My money's usually on the people in the field."

"Thank you for that, Lieutenant." Lloyd turned back to the body. "I don't see anything blocking the airways and I do see marks on the neck that suggest external pressure, if that helps."

"It does. Any way to know where the body went in?"

"Afraid not. I'm not an expert in currents. Any trace evidence has probably been washed away."

"I understand. What about the hands?"

"They were burned."

"Chemical? Bacterial? Something in the water? Something our victim handled?"

Lloyd leaned over and sniffed. He pulled out a baggie and picked at the hand with a tweezer. A flake of skin came loose. He pointed to darkened cuffs on the jacket.

"It's a fire burn. As if he stuck his hands into a hot flame. Or someone did it for him."

"Both hands." Sam stared at the appendages.

"Yes. I don't yet know if the burns were peri- or post-mortem." Lloyd leaned over the body again. "Well, well, what have we here?"

Out came the tweezers again, which Lloyd used to reach into the right jacket pocket on the victim's coat. He sat back on his heels and held up an irregularly shaped object that glinted in the faint morning light.

"You'll find this interesting, I think." He dropped the object into a small plastic bag. "A piece of metal that looks like—well, I'm not sure what it looks like. That's someone else's bailiwick. Shall I give this to your CSI?"

"I'll take that and log it into evidence."

"Fine." He handed her the bag and looked around. "I've still got a few more samples to collect and pictures to take for my report. You can get copies of whatever I have, although your CSI seems to be documenting everything to perfection." He exchanged a lingering look with Carol. Sam could almost hear the hum of the current that ran between them. Two crime scene investigators. Why not?

Lloyd transferred his attention to Sam. "One more thing: We seem to be minus at least one witness."

"Whoever discovered the body took off after he called it in."

Lloyd nodded. "I'm not surprised. Probably fishing illegally. Not that there's much he could tell us." He seemed to tick off an item on a list. "That leaves next of kin to interview."

"He mentioned a cousin in Massachusetts," Gordy said. The detective still stood on the rocks, watching the interplay between the investigator and his sister. "We can handle the interview through the local police."

Lloyd looked down at his clipboard. "Works for me. Just make sure the ME's office gets those notes, will you?"

He looked up at Sam, as if he suddenly remembered who the ranking officer was.

"We'll take care of it," she said.

"Of course. I should be done in another hour. I've already called for a wagon. I'll do my best to expedite the autopsy, Lieutenant. Guess you know how backed up things are in Baltimore. You can thank the opioid epidemic."

"I've heard."

"Anything else?"

"No. You seem to have everything under control." She pivoted to her number one. "Detective Gordy?"

"Right. CSI Davidson and I will need a little time to finish up here. Do you want us to then head over to Arley's place? I think he rents right in the middle of Easton. Or would you prefer I notify the cousin?"

"I'll take care of that. Find Arley's landlord first thing. Tell whoever it is we consider the house a potential crime scene." She imagined yellow tape and curious onlookers in the middle of town. "Don't make it look like one from the outside, though."

"Are we keeping this case or giving it away?"

Sam knew Gordy was asking if Talbot County Sheriff's Office would call in the much larger Maryland State Police to take over. Not that she had an issue with cooperation. Bigger agencies had more resources. During her time as sheriff of Pickett County, Tennessee, she'd requested assistance from state agencies more than once.

Asking for help was not the same as handing off a case, though. Sam had to assume her new boss would give her a chance to demonstrate her ability to lead a murder investigation.

You know what they say about assumptions, she thought.

"That'll be Sheriff Donahue's call," she said.

Chapter 3

It was nearly nine-thirty when she pulled up to the red brick building on Dover Street. Three flagpoles stood sentry at the main entrance, over which hung the Maryland State Seal and lettering that identified the building as the "Public Safety Center." The pumpkin sitting by the door had appeared a few days earlier, just in time for Halloween. Sam guessed Rose had put it there. The office administrator had a thing for holidays.

Directly across the street sat the Town of Easton police headquarters. Sam planned to include the chief of police on any preliminary meetings, although she guessed he'd be happy to stay in the background on the case.

She texted Terry to fill him in.

"First homicide," he replied. "Congrats."

"Not ready to celebrate," she shot back with an emoji of a frowny face. "Talk tonight?"

She got a thumbs up.

Sam walked into her office, dumped her gear, and headed across the hall to her boss's office. Donahue was bent over his desk, taking notes and gesticulating, the phone jammed between his ear and his substantial shoulder. She caught Arley Fitchett's name and something about a garrote.

He looked up and put his palm out to keep her from entering. "Later," he mouthed.

Sam nodded. She backed out and turned away, frustrated. Who would he be talking with about her case? Maybe someone from the Maryland State Police. But why wasn't she part of the call?

Sam knew that before being elected Talbot County Sheriff, Donahue had spent twenty years with MSP, most of it as a criminal investigator. He'd finished as Commander of the

29

Homicide Unit. Unlike many rural sheriffs, he didn't consider the state police rivals but allies with superior technology and more manpower.

Understandable. After all, the organization had a far better track record when it came to solving homicides than most municipalities. Without a doubt, assistance from MSP experts could provide a tactical advantage.

Would they be assisting, though, or leading? Where did that leave her?

Sam didn't think she was prideful. She knew how to ask for help if she needed it. Yes, she was new. Yes, she'd replaced a beloved older figure, just as she had back in Tennessee. On the other hand, she was a damned good cop with plenty of investigative and administrative experience of her own. At least Donahue might run his thoughts by her first.

She shut the door and logged onto her laptop to learn more about the victim. Fitchett's resumé proved easy to put together. Born forty-three years earlier in the coastal Massachusetts town of Wareham. Father a commercial fisherman, mother a librarian. Both passed. No other relatives listed, except for a cousin, Susan Ernst.

Fitchett had snagged a baseball scholarship to a local college just after high school. A torn meniscus sidelined him in the first year. Though apparently bright, he didn't seem interested in higher learning for its own sake and washed out of school soon thereafter. He subsequently enlisted in the Merchant Marines.

He received several commendations during his years at sea. Unfortunately, his lack of education hindered his chances for advancement. After several years, he returned to Wareham and then drifted down the east coast. He ended up on Maryland's Eastern Shore, renting a succession of living spaces and working at odd jobs. He schooled himself in local history and offered himself as a guide for tourists who wanted to explore the "real" Eastern Shore on and off the water. He even had a nautical-themed website. According to several online comments, he was knowledgeable and passionate about finding objects long buried or hidden from careless eyes.

He'd never married. Neither McCready or Gordy could remember seeing him in the company of a special someone, male or female. His name came up as an honorary member of the Maryland Free-State Treasure Club. Sam looked up the website and added the name of the current president, Benjamin Hart, to a list of people she or Gordy needed to meet.

Other than that, Fitchett had exactly one outstanding parking ticket, one warning for drunk and disorderly that never led to an arrest, and even a commendation for rescuing a child who'd slipped off a pier. By all accounts, Arley Fitchett was a good man, willing to work and fun to be around. The kind of man without an enemy in the world.

Except for the person who choked him to death, set his hands on fire, and tossed him into the water.

Sam placed a call to McCready's supervisor, Tanner Reed. Fortunately, the veteran cop was at his desk. "Shouldn't be a problem," he said. "I can get his shift covered. But why do you want McCready? I've got more senior deputies."

"I like the way he thinks," Sam replied.

"Alright, then. Good luck on your homicide."

She thanked Reed and placed a call to McCready. A sleepy voice answered on a yawn. Not surprising, given he'd gone home just two hours earlier after pulling the graveyard shift.

Oh, well, he's young, Sam thought. "Deputy McCready, are you awake?" she asked.

"Lieutenant Tate? Yes ma'am." He snapped to attention. A good sign.

"Deputy—Pat—if you're interested, I'd like your help on this Fitchett investigation. I know you're short on sleep."

"Not a problem, Lieutenant."

"Good. Your role will be to help us learn more about Arley Fitchett. I might also need you to accompany Detective Gordy on a couple of outings. How fast can you get in here?"

He mumbled something, then cleared his throat.

"Sorry. I was pulling on my shirt. Ten minutes, tops."

"Great. Looks like we still have donuts and coffee."

"Works for me."

Sam next called Larry Anson, Wareham's chief of police.

"Arley Fitchett?" he said. "Haven't seen him for years. Murdered, you say? That's a damned shame."

"I understand his parents are deceased, but he has a cousin, a Susan Ernst."

"Sure, she's still in the area. I can get in touch with her if you'd like." Anson paused. "What about the sister, Josie? You able to track her down?"

"Arley had a sister?" Sam asked in surprise.

"Half-sister, actually. Seven or eight years older. Left town when she was seventeen. No one knows where she went after that." He paused. "Maybe Susan remembers something helpful. I'll talk with her and have her get in touch with you."

Sam had a feeling he had a lot more to add. She decided to let it go. "That'd be helpful," she said instead.

As soon as she hung up, her cell phone rang. Gordy.

"Forensic investigator is finished and so are we. Body's on its way to the ME's office and we're headed over to Fitchett's. The landlord will meet us."

"I hope Lloyd is able to get this autopsy scheduled ASAP, Gordy. I know the ME up in Baltimore is swamped with bodies, but ours is garroted and his hands are burned. That could get us bumped to the head of the line."

"You're thinking the cartel is involved?"

"I'm thinking if we make it seem that way, we might get an expedited autopsy."

She could imagine him nodding. "Makes sense. I'll call on the way over to Fitchett's, see what I can do."

"Thanks. I've got Pat McCready coming in to handle some background research for me here. I've cleared it with his immediate supervisor."

"Isn't he one of the kids who ride the graveyard shift?"

"He is. Or he was. I'm going to bring him into this investigation. We have to mentor, Gordy, and quickly. Especially if we want to keep things in-house."

With her immediate obligations out of the way, Sam remembered the plastic bag in her pocket. She planned to log it into evidence. First, she fished a pair of latex gloves and an old-fashioned magnifier from her desk drawer.

She carefully shook the uneven metal object onto a piece of white paper. The piece was worn and tarnished, but she thought it might be silver. It was also old. She could just make out a cross, perhaps a coat of arms, and a date, 1715. It measured about an inch by an inch-and-a-half, crudely hammered into an oblong shape like a shield. It reminded Sam of the Indian heads she and her uncle Kevin found once at Silver Lake Park.

The internet offered up bits of information. The coin was probably a Spanish *cabal* or "cob." Gold and especially silver Spanish coins were a common form of currency in most western countries well into the 19th century. Spain had mints all over the New World. The largest of these was located in Mexico City, which for two centuries produced nearly half the coins used until a more traditional looking milled version replaced them.

The piece was worth eight *reales* and came to be known in popular culture by its colloquial name, "pieces of eight."

She sat back, hands behind her head, and contemplated the find. Why would a cartel hit include an old Spanish coin with the victim? Some kind of message? Everyone knew Fitchett hunted treasure. Maybe whoever killed Fitchett or ordered him killed had a wicked sense of humor to go along with nasty ideas about punishment.

She was lost in thought when Pat McCready knocked on the door, just fifteen minutes after they'd hung up. Sam guiltily slipped the coin back into its protective cover. Not that the bleary-eyed young deputy noticed.

"Ready to work, Deputy?" Sam remembered to add, "Got your coffee?"

"And a donut," he replied with a grin. "Where do you want me to start?"

"Think about everything you know or have heard about Arley Fitchett, then make a list of anyone he might have known or hung out with or worked for or socialized with. Did he keep a list of clients or the folks he took out on one of his treasure-hunting expeditions? Are we certain he didn't have a regular companion or at least a romantic liaison? Maybe someone from out of town? We need to talk with people who've interacted with him recently. I want to know what he was up to the last few days, weeks, months, if possible. We also need to subpoena cell phone records, assuming Fitchett used one. We didn't see it at the scene."

"I'll call Judge Simon. He's a family friend."

The look Sam gave her deputy suggested she was impressed. He blushed and tried to cover it with a shrug. "His daughter is engaged to my cousin," he explained. "I've been over to the house a few times."

"Sounds good. I want that list and any information you can gather by the end of the day, if possible. I'm not interested in gossip, but I do want to get the measure of the man."

"Yes, ma'am."

"Don't work past five. I want you rested. You're now part of the task force investigating this death."

"Is it a homicide?" the young man asked.

"The ME in Baltimore has to confirm. We're going to have a procedural meeting tomorrow. I want you there."

"Really? Excellent." He blushed. "I mean—"

"It's fine, Deputy."

Sam waited until he left and allowed herself a small smile. Supporting subordinates made sense. Besides, she genuinely enjoyed bringing along new officers. She'd grown fond of a promising recruit back in Tennessee. The young woman had been murdered by one of the killers they'd been pursuing.

The memory caused her chest to ache. She allowed the pain to briefly surface. She'd known a lot of loss over the course of her life and buried too much grief along with a father, a brother, a fiancé, and several friends.

Her office phone alerted her to another call. Fitchett's cousin, Susan Ernst.

"Lieutenant Tate?" The voice was soft, with a touch of New England attached to it. "The sheriff just called me. How awful. Poor Arley. He was a good kid."

"I'm sorry for your loss, Ms. Ernst. If you don't mind my asking, were you close with your cousin?"

"Not really. We're related through his father, but I'm ten years older. I was already married with a couple of kids when Arley took off. We stayed in touch, though. Christmas card, the odd letter. And he did contact me when my husband Alan passed." She was quiet a moment. "Does Josie know?"

"We can't seem to locate her."

"I doubt she'd give a damn." Her vehemence startled Sam. "That young woman was pure trash. Went out of her way to be not just difficult but cruel. She hurt her little brother, that I'm sure of. He fought back one time, though. Made quite a mark. Good for him, I say."

They spoke a bit longer. The cousin offered to make funeral arrangements once the body was released.

Sam made a note to ask Shana Pierce, the department's IT specialist and internet sleuth, to try and track down the half-sister. She stood and stretched, wishing she hadn't shortened her earlier yoga workout. Mustn't let that slide.

Back in her chair, she pulled out a pad of paper—still her favorite method of working—and created two side by side lists: DRUGS and TREASURE.

Under DRUGS she wrote:

- Victim: user, dealer, thief, borrower
- Killer: local drug lord, rival, cartel-connected
- Motive: elimination of rival, a warning/example

If his death turned out to be a homicide attached to narcotics trafficking, she could guarantee a three-ring circus that extended far beyond the Maryland State Police. DEA and even the FBI would be involved. She might have an opportunity to work with Special Agent Terry Sloan. She smiled at the prospect and went back to her list.

Fitchett dedicated his life to looking for treasure. What was his latest quest? Had he worked alone or with a partner? Did such people have agreements about who looks where or who gets to keep what? Had Fitchett crossed or cut out an associate? Had he discovered something valuable that someone else wanted or felt entitled to have?

She chewed on her number two pencil, then began her list under TREASURE:

- Victim: treasure-hunter or treasure broker

- Killer: partner, rival, interested third party
- Motive: greed, revenge, business transaction or acquisition

Greed and revenge covered a wide range of possible motives. If Arley Fitchett had something of value, whoever wanted it could have killed him and taken it. On the other hand, setting the murder to look like a mob or cartel-type hit would confuse the issue.

She checked her watch. Midday. Sam was always amazed at how easily she lost track of time. She enjoyed research, which was a strength when dealing with the drearier parts of any investigation. At the same time, her mind sometimes wandered, a habit she hoped to break without stifling her imagination.

"You're thinking outside the box," Terry once told her. He still taught the occasional class in investigative techniques to trainees in and out of the FBI. He instructed his students to make use of intuition as well as logic whenever possible. "We all have the capability to employ different kinds of thinking," he told them. "Trust your brain to use the right combination."

Trust was always where Sam got hung up. She was working on that as well.

Gordy should be checking in soon. She also wanted to see how McCready was coming along.

On the way out, she passed Betty Claiborne and waved. A small woman of indeterminate age, Betty favored cardigans and an outdated hairstyle she nevertheless managed to pull off. She'd worked as the sheriff's personal assistant for six years and had worked for his predecessor at least a decade before that. Her efficiency was impressive, her powers of observation legendary.

The first time she met Sam, she handed her a slim book entitled *Maryland's Eastern Shore: Past and Present.* "Read up, Lieutenant," she advised. "History still matters to a lot of people around here."

Sam had already learned that a number of the locals traced their roots back to before the Revolutionary War. Claiborne was one of the earliest families, dating to the beginning of the seventeenth century.

Now she called out to Sam, "Hold on, Lieutenant Tate. I have an invitation for you." She handed Sam an engraved card on heavy ivory stock edged in burnt umber.

Sam turned it over. "What is this?"

"An invitation to the opening of a new art gallery in St. Michaels. Two weeks from today, I believe."

"How did I get on the list?"

"Lucy figured you might like to go." Lucy Gilden, Donahue's wife, was a wildlife photographer with an affection for the arts. "I know you've got the murder of poor Arley Fitchett to solve, but I'm sure you can do both."

"I appreciate the vote of confidence." She looked at the invitation. "Who's Wallace Bonnet, besides the featured attraction? Is he a famous artist I should know?"

"Not exactly. He subsists by carving wooden duck decoys for the gift shops. Some of them are quite sophisticated."

"That can't be all that lucrative," Sam observed.

"Heavens, no. He's had some help from his very wealthy and very politically connected family, though he downplays that relationship."

"Cultivating the starving artist image." They shared a chuckle.

"The Bonnet name carries a lot of weight here as well as back in D.C.," Betty said. "It got Wallace a lovely property just outside St. Michaels and right on the water."

"Bonnet is an unusual name. He wouldn't be descended from the Bonnet who went from being a rich farmer to a poor pirate, would he?"

The older woman laughed. "You know your history, Lieutenant. In answer to your question, there could be a direct connection. This branch of the Bonnet family has been in Virginia for some time. It's not something they bring up. Old Stede Bonnet was pretty much a failure. James Bonnet, Wallace's father, is anything but. He's quite the mover and shaker in Washington, if you know what I mean."

Sam did not but made a note to find out.

"The owner, Jaqueline Templeton, claims to have roots in Talbot County as well," Betty went on. "I don't recognize Templeton as an Eastern Shore name. Perhaps there's an ancestor on her maternal side about whom I'm unaware."

Sam suppressed the urge to giggle. "Could be," she said.

"Well, she doesn't seem to be lacking in funds. She's made a name in D.C. both in real estate and with her pricey store. She'll likely attract the same sort of clientele here."

Betty jotted a note on a pad that sat on her impossibly neat desk.

"I'll RSVP for you and a guest, shall I? This crowd may be a little more high-tone than we're used to seeing here." She looked Sam up and down. "I have the name of a place you can shop if you need something to wear."

"Um, yes, thanks."

"Oh, one more thing. Sheriff wants to see you."

"What, now?"

"His exact words were 'I'd like to see her as soon as she has a minute.'"

"Let me just finish up." She pointed over her shoulder. "Be right back."

Sam went to find Pat McCready. He was on the phone, nodding vigorously and scribbling notes. At least someone was getting something done.

Just then, her cell rang. Rather, it played her latest ringtone, a gentle song by Lyle Lovett about a boat. She glanced at the number. Gordy.

"You still at Fitchett's house? What'd you find?"

"More than I can explain over the phone, Lieutenant. How soon can you get here?"

"I'll be right over."

She ducked into her office for her jacket. Almost without thinking, she grabbed the bag containing the coin and pocketed it. On the way out, she stuck her head into Donahue's office.

"Sheriff, Gordy and Carol are over at Arley's house. I'd like to head over there before I sit down with you, if you don't mind. I'm sure I'll have a lot of pertinent information to share with you when I get back."

Donahue looked at her for a second or two, then nodded. "Sure. Make it end of day. Give us both more time."

Sam nodded, backed out, and sprinted for the door, thinking about the abbreviated conversation, especially the last line.

Dear Teresa,

Before I set foot on this vessel, I held a somewhat romantic image of life at sea. The sad truth is my notions were formed entirely from reading and from third-hand tales overheard in the company of my father's squire. I was woefully unprepared for life at sea, yet the men have been uncommonly kind.

We are twenty-two in total. These include the Captain, a man by the delightful name of Phineas Digg. He is served by a quartermaster, a boatswain, a first and second mate, a rigger, a cook, a cabin boy, and ten able seamen. White, Brown, and Black work in harmony, thanks in no small part to Captain Digg's even-handed and temperate stewardship.

Also onboard is a surgeon, Dr. Thaddeus Bell. He is already proving a delightful conversationalist; I suspect we shall become great friends. Last but not least is a distinguished gentleman of some years by the name of Frederick Claiborne. He tends toward solitude, though he has joined us at the captain's table for most dinners. I am given to understand his family has relations who live along the Chesapeake Bay. I hope to learn more as the days go by.

We eat well enough and so, it appears, do the sailors. Beef, salted pork, peas, cheese and butter are plentiful, as is jam for biscuits. We seem to have plentiful quantities of tea and beer, and wine for those of us lucky to dine at the captain's table.

Captain Digg has included a quantity of lemons as part of our diet. He is in possession of the novel idea that the sour fruit may prevent scurvy, a most unpleasant disease that affects primarily men at sea. In this he is supported by Dr. Bell, who insists that everyone on board partake of a sour spoonful every day. I cannot speak to cause and effect, dear Teresa. Time will no doubt tell.

I would be at pains to describe how much work is required to keep the boat upright and in forward motion. Whereas I sit scribbling, the men appear never to stop moving, raising and lowering the sails, cleaning the privy, swabbing the decks, repairing rips and tears to the wood or canvas.

We are oft accompanied by all manner of finned creatures. Smaller fish join us early in the day and porpoises appear at dusk. The odd shark will circle the boat looking for food. Seagulls perch on the mast as if on lookout and a pelican landed on the deck the other day, apparently to sun himself. Yesterday, we saw a school of whales! I will freely admit to you that these animals provide a great deal of relief from the wretched monotony of water.

The weather is not always with us. We have encountered our share of storms. The ones at night are the worst. The crew is forced to work nearly blind, so thick is the black that envelops us. I am grateful my task is to stay below and keep my meals in my stomach during these sieges.

Of greater concern is the possibility of losing the wind. If that should happen, we could not move. The men have talked of privation and madness after weeks aboard a becalmed vessel. I pray we will be spared that experience.

As for man-made perils, Providence has seen fit to spare us thus far. The pirates who sail the Atlantic tend to focus their activities closer to land. In truth, they are nothing more than privateers who practice a form of sanctioned thievery. Many are retained by various Private Entities and by the governments of Certain Countries, including, yes, our own beloved England, in order to provide protection or discourage competitors. Frankly, we carry little that might warrant attention, save for the most precious gift I am charged with transporting. About that I shall write more in a future letter.

Fondly,
William

Chapter 4

The place Arley Fitchett had called home was a modest single-story white-washed wood-framed bungalow that looked as if it dated from the mid-thirties. Located at the edge of the Easton city limits, it was perhaps 900 square feet. A trimmed front lawn and a brick walkway led up to a tiny front porch with a rocking chair and a table. A clay pot with a drooping purple and green sedum suggested an effort to give the place some life, though the plant clearly needed water. Off-white curtains, tightly closed, hung in the windows.

Sam raised a hand to the siblings who stood at the open front door in latex gloves and paper booties. "I gather you interviewed the owner already?" she queried.

Gordy nodded. "George Boyd. He had to get back to his sick wife. He was distraught, insisted Arley Fitchett was a good tenant. Paid on time and was quiet. Made just one request, that he be allowed to use part of the small storage unit in the back. Promised to empty it out before he left."

"Fitchett was planning to move?"

"He told Boyd he was close to being able to afford his own place." Gordy shrugged. "Nothing about where or when."

"He expected to come into some funds," Sam said. "Well, let's see what his current residence has to tell us. Lead the way." She pulled on gloves and booties and followed her officers inside.

The tiny house was well-ordered, if a bit shabby. A comfortable fabric chair sat in front of an older-model television and perpendicular to a well-worn sofa with throw pillows. Sam lifted the corner of an oval braided rug that covered a scuffed but clean wood floor. A carved duck decoy sat on a side table next to a pull-chain lamp.

Two large oil paintings, one on each wall, looked to be by local artists. One depicted a waterman hauling an oyster cage into his boat early in the morning, judging by the muted colors. In the other picture, sailboats navigated the bay on a sunny afternoon.

Fitchett kept the place very neat. No dust bunnies, no filled ashtrays or empty glasses. Sam stared at the floor, at the front door, at a pillow on the couch, then over at Gordy and Carol. "What do you think?"

"I think someone was here," Gordy said. "Little things. The pillow is upside-down. The rug is off-center. The closet by the front door isn't quite closed. The pictures are crooked. If Arley was as orderly as he seemed, he'd automatically straighten up."

"I ran my LUMI over the entire house," Carol added. "I didn't find any stains or fluid patterns. Just one set of fingerprints belonging to Fitchett. But there is the faintest outline of a footprint. Much larger than Fitchett's size ten."

"A careful visitor who came to the house following Mr. Fitchett's demise," Sam said. "Which doesn't seem to have occurred here. What was this visitor looking for, I wonder?"

"Maybe what we pulled off the back of a shelf in the next room," Carol said."

The three of them crowded into the galley-style kitchen, narrow enough that one could almost touch the opposite walls at the same time. No dishes in the sink, cabinets closed, except for one. On the impossibly clean counter sat a microfiber sports bag. Inside she saw a box of three-inch vials, a collection of small plastic zip bags, a small blade, a digital scale, and a roll of $100 bills.

"Your basic drug supplies." Sam shook her head. "Not terribly well hidden. Are we supposed to believe Arley Fitchett was a user or a dealer?"

"There's nothing in here to suggest he used," Gordy observed. "No bongs, papers, pipes, or syringes. He's got maybe three thousand total in cash. It's more like a go bag for a small-time dealer."

"Something doesn't feel right," Sam muttered. "Is that all?

"Not by half," Carol said with obvious delight. "The real story's back here."

The siblings led Sam through a tiny windowless bathroom and another room just big enough for a bed, a tiny bureau, and a desk. Again, nothing amiss except for a drawer handle flipped up. They went out the back door to the fenced-in dirt yard with a tiny, well-tended garden. Gordy pointed at a pole. "Night light is triggered by motion," he said.

"That's where all the fun is," Carol said.

A couple of strides took them to a newish-looking ten by ten shed, one of those aluminum-sided easy-to-assemble models, gray with white trim and a double front door. The lock on the front had been broken.

"Arley's visitors weren't as careful out here," Sam said.

"Landlord said Fitchett hid the key around here," Gordy observed. "He wasn't sure where."

The small structure was filled to capacity with the discarded junk of ordinary life. An ancient seated lawn mower did its best to block the entrance. A wobbly-looking bike leaned against the wall next to a wooden bench loaded with rusty tools. Dented patio furniture was half piled on a couch that had seen better days. Several lamps and chairs, were pushed into a corner. Wicker baskets of various sizes hung overhead. Boxes were piled everywhere, some sealed and some opened and overflowing with bric-a-brac. A black metal filing cabinet at the rear sat with open drawers and files askew.

The place looked like a pawed-over flea market.

"Check it out." Gordy hoisted a well-worn bat in his hands. "Louisville Slugger. These things last forever. You said Fitchett played ball?"

"Briefly." Sam looked at the rifled papers. "Did they find what they were looking for?" she asked.

"I doubt it," Gordy replied, carefully leaning the bat against the wall. "But we did."

The back wall seemed to be solid, just a couple of industrial hooks from which hung a ladder and a spade. Gordy pulled the tool's handle and the wall moved.

"That's pretty neat," Sam admitted. "How'd you think of that?"

"I read a lot of detective novels," Gordy deadpanned.

Behind the false wall was another, not quite big enough to be considered a closet, much less a room. More like a cubby hole or a secret hiding place.

"Arley built this?" Sam asked. "I'm impressed."

The back wall was covered with clipping, scribbled notes, prints, pictures, and print-outs. Two maps of the Chesapeake Bay area, one current and one centuries old, were circled with red magic marker. A couple of colorized sketches of old-fashioned sailing vessels were flanked by images of historical figures, each helpfully identified by name.

Two articles had been cut from print editions of the local paper, the *Star Democrat*. One featured an interview with "prominent Eastern Shore appraiser and noted historian" Dr. Charles Fox. The other announced an upcoming event featuring the work of local artist Wallace Bonnet.

"I just got an invitation to this event," Sam said.

"That's supposed to be a hot ticket, Lieutenant," Carol observed.

"I'm treating it as a work assignment. Let's focus on this display right now."

Red string ran from one piece to the next, connecting the various items to one another. Everything led to a centrally placed drawing of a bird, maybe a wren or a sparrow, sitting on a human hand. The artist had also sketched an ornate container or cage in one corner. To Sam's untrained eye, it was skillfully rendered. Even though she was looking at a photocopy of an old drawing, she could make out details indicated by brush strokes and shading.

The entire display reminded her of an evidence board. Not one created by the police but rather by someone with something to prove. A conspiracy theorist, perhaps. Or a treasure hunter.

"I'll start with what I know," Gordy began. "The ships are eighteenth-century sailing vessels. The smaller one's called a Bermuda sloop. Used mostly as a trading ship. This other one's a frigate. Might be a hundred or more guns on one of those. Definitely a battleship."

"You play with boats as a kid?" Sam asked.

Gordy laughed. "Our dad was a maritime history buff. I'm willing to bet these characters came from the same time period. Fortunately, Fitchett labeled the images for us." Gordy leaned in. "The bearded guy is Blackbeard. Every school kid knows about him. He would set his beard on fire to frighten his victims into surrendering. The well-fed guy next to him is Stede Bonnet."

"The Gentleman Pirate," Sam murmured. "Who may or may not be Wallace Bonnet's ancestor."

"No kidding?" Gordy commented. "Moving along, we have John Hart. Why does that sound familiar?"

"I remember," Carol volunteered. "He was the provisional governor of Maryland when Protestants kicked out the Catholic Calvert family." She grinned at her brother. "One of us was paying attention in history class."

Gordy snorted. "Good for you. Who is this younger man, William Calvert?"

Carol shrugged. "Maybe a relative."

"Arley was interested in eighteenth-century ships and people, including a notorious pirate," Sam observed. "What's stored in the boxes below?"

Gordy trained his flashlight on the open containers. One box had equipment—rope, lantern, hand shovel. "Tools of the trade, maybe," he said. "You might find this interesting." He handed Sam his flashlight and hoisted a second box to a narrow bench pressed to the wall.

Sam riffled through the contents. "Receipts, correspondence, and what have we here?" She pulled out a manila envelope and removed a cellophane-encased paper.

"That's one of two letters we found," Carol volunteered. "Both very old, at least if the paper and the dates are to be believed."

"1718," Sam read. "What about these other letters?"

"Photocopies, all dated 1718," Gordy replied.

"They're all written to someone named Teresa," Sam said. "And all important to Arley Fitchett, apparently."

"I saved the best for last." Gordy reached down to the lower shelf tucked under the bench. "Ta-da. A laptop. Fortunately for us, Mr. Fitchett was a cautious man."

Sam nodded her approval. "Perhaps he was expecting company. I'll take that back with me so that Shana can find out if there's anything useful on it. I don't guess you found a cell phone?"

"No such luck," Gordy said.

Sam turned back to the wall, arms folded. "How does the bird figure into all this?"

"There's writing on the sketch," Carol pointed out. She pulled a small black box with a glass lens and two light sources out of her bag. "It says 'Bird in Hand.' I can make out a signature. G. Gibbons. And here's a note next to it, maybe in Arley's handwriting? Let's see. 'Copper cage preserves wood.' Huh. Next, we've got 'five-carat Kashmir sapphire' and 'wood is sapele.' Not sure I pronounced it correctly."

"Sapele," Sam said. "It's an exotic hardwood, found mainly in Africa. Similar to mahogany." She noticed the siblings staring at her. "I have a friend in Nashville who makes guitars."

"Is sapele rare?" Gordy asked.

"Maybe back then. Not anymore. That stone might be, though."

"Found a Grinling Gibbons." Carol was looking at her phone. "The portrait here matches our thin-faced friend on the wall. He's listed as Master Woodworker to the royal court from 1710 to 1727."

"This could be a sketch of his work," Gordy said. "Pretty fancy, even for a king's woodworker."

"And clever," Sam added. "Look at the container. At least I think it's meant to hold the carving. Copper naphthenate protects untreated wood against deterioration. That's a twentieth-century discovery, as I recall. Our master woodworker was well ahead of his time."

"Do you think our bird made a trip across the Atlantic in 1718?" Carol asked.

"Anything's possible," Sam replied. "Carol, do you have the pictures you need?"

"Yes, ma'am. Every possible angle."

Sam's moss-green eyes swept the tiny room. *What were you after, Arley Fitchett, and did it get you killed?*

"Bag it and tag it all. Take this as well." She handed over the coin. "Martin Lloyd retrieved this from the victim's pocket. I meant to give it to you."

"Well, would you look at that?" Carol exclaimed. "A Spanish *cob*. We used to go hunting for these when we were kids. They were standard currency in the English colonies."

"Show-off," her brother muttered.

Carol ignored him. "Still a lot of them lying around. This one's in pretty good condition." She took the small bag and stared at the wall. "An old Spanish coin in Arley Fitchett's pocket and a group of eighteenth-century references on his wall. Think it's a coincidence, Lieutenant?"

"I don't believe in coincidences."

"Do you believe in buried treasure?" Gordy asked.

"Doesn't matter what I believe, Gordy. We're not hunting for treasure; we're hunting for a killer."

Chapter 5

Sam sought out Pat McCready as soon as she got back to the office.

"Hey, Lieutenant. How's it going?" The young deputy looked and sounded energized. Sam suspected adrenaline and caffeine in equal measure.

"It's certainly going; I just don't know where. Have any of your searches turned up the names Charles Fox or Wallace Bonnet? I'm interested in whether they had more than a passing acquaintance with Arley Fitchett—or each other."

"Funny you should mention those two in particular, Lieutenant. I got Fitchett's phone records. In the last thirty days, there's been a lot of back and forth between Fitchett and the number I traced back to Fox's office. He's some kind of bigshot appraiser, goes into rich people's homes after they've passed and figures out how much their stuff is worth. He also wrote a book on Maryland during the eighteenth century."

"What's his connection to Fitchett?"

"Good question. I've got records of maybe half a dozen texts. Mostly short. Two calls, each lasting a couple of minutes."

"What about Bonnet?"

"A couple of quick texts. Something from Fitchett about a 'stupid idea for a show' when he—I guess Fitchett—was 'so close.' Bonnet responded with 'good for you.' Sounds like a brush-off."

"Let's not get ahead of ourselves. What else?"

"Arley made one call to Sotheby's in New York. I called that one." He looked apologetic.

"Smart. What did you learn?"

McCready brightened. "Arley was trying to reach an appraiser to discuss what he called 'antique items of value' he might be interested in putting up for sale. He didn't get through to any major players, I guess, but the assistant I talked to said they would have sent him to an independent appraiser."

"Arley Fitchett had something he decided was worthy not just of Charles Fox's time but also Sotheby's. Hmm. Anything else?"

"Just working my way down the list, although there aren't that many numbers. A salvage company Fitchett hired. A Chinese takeout place. The Lowe's out on Glebe Road. Also, texts tied to three different numbers, none of which go anywhere."

"Except maybe three burner phones. Keep looking. And text me both Fox and Bonnet's telephone numbers."

Sam next went looking for Shana Pierce. A pretty, petite young woman with pale, nearly translucent skin, she wore her jet-black hair short with long bangs streaked purple. Large blue eyes were always heavily lined and shadowed, though she was otherwise make-up free.

The young woman was aptly named. Five holes graced one ear, three in the lobe and two in the cartilage. A tiny ring decorated one nostril and a delicate hoop hung at the edge of her lower lip. She'd recently removed her tongue stud.

"These are only the ones you can see," she'd confided in Sam when they first met. "I can show you the rest." She looked at Sam's left ear, with its three small studs.

"I'm good," Sam assured her. "I'm just surprised you don't have any visible tats."

The girl reacted with shock. "Eww, no. I can't stand the idea of ink on my skin. I don't know why anyone would do that." For good measure, she shuddered.

Sam had worked hard not to laugh.

Idiosyncratic or not, Shana was not just reliable and thorough but also fast and creative when it came to breaking firewalls, catching hackers, or decrypting files. Sam knew someone through Terry who worked as a cyber-security expert for the FBI. Sam admired the woman's outlier attitude almost as much as her formidable skills. She thought it might be fun to get Paula Norris and Shana Pierce in a room together.

Sam handed over the MacBook. "I have no idea if this is password protected."

"A password-protected personal computer?" She snorted. "Come on, Lieutenant, where's the challenge in that?"

"I'm sure there'll be something more exciting for you down the line," Sam said with a laugh. "What I need now is a speedy turnaround."

"What are you looking for?"

"Internet history. Visits to sites, chat rooms or forums that are about the Chesapeake Bay, eighteenth-century sailing, missing artifacts, or treasure hunting."

Her blue eyes widened. "Like pirate treasure?"

"Like evidence, Shana. Also, any emails over the last couple of months, especially to or from either Charles Fox or Wallace Bonnet. Anything with the words treasure, antiquity, discovery." She paused. "Or something about a carving of a bird. I assume even if he cleared his cache—"

Shana rolled her eyes.

"Sorry," Sam said. "I know you can find it."

"That's quite an eclectic list, Lieutenant."

"Should keep it interesting." Sam smiled. She liked this offbeat girl. "How soon can you get me something?"

"Depends on how much reading I have to do. Which means I need to get to work, Lieutenant." She rubbed her hands. "This'll be fun."

Sam left Shana and went back to her desk to schedule appointments to interview both Charles Fox and Wallace Bonnet. She was able to reach Fox's assistant, who told her he was out of town until late Sunday, but she would let him know to expect two Talbot County law officers early Monday morning. No luck with Bonnet. Instead, she reached an answering machine with a wryly cheery voice asking for a succinct and, if possible, witty message.

By the end of the day, she had a report from Shana.

"Mr. Fitchett didn't use email much," Shana told her. "He had quite the internet history, though. Mostly things you already pegged." She handed Sam a neatly bound report. "I was going to transfer everything to you digitally, but I wasn't sure if you preferred, you know, paper."

"Digital is fine, Shana."

At 4:30, Sam popped her head into Donahue's office.

"Seems as if you've had a busy day Lieutenant," he said. "Come in and catch me up."

She did, beginning with the forensic investigator's preliminary findings. She went on to describe the secret display at Arley's place, and ended with the information she collected from Shana and Pat and her plans to interview Fox, Bonnet and half a dozen people who either worked with or drank with Arley Fitchett.

"Only thing we need now is the post-mortem," she concluded. "Not easy to move those along, although our forensic investigator is doing his best."

"I might still have some pull," Donahue said. He looked thoughtful. "You think it's a treasure hunt gone wrong rather than a drug-related murder?"

"I'd prefer to wait until I've gone through more of the evidence. Seems that way, though."

"Uh-huh." Donahue seemed preoccupied. "You're working with Gordy and that kid, right?"

"Yes, sir." She waited for the other shoe to drop.

"Talbot County had just two murders last year. A domestic incident and a low-level dealer who got into it with his supplier. Both cases were pretty straightforward and easily closed by your predecessor. This—" he waved his hand— "is an execution. Not exactly an ordinary homicide. And it comes right in the middle of a surge in drug-related incidents."

"I've worked on cases like these before, Sheriff. It's why you hired me." The words came out more abruptly than she intended.

"Yes. You have extensive homicide experience. So do I and so does Gordy. Tanner Reed worked our side of the block before he moved over to less stressful cases. After that ..." He gave her an expectant look.

"Our bench is shallow."

"It is. Sometimes rural communities and small towns need to bring in other help, use the resources of other agencies. You know what I'm talking about, Lieutenant. You ran into a similar situation back in Tennessee."

"With all due respect, sir, we were after a serial killer who'd operated over six years across several states. And this department is bigger."

Donahue seemed not to have heard her. "We've got good people," he said. "But every homicide comes with pressures, political and otherwise. Cooperation is always seen as a sign of progress."

Especially when D.C. bigwigs are snapping up coveted Eastern Shore property, Sam thought.

"Problems only come up when county sheriffs let their egos get the better of them and insist on taking the lead on cases their departments can't handle," he went on. "I like to think we're a little more flexible than that."

"Are you're calling in the Maryland State Police?"

"I'm not calling in anyone, Sam. This is your case, okay? But consider this. First off, we don't know where Fitchett died. Maybe not in Talbot County. Second, if this is a cartel hit, we're gonna have a whole lotta people up our butts. I don't think having a little cover is a bad thing."

"Sheriff, I get where you're coming from, I really do." Sam eased her way around her words. She wanted to argue, oh, did she ever. She forced herself to sound calm, to feel calm.

"We've been at this less than twelve hours," she continued. "We need a little more time to sort through the evidence, interview the locals, study the autopsy report if we can get it expedited. Obviously, we want to solve this, but let's see if we can stitch it up in-house."

"I'll give you until Monday night." Donahue said with finality.

Sam fought to keep her expression neutral. "Fine."

"Lieutenant, even if I extend an invitation, you'll still be in the driver's seat. Whoever comes in will stay in the background, there when you need them. Kind of a consultant. Strictly standby."

Not a chance, Sam thought.

"Happy for the help," she said.

Chapter 6

White Birch Manor made Sam think of those creepy movies that feature evil doctors and patients in peril. Not that her mother's permanent home, with its spacious grounds, abundant foliage, attractive pathways, and ample benches, earned her discomfort. The privately-run institution was considered the best in Delaware and one of the top ten in the country. Yet visiting always made her uneasy.

Guilt, she knew, mixed with concern for her mother's welfare. Her aunt Gillian had shouldered so much responsibility following the wedding-day shooting that killed Sam's father and brother and made her mother an invalid. Gillian and her late husband had nurtured their niece, had tried to give her a normal life.

And what did Sam do? She left home at eighteen. She changed her name, kept her distance. In the intervening years, she advanced her education, cycled through several careers. She loved her aunt and uncle; she was just trying to obscure the awful memories of the event the destroyed the rest of her family.

When Gillian died, Sam hadn't hesitated to upend her life to take over as her mother's guardian. A settlement from the gunman's relatives paid for the best care possible. Yet the daughter still felt inadequate to the task. The visits to her mother were never less than bittersweet, a persistent reminder of all that had been lost.

She'd shared all of this with Terry even before they'd become a couple. Sam struggled to absorb that notion. The affair still felt new, almost fragile. Though they were geographically closer, their jobs kept them apart more than either of them liked. Terry's career was on the fast track after stalling out for several years. Sam meanwhile tried to adjust to being a smaller fish in a larger pond.

"I want you to meet my mother," she blurted out as they got ready for bed one sticky Saturday evening in Terry's tiny Capitol Hill apartment just a few months earlier. Washington, D.C. was no place to be in the summer, but Terry had meetings all weekend.

"I'd like that," he said. And waited.

"I know you've got a lot on your plate."

"Pick a date, Sam," he said and took both her hands in his. The gesture was old-fashioned and so sweet it made her heart ache.

"I will," she declared even as she fought the desire to walk it all back, not only the invitation but the implied intimacy.

By late September, Terry was swamped. She didn't mention her offer again and neither did he. She didn't want to think what that meant, so she chalked it up to busy schedules and continued her weekly visits to White Birch Manor.

Now that she faced a case she wanted to work and a boss who might doubt her ability to work it, she welcomed his support. There would never be a good time to introduce Terry to her mother, she reasoned. She asked him straight out if he could get away Sunday, and he immediately agreed.

Terry came up the day before, his laptop in tow. They ate in that night; he studied and she went over her notes. McCready had come up with a list of fifteen people with whom Arley Fitchett had some interaction in the last six months. Most of them seemed like passing acquaintances or casual connections. Sam kept coming back to Fox and Bonnet. She felt as if she were spinning her wheels.

Sam rose early on Sunday and spent fifteen minutes on the front porch. Ten sun salutations. Mountain pose. Step back into warrior one. Move to downward dog and then to plank.

Lower down, cobra, push back to downward dog to mountain pose. Same on the other side. Rinse and repeat. She followed the workout with a short run. She returned, feeling virtuous, to find Terry cooking breakfast.

"All you need is a dog," Terry said. "He could join you for yoga—I've seen that on YouTube—then on your run. He could be here when you came home, especially in the dark."

"You're not up to the task?" She tried to sound breezy, offhanded. The last thing Terry deserved was a needy girlfriend. She had the impression his previous love interest had nearly suffocated him.

"More than up to it. But you know that as much as I believe you to be the most accomplished, adaptable woman on the planet, I worry. If this new case involves the cartel—"

"It doesn't," Sam sang out from the other room. She walked into the kitchen clad in jeans and a sweatshirt with a Chesapeake Bay logo. "Besides, I'm badass enough to handle live drug dealers or dead pirates." She walked over and wrapped her arms around him from behind.

He stayed at the stove, his back to her. "Are you still having those bad dreams?" he asked.

She tried for a seductive purr. "Did I keep you up last night?"

"I'm serious, Sam. Like I said, I worry."

She broke her hold and began to set the table herself. Her nightmares persisted, though less frequently than when she had hunted the serial killer back in Tennessee. The dreams manifested as unnamed threats, wedding themed, to be sure, but also familiar tropes in which she failed a class, missed a train, lost her way, or found herself in a dark, close place.

But how do you go back to therapy when your previous psychologist mysteriously disappears and is later shot dead in

59

a parking lot, likely because of something she did or did not figure out about you even before you did?

Terry put down the pan and turned to her, his face grave. "Please don't blow me off about this, Sam. Let me at least get you the name of a therapist."

"Fine. Now can we eat?"

After tucking away a substantial breakfast and enjoying a shower that almost derailed their travel plans, they headed out. They chatted along the way, mostly about Terry's work. He was back with the FBI's Criminal Investigations Division, which primarily handled cases centered on financial, violent, and civil rights or corruption crimes. Mob activity figured prominently in the investigations. The division even partnered with specialized sub-divisions, such as the Art Crimes Team, which handled the criminal side of art and cultural property theft.

"Would Art Crimes hunt down an antique wood carving that went missing three centuries ago?" Sam asked.

"Not unless a legitimate entity like the British government reports it stolen and asks us to help recover it," Terry replied. "Don't get me wrong; antiquities theft is a multi-billion-dollar enterprise. But I'm talking about recently pilfered and catalogued items, not pirate booty from the eighteenth century."

"What if the eye of the bird turned out to be a rare sapphire?"

"That would certainly make it more enticing. Still not our department. Have you contacted the UK government?"

"I've got a call in to someone from the British Museum. I want to start by establishing the veracity of the letters. As a bonus, I'd like to know if there's a record of a wood carving made at the request of Charles Calvert."

"What's your boss say about all this?"

"He'd like to declare it a drug hit and call in the Maryland State Police."

"Ever met someone from MSP? Those guys mean business."

"Yeah, well, so do I," Sam huffed. "I just wish Jake would give me a chance to prove it." She shook her head. "On another topic, any news about Arthur Randolph or the mystery person trying to access files on the old case?" Randolph, the gunman who had killed her father and brother, had died the previous winter just after his release from a psychiatric ward in upstate New York. The cause of death had been ruled as natural.

"None. Which is to say, case closed. His mother isn't returning my calls. Not that I have any business making them."

Terry had learned around the time of Randolph's release that someone had requested to see related case files. He tried to find out who had access to the sealed records. He hit a wall.

"Hard for me to pursue anything without authorization, Sam."

"I know." She patted his hand.

"I'm not giving up. I want to know who's interested in the testimony and I'm more than a little curious about the timing. Why now?"

"Maybe the relative of another victim has finally healed enough to review what happened, get some closure." Sam rubbed the spot between her eyes, trying to ignore the anxiety the conversation caused. She regretted bringing up the subject. She didn't want to dwell on her elusive memories, her buried pain, her hidden pockets of grief. Not when she was on her way to visit the living reminder of all she'd lost.

Terry, ever empathetic, picked up on her distress. "We don't need to hash this out right now," he told her. "We can figure out what kind of dog to get you."

"How about one that can fetch coffee?"

They arrived at White Birch Manor at eleven. A neatly trimmed path led up to a red brick building that managed to look both regal and accommodating at the same time. The main house, they called it. A small building just behind it presumably lodged the onsite staff. Nothing else, no small homes or apartments, no separate facilities for inhabitants wishing to pursue an independent lifestyle within a community. No one lived independently at this facility.

Sam signed in and led Terry down a corridor that smelled pleasantly floral and just short of cloying. Sunlight streamed through clerestory windows. Soothing music played. No blaring TVs or bleeping signals for help, no residents weeping unconsolably or causing a fuss. Not today, not at this hour.

She breathed deeply, fighting nerves. Sam Tate, who'd faced down any number of evil-doers and low-lifes, felt as if she were about to introduce her boyfriend to her parent for the first time. Which she was. She also knew Terry was in for a big surprise.

"Mom," she said as she knocked on the door and gently opened it. "I've come with a special friend. This is Terry."

Her mother sat in a wheelchair, a blue sweater over her shoulders, her face to the window. At their entry, she turned to smile. And, as Sam expected, Terry's mouth fell open, though he quickly recovered.

No one expected to see such a beautiful woman in a place like this. Colleen Murphy Russo, at sixty-six, looked decades younger, more like Sam's older sister than her mother. Her skin was porcelain, unblemished and unlined. Her luminous blue-gray eyes shone as if lit from within. Her lips were soft. Her expression was flat yet relaxed, even pleasant, like a doll Sam once cherished. It was as if time stopped the day she took a bullet to the head.

Colleen's hair was the envy of most of the residents, not to mention the staff. Abundant ginger curls with only a few stray silver threads here and there tumbled to her shoulders. Sometimes a staff member would tie it back with a bright ribbon. When she'd first arrived, a nurse recommended to Gillian that her younger sister's locks should be cut shorter for safety reasons. Gillian put her foot down. The luxurious tresses remained. Colleen enjoyed having them brushed and never lacked for volunteers.

"I can see the resemblance," Terry whispered, smiling at the older woman.

"Really?" Sam pushed back her mahogany curls. She felt an unfamiliar sensation and realized she was blushing.

Terry squatted in front of Sam's mother and took her hand. "I can't tell you how pleased I am to meet you, Mrs. Russo. Sam—Sophia—talks about you all the time."

Sophia. Sam's birth name. It sounded odd coming from Terry. As if he were crossing from her present into her past.

Did her mother smile? Unlikely. Except Sam could have sworn she saw a gleam in those wide eyes.

Terry kept up an easy patter as he pushed Colleen out of doors and up and down the pathways. Sam walked beside them, a bounce to her step. She felt buoyant, as if she'd been freed from jail or granted a reprieve. Or glimpsed a happier possibility.

They stayed another ninety minutes, then chatted with Colleen's doctor, who was there on a rare Sunday visit.

"Your mother is remarkably healthy, all things considered, Lieutenant Tate," he began.

"Sam."

"Of course. Sam. We're continuing physical therapy so that she's able to maintain whatever strength she has, maybe even increase muscle tone. In case she regains upper body motor skills."

Sam raised her eyebrows. "How likely is that? I mean, it's been twenty-six years."

The doctor looked surprised at the question. "The brain has untapped capacity to grow and heal. There are new breakthroughs all the time. We don't give up hope here."

Not when you have customers who pay so well, Sam's inner voice whispered. She instantly chastised herself. They were all doing what they could.

As they made ready to leave, the nurse stopped them. "Your mother's become a bit agitated, which is unlike her. I wouldn't normally advise this, but maybe you could stick your heads back in there, just for a minute."

"Sure," Terry said.

Colleen was sitting upright, her face slightly flushed and turned away from the nurse who was trying to feed her.

"Mom, you okay?" Sam squatted down beside the wheelchair. "You want me to get you something else? Or I could eat with you."

Colleen raised a hand to Sam's face. This time she definitely smiled. The gesture was so unexpected that Sam almost fell back onto the floor. She laid her hand gently on her mother's.

Colleen Russo stared at Terry, who'd come to stand beside her. Her eyes cleared, her expression became determined. She grabbed Terry's hand and squeezed until he flinched. In a low voice no one remembered hearing for years, she spoke two words.

"Find him." Then she turned her head and looked out the window.

Chapter 7

Charles Fox sat at his polished oak desk in a sunlit room that overlooked a leafy enclave off Main Street. His office was on the first floor of a well-maintained Victorian. He'd avoided most people's penchant for stuffing those sorts of rooms with antiques of various provenances. He'd restored the elaborate molding and the wall sconces, replaced the windows, and covered them with clever shades that allowed him to view out while keeping prying eyes from looking in. He'd brought the fireplace back to working condition, painted the walls in creamy beige, added a high-end Oriental rug, and chosen a few timeless, well-crafted pieces of furniture with good lines. The room conveyed taste and wealth in equal measure.

Fox splayed his soft pink hands across the photographs of a different set of rooms, all of them crammed with the contents of a lifetime: lamps, rugs, tables, chairs, settees, fixtures, paintings, vases. Certain items, like the exquisite gemstone necklace or the perfectly preserved mink coat, had been separately photographed. His laptop sat to the left of the images, the list of sellable items divided between those appraised and those which had yet to be appraised.

The Reynolds estate was one of the last of its kind and considered one of the most valuable. The name was associated with a Maryland dynasty dating back to the mid-seventeenth century. The house had been in the family for two hundred years, but the current generation had no interest in genealogy or history, only in present-day prosperity. Fox already knew some of the items would bring millions at auction, which would boost his already substantial fee that much higher. He should have been elated. He didn't care about any of it.

He feared he'd lost an opportunity that couldn't be measured in mere dollars, although those would have been considerable. How he'd yearned for the chance to enhance his reputation, boost his capital, so to speak. No longer forced to paw over and assign value to the mildewed possessions of the dead so that the living could throw them aside. No longer required to live in this backwater town where stagnant old money met politically-inclined new money, and culture consisted of lectures about wildfowl migration or the history of oyster fishing.

Once within his reach and now lost forever. Unless—

The discreet knock at the door interrupted his train of thought. The comely young woman he'd just hired popped her fair head inside.

"What?" he demanded, unable to keep the irritation out of his voice.

"A Lieutenant Tate and Detective Gordy are here to see you. I made the appointment yesterday after speaking with you."

"Yes, yes, I remember. Give me a minute, then show them in." As she closed the door, he ran a hand through his thinning sandy hair and swept the images on his desk into a manila folder he put to one side. He hoisted his bulk out of his chair and endeavored to arrange his features into a pleasant expression.

The two neatly-dressed officers who entered were more attractive than he expected. The man was lean and watchful with heavy eyebrows, thin lips, and a sooty stare. The woman, dressed in blazer and slacks like her counterpart, was also eye-catching, not conventionally beautiful but almost exotic, with her strong features and abundant dark hair. Her remarkable eyes—green shaded with gray—gleamed like twin lanterns above her prominent cheekbones.

She stepped forward, her hand outstretched. "Dr. Fox," she began, "I'm Lieutenant Samantha Tate, Criminal Commander with Talbot County Sheriff's Office. This is Detective Bruce Gordy. Thank you for seeing us on such short notice." She spoke softly, with just a whisper of an accent that suggested Appalachia.

For his part, Fox made a point of projecting professional assurance. "I'm always happy to help. Can I get you some coffee or water?"

The two officers declined. Fox waved them into a pair of leather armchairs, settled himself behind his desk, folded his hands, and attempted to smile. He looked from one to another. "Criminal Command. Sounds ominous."

"Homicide usually is," Lieutenant Tate replied.

Fox's eyes widened. "Someone was murdered?"

"Arley Fitchett." She was watching him like a hawk.

"Arley Fitchett? When? How? For God's sake, why?"

Gordy and Tate exchanged a look. "I suppose it will be in the papers soon enough," the man said. "Arley Fitchett was strangled with a thin wire. Garroted. His hands were badly burned. He was tossed into the bay."

Fox realized they were both studying him to see how he might react. His shock was real, though. He sipped from his cup of cold coffee to steady his nerves.

"What a violent way to die. Not the kind of thing one associates with our part of the world. Who kills like that? Assassins? Mobsters? Drug lords?"

"That's what we're investigating," Gordy replied. "You knew Mr. Fitchett."

"Everyone in Easton knew Arley Fitchett."

"But you two were communicating over the last few months, according to phone records. Your assistant told us he came to your office at least once."

Fox made a show of thinking. "Now that I recall—"

Tate cut him off. "What is it you do, Mr. Fox?" She looked around the office.

"I'm an appraiser for high-end residential estates. There are a number of houses that come on the market when their owners die that contain pieces of some value."

"Paintings, jewelry, rare books, those sorts of things?"

"Exactly."

She nodded agreeably. "Interesting career path you've taken. You have a PhD in early American history, don't you? Didn't you try teaching?"

"I see you've studied up on me. Believe it or not, Lieutenant, I find dealing with even the most avaricious family members easier than coddling students or competing with faculty. This line of work pays better."

Gordy looked down at his notepad. "You and Mr. Fitchett talked or met several times, correct?"

Fox decided to be forthright. "Arley sought me out several months ago because he wanted me to appraise and help him sell a group of letters he believed had historical value. They were purportedly written by the first cousin of the fifth Lord Baltimore. The man was traveling aboard a ship bound for Annapolis when it disappeared in 1718. I told Arley that as soon as he had all the letters in hand, I would take a look. He said he was working on it."

"We found two letters at Mr. Fitchett's home that might be several hundred years old, along with photocopies of other letters." Gordy said. "They read almost like a diary of a sea voyage."

Fox considered. "Interesting. I would love to see those. Assuming they're real, they constitute a living record of the times. A private collector, a museum, or a university might be willing to pay quite handsomely. As I said, I offered to act as broker. What happens to them, by the way?"

"They're evidence in a murder investigation," the detective answered. "They'll probably be claimed by the British government."

"The later correspondence mentioned a particular object that the author considered valuable," Tate said. She fixed her startling green eyes on him.

Fox shifted in his chair. "If by valuable, you mean something to be traded, it's quite possible the ship carried such things for the purpose of barter."

"What about a carving, meant as a gift?" Gordy laid a photocopy of a sketch in front of Fox.

The appraiser looked at it. His breath caught in his throat. He was aware the two law officers stared at him, measuring his reaction. With some effort, he assumed a puzzled expression and made himself push the copy back across the desk. "A drawing, quite old, I should guess. Bird in Hand. What is its significance?"

"Fitchett had it in his possession. Does it seem familiar?"

"Now that you mention it, it does. The fable of Bird in Hand is well known to some of us whose studies focus on this region. According to the legend, it was stolen by pirates who made their way to the Chesapeake Bay and hid it somewhere. There's absolutely no evidence anything of the sort ever happened, but that hasn't stopped amateurs from splashing through the marshlands along the shoreline, absolutely certain that every Spanish coin they turn up puts them one step closer to buried treasure. This is the first time I've ever seen it rendered, though."

He made a show of studying the sketch more carefully, then looked up. "Please tell me Arley Fitchett didn't lose his life in pursuit of a fiction," he said. "The man seemed more rational than that."

"Is it conceivable such a piece existed?" Tate asked.

Fox sat back in his chair and folded his arms. "Many royal woodworkers were skilled artisans who benefitted from the largesse of the court, Lieutenant. An adroit practitioner might have had talents in related arts, such as drawing or painting. He might have made furniture, molding, or toys for the royal children. Or one-of-a-kind gifts for various friends of the court."

"Did Arley Fitchett mention working with other people, Mr. Fox? Partners, benefactors?" Gordy again, still taking notes.

"He did not. Obviously, I asked him how he came to own the letters. Arley told me an acquaintance of his had come across the correspondence at an estate sale in Surrey over in the UK. The man, knowing of Arley's passion for the history and lore of the area, offered to sell the lot to him for a substantial fee. All this is second-hand, you understand. I never got the name of the English connection, let alone spoke to him. Nor do I have any idea how Arley intended to finance such a purchase."

"You didn't see the letters?"

"I was waiting until he had the entire collection. I certainly didn't realize he was hunting for some sort of antique."

"Do you know if the artist Wallace Bonnet had business or personal dealings with Mr. Fitchett?" Tate asked. "Perhaps they discussed the carving?"

"Bonnet?" Fox said with a dismissive wave. "Please. The man scarcely rises to the level of carpenter, let alone artist. He's made some halfway decent tables and chairs on consignment and a number of those hideous duck decoys the tourists and opportunistic shopkeepers insist on calling folk art. He also has an enviable multi-million-dollar property complete with a separate studio in St. Michaels and an exhibit opening in town next week. I would guess his father's considerable wealth underpins his so-called career. I hope he wasn't the one who put Arley up to this foolish quest."

Samantha Tate stood up in one fluid move. "I want to thank you for your time, Mr. Fox. We've learned quite a bit today." She reached for the sketch.

"Do you think you might leave the drawing? I might be able to ascertain its historical accuracy."

Samantha Tate smiled. "Of course. We've made copies."

Fox accompanied them to the door and gave them each a hearty handshake. As soon as they exited, he rushed back to his desk and fell into his chair, breathing heavily and staring at the sketch. His fear over Fitchett's manner of death gave way to a sense of elation. The man proved to be intrepid but also foolish. Probably made promises to the wrong people. Fox would not make that mistake. He had knowledge and resources. He simply had to reach the London buyer, whose name Fitchett had helpfully supplied. Or maybe he could find another way to get his hands on the rest of the letters. Then on to the item itself. He had to move quickly. At least he knew what to look for.

Dear Teresa,

I feel as if the very fact of my last letter has brought a Curse upon this ship (although I do not believe in such things). We are becalmed. Having forsaken the unpredictable headwinds for a more southerly course, we now find the wind that had powered our sails these two weeks quite disappeared off the face of the Earth. 'Tis but our fourth day, not yet cause for great concern. Even after a relatively short time, though, I can see its effect upon the men.

The captain and first and second mates are huddled below deck, examining charts and deciding what recourse may be available to us. I do not know what is to be done except to trust to Our Lord and the skills of our most able crew.

As I have even more time than usual, having been deprived of my opportunity to watch the men at work, I have decided to examine the gift I bear. I must do so with utmost discretion, as I am charged by my cousin with delivering it in person to its future owner without bringing undue attention to either the piece or its intended recipient.

The piece is a carving commissioned by Lord Baltimore and executed by the Royal Court Woodworker, a Mr. Grinling Gibbons. I should not have imagined that a piece of wood, however artfully molded, could change the dynamics of a political or personal relationship. But as I have learned, my cousin has developed his own approach to the art of trading favours and securing alliances.

Having cast mine own eyes upon the piece in question, I daresay it commands the power to bring to heel anyone into whose possession it falls. I took the liberty to show it to Dr. Bell. That gentleman insists it is unlike anything any English artist has hitherto been inspired to create.

Not being inclined towards the Arts, I cannot vouchsafe that observation. Nor am I acquainted with other works created by Mr. Gibbons. Yet even to my untested eye, this Bird is a singular piece. I trust my efforts to describe it will meet your more refined standards.

A small bird rests within the palm of an outstretched hand that appears to belong to a young woman. The bird is delicately rendered, life-like and yet not ornate. A few deft cuts indicate a wing here, a beak there. The simple lines suggest a degree of life I would not have believed possible in an inanimate object, as if the bird might take flight at any moment.

The figure has been wrought from an exotic wood, deep brown in colour with a touch of red and a subtly varied grain that give it further depth. Doctor Bell has identified it as sapele, a sort of mahogany found in the East German African colonies. Although I cannot fathom how he knows this, I am learning that Thaddeus Bell is in possession of a great many facts as well as countless theories.

Mr. Gibbons has created but a single eye so piercing one feels one is being watched by a wild animal. The brightness of the orb is enhanced by the use of an impressive gemstone of deep penetrating blue. Captain Digg, whom I confess has also seen the item, has identified it as a rare sapphire from the northern part of India.

The carving is housed within a closed cage made of a reddish metal and fitted with a lock whose key I keep on my person at all times. It cannot otherwise be opened. A fine silk cloth covers the cage, in order to give the illusion of transporting a live creature.

All in all, a most remarkable, not to say extravagant, gift that speaks of profound gratitude. Governor Hart deserves no less. He has been stalwart in supporting our family when others have vowed harm to the Calverts, and his loyalty has not gone unnoticed.

As I write this, I sense upon my neck the faintest stirring of air. It may be my imagination at work. One can only hope.

I think of you constantly. Until my return, I hope my words may provide some amusement.

Your loving fiancé,
William

Chapter 8

She dreamed of a man with a black beard dressed in a brown suit who stood on the foredeck of a huge frigate lined with cannons. In one hand, he held a semi-automatic pistol, in the other, an old coin.

"Choose," he commanded above the roaring of the wind.

"No!" Sam yelled and bolted out of bed. She stood shivering in the cold damp air that made its way in via the old cottage's leaky seams. She normally loved being near the water, loved waking to the briny smell of the bay and the plaintive cries of the waterfowl. Sometimes, though, when the fog descended, she felt closed in, held down, cut off.

She flipped on the lights, yanked on a sweatshirt and her well-worn Nikes, and forced herself out for a run, her mind in hyper-drive.

The interview with Fox left her with more questions than answers. She felt certain he was keeping something from her. He had more than a passing interest in the drawing, to begin with. Perhaps his interest lay beyond the letters Arley offered him.

What was the likely fate of a small wooden carving on board a missing ship? Pummeled by the elements? Buried by sand, silt, and shells? Broken apart, its gemstone lost, or found and sold? But what if it had made it off the ship and ended up in the hands of its intended recipient? Or what if it had been seized by bandits and hidden in a cove or sold to the highest bidder? What if it survived, tucked away in an attic or displayed on the mantle of the latest unsuspecting owner?

Too many *what ifs*.

Wasn't that just what motivated true believers? The what ifs, the might haves, the impossible dreams. It didn't matter if

Bird in Hand existed, only that one or more people thought it did, beginning with Arley Fitchett.

She headed into work and was surprised to bump into Martin Lloyd on his way out of the building. It was not yet eight o'clock.

"Are there any dead bodies I should know about, Mr. Lloyd?" she asked with a smile. She wasn't surprised to see the tall man blush.

"No, nothing like that. I was just, uh, dropping off ..." He stopped, flummoxed.

"I'm sure CSI Davidson appreciates the ride," Sam offered.

"Yes, well, I've got to get up to Baltimore." Lloyd regained his composure. "Nice to see you, Lieutenant Tate."

Armed with her first coffee of the day, Sam reviewed her to-do list. She first called her contact at the British Museum, a young woman named Rita Khatri.

"Any word on when you might get those letters to us?" she asked "The pictures look promising."

"They're still a part of our murder investigation, but I will make sure you get them when we close the case."

"Hope it's soon," Khatri said. "We rarely get our hands on historical correspondence these days, especially anything that predates the mid-eighteenth century. British ships weren't required to keep official logs until a century after that. I'm afraid a lot of anecdotal records, diaries, letters, and such are in the hands of private collectors."

"I appreciate your interest," Sam told her.

Khatri laughed. "Oh, I haven't given up, Lieutenant. I would very much like to know the fate of the unfortunate little ship that attempted to sail to the New World."

Sam thanked the woman and hung up. She tried to quell her frustration. After all, she wasn't in the business of learning the fate of the elusive ship or its even more elusive treasure, except insofar as it helped identify poor Arley Fitchett's killer.

She looked up, startled by the sound of a knock. A quick glance at her watch told her four hours had passed.

"You were somewhere else," Betty observed.

"Sorry, just working the case. Guess you didn't knock just to remind me to get lunch. What's up?"

"Sheriff has a visitor he wants you to meet." Betty cocked her head in the direction of Donahue's office.

"That sounds a little ominous," Sam said, pushing back from her desk.

"I'm just the messenger."

"Lieutenant Tate," the sheriff said as Sam hesitated at his door. "Come on in." His smile seemed unnaturally wide. "I'd like you to meet Detective Sergeant Francis Weller from the Maryland State Police's Criminal Investigative Bureau."

She stuck out her hand. "Hello, Detective Sergeant Weller."

He hesitated a bare second as if to appraise her before offering up a firm handshake. If her powerful grip surprised him, he showed no sign of it.

"Call me Frank, Lieutenant Tate. Or Weller."

Donahue had stressed the word *detective*. Instead of the military-style uniform Sam knew was typical of MSP, the investigator wore a well-cut navy jacket, a subdued tie, and pressed gray slacks. He appeared to be somewhere in his mid-forties, about Sam's height, muscled through his upper body like a boxer. His light brown hair was shot through with gray and numerous fine lines spread out from the corners of his wary brown eyes. The strong jaw might have appealed to some women. Sam couldn't get past his scowl.

"Sam or Tate is fine," Sam said.

"Sam Tate. Should be easy to remember one or both of those names."

Donahue slapped Weller on the shoulder. "Frank joined MSP about six years behind me."

"And moved through the ranks a lot more slowly," Weller replied. Sam caught the edge in his tone and looked at him more closely.

Donahue laughed. "Well, they finally kicked you part way upstairs, didn't they? The man is a first-rate investigator, Sam. It's just taking the brass a long time to realize it."

"Something about following direction," Weller replied. The men laughed, sharing what was obviously an inside joke.

"At least the CIB—that's their Criminal Investigative Bureau, Sam—gives you some juicy assignments, Frank. How did we get so lucky?"

Weller smiled. "I figure you called in some favors. They remember you fondly over at MSP."

Sam bit her tongue so hard she had to keep herself from crying out. The back and forth male banter did not inspire confidence. She felt left out, pushed to the side.

"Tell me, Frank," she began, more brightly than she intended, "what brings you over here?"

Donahue cleared his throat. "Frank has a lot of homicide experience, Lieutenant. He's also very familiar with cartel operations in and around our neck of the woods. I thought it might help to have him as a sort of observer, add his expertise and knowledge while we sort out jurisdiction."

"Jurisdiction? It's a local homicide investigation." The words were out before she'd fully considered them; she only hoped it didn't sound like a protest. "Besides, we don't yet know if it's—"

"A homicide, Lieutenant Tate?" Weller cut in. "Or is it motive that's got you stumped? Either way, if you know something I don't, maybe we can wrap this up quickly and get back to other business. Unless you think it's a serial killer. I understand you have some experience with that, even had one working as your assistant back in Tennessee, was it?"

"Frank," Donahue warned.

Sam eyed the investigator. "You're right Detective Sergeant. Kaylee Simpson was on staff when I was sheriff of Pickett County. Until we took her down along with her son and ended a six-year killing spree that extended across three states. You might also know I was previously a Nashville detective with one of the highest close rates in the homicide department."

She gave him a tight smile. "As for any information or working theories I have, I'm happy to share all of it with you once we set up the task force. I imagine you have some familiarity with how those work. Lots of cooperation involved."

She sounded matter-of-fact, even pleasant. Nevertheless, she figured her words had an effect. She saw Weller wince.

"Clearly, there's a lot of experience represented in this room," Donahue interjected. "Apparently, there's also a decent amount of ego. So, here's how it's going to work. Tate, you will run the investigation for now. Weller is here as an advisor, one with a lot to offer." He gave Sam a pointed look, then transferred his gaze to Weller.

"The case technically belongs to this office," he continued. "However, we are using the full resources of the Maryland State Police. I don't give a damn about politics or PR, but I do want to reassure the people of my county. This homicide could be local or something larger. Whatever we do, we won't call in the FBI. They couldn't find their—well, Frank knows how I feel. No offense to your friend, Sam."

"None taken." *Had she told him about Terry?* she wondered.

"Lieutenant Tate's got a detective with a background in homicide investigations, along with a young deputy who knows everything there is to know about Easton."

Weller looked skeptical.

"Arley was something of a local legend," Donahue explained. "As the lieutenant reminded me."

"I see."

Down to two words and still snide, Sam thought.

"Frank, you do whatever you need from your side, but keep the lieutenant in the loop at all times, okay? I'll stay in touch with your commander, but for now, information on the investigation comes to me. If this is a one-off in Talbot County, I want to know. If something else is going on, I still want to know about it. Again, Tate here is team leader. We clear?"

"Yes, sir," Weller replied. Sam marveled that a county sheriff could command such respect from a senior investigator with the mighty Maryland State Police. Then she remembered Donahue had been an MSP statewide CIB commander before coming over to Talbot County. Weller clearly appreciated the chain of command, even if he couldn't find a place in it.

They walked out at the same time. Sam pondered what she should say. She wasn't about to apologize for his hurt feelings about playing second fiddle to a county lieutenant, assuming he had any. Still, if the sheriff had picked up tension, she bore some responsibility.

"Look, Detective Sergeant—"

"I need something to eat. Grab your people and a conference room and we'll start in an hour." Weller headed for the door.

"You want to meet today?"

He stopped, turned. "You don't?"

"Detective Gordy and I have just begun interviewing people of interest. We need to go over our notes. Besides, I doubt your people can get here that fast."

He looked at her, his expression a mask. "I don't need people here, Tate. Yours will do just fine." He made a show of looking at his watch. "Are we doing this?"

Does not play well with others, Sam thought. She felt backed into a corner. It didn't suit her.

She took a breath, forced another smile. "Tell you what, Detective Sergeant. I imagine you have a lot of other cases you're working on. Why don't you head back to your office and let *my* people finish their assignments? I'll pull everything together over the next few days. Then we'll meet first thing Monday. Let's say eight o'clock. I hope that works for you, what with Bay Bridge traffic and all."

She turned on her heel without waiting for his response. She was none too pleased with her reaction to Weller. She'd run into his kind plenty of times, men resentful of the powerful women with whom they had to work. She'd learned over the years to stand up for herself without revealing how pissed off such men made her. Losing her temper could leave her with a reputation as a bitch. Unfair, but true.

Nor did it matter that the man might have a chip on his shoulder. Clearly, he had his own problems with command. Maybe his lack of advancement rankled him. She could tell him a thing or two about accepting setbacks, not that she wanted to. She simply didn't want his sour attitude to affect the team's work—or her own.

Chapter 9

Terry Sloan lifted his arms to stretch, narrowly missing the cold coffee that sat at his left hand. He yawned expansively. Jesus, what time was it? He squinted at the clock on his computer screen. 1:15 in the morning. AM, also written a.m., am, or even A.M., although his schoolteacher mother would have screeched at that usage. Ante meridiem or "before midday." How many people knew that? How many people cared?

And don't you have far better things to think about, Sloan?

He yawned again and stood up, carrying the cup and a carton of whatever he'd had for dinner to the kitchen. The window over the sink had the best view, a picture-perfect shot of the Capitol. Despite his exhaustion, he paused to admire the domed building. Within its sturdy walls, the business of democracy was presumably conducted. There were days he wondered how resilient the structure or the democracy it represented really were. Not too many, though; not helpful in his line of work.

Late night was his only opportunity to deal with anything unrelated to work and school. He'd been swamped with both, especially on the heels of his move back from Tampa. For the moment, he worked as a supervisory special agent within the Criminal Investigative Division, a job he relished. The Master's Degree in Criminal Justice he'd earn in eighteen months would lift him into the ranks of the Bureau's executive positions. Less field work, sure. Possibly more politics. But something approaching normal working hours.

Was he ready for it? He would turn thirty-nine next month. Still young enough to start a life. Start a family. He'd mourned his wife and unborn son for more than seven years. Time to move ahead.

With Sam? He wanted that; he really did. Did she? He thought she might, but he couldn't be sure. She'd lost her family as a child. Changed her name, served her country, forged a career as a homicide detective turned sheriff. Hell, she'd lost her fiancé in a car crash. She seemed to process personal pain by ignoring it. Was someone who tried to hide her past from herself as well as others ready to make a commitment to the future?

The problem with the past, Terry had learned, is that it never stayed there. Quite apart from residual trauma, something specific nagged at Sam. Something that continually made its presence known but not its content. A particular memory lodged in her subconscious that might represent an unresolved issue or a dangerous piece of information.

The suspicious deaths of both Sam's former therapist and Arthur Randolph worried Terry as well. So did the as-yet undiscovered identity of the person looking at the sealed courtroom transcripts of a case that should have been closed for good.

And what were they to make of her mother's urgent, if cryptic demand to "find him." Find who? What did Colleen Russo recall from deep within the recesses of her damaged mind?

He moved back to the computer, staring with scratchy eyes at the notes he'd typed up. Twelve people stood on the rose-petal-strewn dais the day of Sam's brother's wedding. Randolph had gunned down all but four with his efficient German-made pistol. Two of the survivors had subsequently died. The bride-to-be, Nicole Wozniak, testified at Randolph's trial. Two years later, she overdosed. A groomsman, Don Platt, also gave testimony. He hanged himself within the month.

Terry winced, caught himself rubbing his forehead in an unconscious imitation of Sam.

That left two. Sophia, as Sam was once called, had been the youngest member of the wedding party at age nine. She gave her testimony in a closed session with only the judge, her aunt and uncle, and a court-appointed child psychologist present. After that, she refused to talk for a year.

Wyn O'Brien, the best man, was twenty-one when he disappeared just before the trial. Born Winifred, he'd self-identified as male from an early age. Both Sophia and the young man had clearly been traumatized by the events of the day. Yet they might be the only two who, with their unique vantage points, would have seen everything.

Back to the computer, where he had an array of files open concerning "the wedding massacre," as the news media had dubbed the incident. Ballistics, witness statements, even autopsy reports.

Everyone assumed Randolph acted alone. What if that weren't true? His mother indicated the troubled man always insisted he was not solely to blame, as if someone else shared responsibility for his heinous actions. But who? And why? Had one of the guests been targeted? Maybe the cousin, Johnny, who Sam described as a "bad boy" type. Would a hitman choose a crowded ceremony as a perfect place to assassinate his victim? Would he partner with or recruit an emotionally unstable man to create a distraction? Terry couldn't wrap his sleep-deprived brain around the idea.

One thing was certain. Wyn O'Brien may have known more than anyone ever considered. Which meant Terry had an important task to add to his list: He had to find the best man and find out what he'd seen.

Chapter 10

Sam got in early to set up the conference room. Donuts, coffee, and six handouts, just in case. She'd asked Bruce Gordy and Pat McCready to the team meeting. At this point, she had no idea if Weller would show up alone. Maybe he'd want to bring his own people after all, add to his side of the table.

Thinking in terms of "his" and "her" sides of the table wasn't the way to foster teamwork. She knew that. Weller seemed to bring out her less-than-cooperative spirit.

McCready and Gordy arrived at 7:45 and headed for the food. Gordy had dressed in a variation of his standard attire, blue denim shirt and brown leather jacket. He looked around, his pewter eyes alert.

"Who are we waiting for?"

Sam poured herself a cup of coffee. "Frank Weller from the Maryland State Police."

Gordy's eyebrows shot up. "Weller? The guy's a legend. Unbelievable close rate. Talk about a first-rate detective. Serious problems with authority, though. For anyone else in MSP, that would have been the end of it. He's that good. Is he still a detective?"

"Detective Sergeant, apparently."

Gordy smiled. "He finally got promoted after twenty years. What do you know?"

Sam was curious in spite of herself. "Does he have family?"

"All gone. Older brother was killed in Iraq. Younger sister overdosed on meth. The parents checked out shortly thereafter."

"That's rough. So, not married."

"Twice, actually. One ended in death, one in divorce. His kid died just after birth of some rare heart condition. The guy's had enough hardship to fill a novel."

"That explains it," Sam said, half to herself.

"Explains what, Lieutenant Tate?" Frank Weller had entered the room at eight o'clock precisely. Sam wondered if he'd stood outside the door in order to time it perfectly. He looked pulled together, clean-shaven and almost dapper in an olive blazer and gold tie. Obviously, he cared about the impression he made. He still wore a glower, though.

"Good morning, Detective Sergeant Weller. And you've brought another associate, I see. Whoops, no, you've brought two." *Way to even the odds*, she thought.

A compactly-built man with dark eyes and thick hair stood beside Weller. His denim shirt, gray vest, pressed slacks, and square black-framed glasses suggested an eager-to-please graduate student. He tucked his tablet under one arm and extended a hand.

"Tyler Caine," he introduced himself with an engaging grin. "I'm with the Maryland State Police's Forensic Sciences Division. Just here to observe, see if I can be of help."

"Tyler is one of our top forensics guys," Weller put in. He reached behind to wave forward a slight young woman with short streaked hair, a deep blue blazer over a white tank top, and what appeared to be expensive mid-heeled boots. On second thought, not so young. The hard expression suggested she was closer to Sam's age.

The woman stuck out her hand to pump Sam's once and dropped her arm back down to her side. "Sarah Pollack," she said. "CIB investigator. I work with Detective Sergeant Weller."

Seems Weller did have people. Or maybe he'd taken on a protégée. One who admired or worse, mirrored, his brusque style. At least Tyler Caine seemed slightly more pleasant.

"Welcome aboard," Sam replied. She made sure to smile. "If no one else is coming, we can get started. To begin with, I've just learned that Arley Fitchett's autopsy has been scheduled for next week. I understand that's nothing short of a miracle."

"I heard yesterday from my commander," Weller said. "Someone in the state government probably helped speed things up."

Sam felt her temperature rise. She'd only found out this morning, just before the meeting.

"I'd guess there are a couple of heavy-hitters in D.C. who want to know what we're dealing with as well," Weller continued. "No one likes the idea that the cartel is invading the Eastern Shore, especially not the politicians with expensive vacation homes out here."

Was he deliberately trying to irritate her? Otherwise, why push the cartel theory right off the bat?

"Is it really that busy at the ME's office?" McCready asked.

"The backlog is worse than you can imagine," Weller told him.

McCready looked at Sam. "I'd like to observe the autopsy, Lieutenant."

Before she had a chance to respond, Weller jumped in. "It won't be necessary, Deputy. It's not like in the movies where the detectives stand in the examination room and hover over the body. We won't even be in the autopsy suite. We can send Caine up to observe. He's in tight with the OCME and he knows the drill. You okay with that, Lieutenant?"

Sam dug her nails into her hand. *Play nice*, she reminded herself. "We're all one team, Detective Sergeant," she replied.

"Do we know who's handling the autopsy?" Gordy asked.

Sam consulted her notes. "Bakir Turabi. Do you know him?"

Gordy nodded. "Turtle. Yeah, I remember him from my time with Baltimore PD. We called him that not because he's slow—far from it—but because the only time he came out of his shell was when the subject was forensic autopsies. He's top-notch, Lieutenant."

"Good to know." She didn't look at Weller. "Let's move along, then."

Caine thumbed through the report with undisguised enthusiasm. "I'm very curious about this evidence board you uncovered," he said. "And I understand there's a gold coin from the eighteenth century found in the victim's pocket. Is that something the cartel would leave behind?"

"Might be a way to signal that they knew all about their victim," Pollack suggested.

"Maybe," Weller replied. "It seems as if some folks inside this department believe Mr. Fitchett was murdered by pirates."

Pollack laughed. McCready flushed. Sam had a retort ready, but Gordy got there first.

"What we believe, Detective Sergeant, is that actual evidence is a good place to begin. Or maybe the Maryland State Police Department has a different approach these days?"

Sam appreciated Gordy's barbed response. However, she was charged with keeping the peace, even if she felt like tossing out her own sharp-tongued rejoinder.

"Why don't we go through what Detective Gordy and CSI Davidson have collected and what Deputy McCready and Specialist Shana Pierce have pulled together about our victim?" she said. "We should be able to at least establish a working theory concerning manner of death and then zero in on determining our perpetrator's motive."

Sam had already reviewed Shana's notes. Fitchett had visited websites related to Chesapeake Bay history. He'd downloaded several documents detailing currents and tides at different times of the year. Some of them dated back more than three hundred years. He had an email from the Easton Public Library about an overdue book on the history of Maryland and another about a book on eighteenth-century art. He'd also spent some time online looking at fine art auction houses and eBay.

"Pricing the market," Weller observed. "Hoping to sell something. Makes sense if he needed the money to support his habit."

Sam ignored him. "I'm going to ask Deputy McCready to summarize what he wrote up about Mr. Fitchett. You have a copy of his report in front of you as well."

"Arley Fitchett was seen around town as a hard worker," McCready began. "He did a lot of odd jobs, mostly as a tour guide and off-season work at the fishery. Sometimes he'd sign up to be part of a team that hunted for old wrecks or treasure at the bottom of the sea. Went all around the world. He was a friendly guy, liked to talk and drink, although he didn't give much away. He was very serious about treasure-hunting. He even belonged to the Maryland Free-State Treasure Club, but it was more like an honorary membership. They're mostly weekend hobbyists. Arley aimed higher."

"Thank you, Deputy," Sam said. "I'm sure we'll circle back to you. Detective Gordy and CSI Davidson went to the victim's house. I'll let him summarize."

"The same day as the body was found, we entered the house Arley Fitchett had been renting in Easton. The evidence—" he glanced at Weller— "indicated someone may have entered the premises to search for something. Items were out of place, we found an outline of a footprint in the rug that didn't belong to Fitchett. But the real excitement was in the back."

Gordy summarized what they discovered in the shed behind the house. "The materials we located at Fitchett's place suggest he was looking for a particular piece of art," he said. "A wooden carving of a bird. It may have been aboard a ship bound for Annapolis in 1718."

"What happened to it?" Caine asked.

"We don't know," Gordy replied. "Fitchett had collected correspondence that was supposed to be from someone onboard the ship. Problem is, the letters are photocopies, except the first two, which need to be authenticated. Fitchett was in touch with Charles Fox, a local appraiser, about reselling the originals as soon as Fitchett could procure them from his London contact."

"Wait a minute." Pollack put up her hand. "You're saying Fitchett had a lead on a set of old letters that might point to the existence of this valuable carving he was looking for." Pollack shook her head. "I can see a historian getting excited about that but not too many other people. I mean, who knows whether the piece of art or whatever even exists?"

"Fox knew about the carving, Bird in Hand," Sam said. "Called it a tall tale, but he couldn't hide his interest in it. Fitchett was also in communication with Wallace Bonnet, a local artist and sculptor with a big show coming up. We don't yet know how that ties in."

"You think someone else besides Fitchett was obsessed with a three-hundred-year-old piece of wood? Someone willing to murder him?" Pollack snorted. "That's seriously far-fetched."

Gordy bristled. "Listen, Detective Pollack," he began.

"What about Fitchett's bank account?" Weller interrupted. Everyone turned to look at him.

"He had one, at Shore United," McCready replied. "His account shows an average amount of activity. Small deposits, except for $31,000 he got from the treasure-hunting crew that went over to Africa for a couple months." McCready looked at Gordy. "Everybody'd heard about that trip. Anyway, no surprises."

"How much cash did you find at the house?" Weller persisted.

Gordy stared at Weller. "A couple of thousand, why?"

"Don't get me wrong, folks. The history lesson is fascinating. But let's stick with the present day, shall we? A couple of thousand might be enough for a score. Not sure it would finance letters that doubled as treasure maps. Not that I know what those things are going for. And why was the cash kept with the drug kit that you mentioned—" he made a show of paging through the papers in front of him— "you found in the kitchen of the house. Did Mr. Fitchett have a history with drugs?"

"Nothing recent," McCready interjected. "A little dabbling in high school. Apparently, he cleaned up when he joined the merchant marines."

"Apparently," Weller murmured.

"We've already established that someone was in the house after Fitchett died," Gordy added. "We think the drug stuff was planted as a misdirect to make us think the cartel is involved."

"Really?" Weller loaded the word with disbelief. "Are you also suggesting that Mr. Fitchett's execution by wire was an elaborate ruse designed to fool the unsuspecting police into assuming drugs are somehow involved? Because I'd like to see the evidence to support that theory, Detective Gordy."

Sam put up her hand. "If we've caught everyone up to date, let's go back and see if we can agree on the timeline. Then we can decide how to proceed."

By the time the meeting ended ninety minutes later, Sam realized Weller hadn't budged from his assumption that Fitchett's death was connected to the Sinaloa cartel. The victim, in his view, either used drugs, dealt drugs, or borrowed money from the organization. He owed, he didn't pay, he was made into an example.

Weller's intransigence disappointed Sam. Regardless of her distaste for his style, she figured him for a smart investigator. No one was asking him to believe in buried treasure or even the existence of a three-hundred-year-old artifact hidden somewhere on the Eastern Shore. But what if Fitchett and a handful of others were convinced the stories were true? What if they were willing to search for it, pay for it, or kill for it? Would she be able to persuade Weller to consider a less straightforward set of circumstances, even if those complicated the case?

Chapter 11

The meeting rankled Sam over the next week, try as she might to pretend otherwise. Even more obvious was the fact that Weller obviously planned to "do his own thing" with regard to the case.

"I'm just here to counsel," he said. "If you want to continue to interview local people you think had run-ins with the victim, I leave you to it. You don't need our help. We have plenty else to work on. If you need anything before our next meeting, give a holler."

She had little doubt he was pursuing the drug angle, perhaps in connection with a case belonging to MSP. As for the next meeting, Sam hadn't scheduled one. She was waiting for a chance to interview Wallace Bonnet. Yes, the man had an opening coming up, but that was no excuse. She even sent Gordy by Bonnet's home, but he was conveniently absent.

Sam had plenty to do besides the Fitchett murder. Other crimes fell under the purview of Criminal Command. She had an ongoing domestic violence case that depended on cooperation from an understandably reluctant wife. The deputy assigned to help the distressed young woman was a fifteen-year veteran named Rhonda Pullman. The trick, if that was the right word, was to gain trust and project assurance without promising anything out of the department's control, i.e., the behavior of the abuser.

Talbot County was also experiencing a rise in burglaries, all of them tied to one particular gang. The members had recently moved from breaking into unoccupied vacation houses during the week to entering the house regardless of who might be present. During a couple of especially bold Saturday night heists, the homeowners were smacked around and tied up. Sam and Donahue feared more violence would follow.

Finally, she had resumes to review from three applicants hoping to come in as detectives. Donahue decided Sam's unit needed to expand quickly. He was fine with mentoring McCready, but he also wanted to add a couple of law officers with homicide experience. She agreed with his assessment; she'd been hired with the expectation her division would grow. She simply hadn't expected to deal with a grisly homicide at the same time.

With great power comes great responsibility, she reminded herself. Somehow, quoting Spider-Man didn't make her feel like a hero.

Gordy stuck his head into her office at the end of the day. She was leaned into her monitor, her drugstore readers perched on the end of her nose.

"What's got you chained to your desk?" he asked.

Sam closed the file she'd been reading. She hadn't discussed the department expansion with her only detective, although she intended to do that sooner rather than later.

"Boring digital paperwork. Come in, have a seat."

Gordy plopped into the chair opposite Sam. "You look very administrative," he observed.

"I look old," she retorted, pulling off the glasses. "Or at least harried. I found a few more gray hairs this morning. It isn't fair, not while I'm still in my thirties."

"It's the job," Gordy told her. "Or maybe it's this case in particular. I guess you saw the preliminary autopsy report on Arley Fitchett."

Sam rubbed her head. "Nothing helpful. It would have been nice to get answers to some of our questions besides the obvious: Fitchett was strangled with a metal wire and his hands were set on fire about the same time and before he went into the water."

"Before he died, right?"

"That seems to be the conclusion," Sam responded. "So?"

"A garrote is the perfect sneak-up-from-behind weapon. It's about the surprise. I can't see a professional hitter using it after he set his victim's hands on fire."

"Then it was staged to look like a hit by someone who wanted us to think cartel-style execution."

Gordy nodded. "Right. Except the cartel is usually more efficient, especially in this country. I'm not sure why burning the hands was so important. If anything, it's risky. Raises too many questions."

"Ritual? Message?"

Gordy shrugged. "Can't say just yet. What do you make of the old scars on Fitchett, by the way?"

"I'm guessing he was tortured or abused as a kid. I got the impression from the cousin that he had a difficult upbringing. It's not all that uncommon."

"Sadly, no. Meanwhile, any luck reaching Bonnet?"

Sam rolled her eyes. "I got one message he left at the office. Said he'd respond as soon as he gets beyond this opening. Little does he know I plan to corner him tomorrow night. Are you going?"

"I wasn't invited." Gordy laughed at her chagrined expression. "Don't worry about it, Lieutenant. Art openings aren't exactly my thing."

"Not sure they're mine, but at least I'll be able to keep an eye out for the man of the hour. We can plan on doing a more thorough interview together."

"Don't you want to bring in your partner or consultant on that?"

Sam snorted. "Detective Sergeant Weller seems to have other cases to work on. More likely, he isn't interested in interviewing any of our suspects. Not that all of them are being cooperative."

"Good luck with that." Gordy rose. "If you don't need me for anything, I'm out of here." He offered a small salute and left. Sam felt her shoulders relax. Never mind Weller and his crappy attitude. She had good people working for her. With her.

* * *

She finished at seven, then remembered she had nothing to wear to next evening's event. She'd put off shopping, put the idea of a dress completely out of her mind, in fact, until Betty popped in to ask if she'd stopped into Allure. It took Sam a minute to realize the older woman was referring to a trendy St. Michaels boutique.

"Here's a reminder," she said, placing a black and white card with the silhouette of a woman on the desk. "Go."

Now, Sam looked at the card. Open Wednesdays until 8pm. If she left now, she'd have forty-five minutes, which was more time than she could imagine shopping for anything except maybe a firearm.

The place was empty. The sales associate, who'd been looking down at his phone when the door opened, was surprised to see a uniformed individual. He raced over. "Hello, Officer," the young man gurgled. "Nice to see you. Did I address you correctly? I hope you're not here to investigate any wrongdoing. If anything, I could probably stand to do a little more wrong in my life. Not that I want to commit any crimes or anything."

He was babbling, Sam noted. People did that in the unexpected presence of a law officer.

"I'm Lieutenant Tate with Talbot County Sheriff's office," she told him. "I'm here to shop, not investigate. I need something for a gallery opening here in town."

The change in the clerk's face was immediate. "You're so lucky you're going," he gushed. "You do realize it's literally the biggest thing to happen around here. And trust me, a lot has been happening in this town lately. Hah, I guess you'd know. Okay, let me get you all set. My name is Justin, by the way."

Within two minutes, he'd picked out a sleeveless black dress and sent Sam to the changing room. Before she had time to slip into the outfit, he came back with a pair of strappy shoes, a gold-tone lanyard-style necklace, and a cuff-style bracelet.

Justin had a good eye, she had to admit. Everything fit, and everything worked. When she emerged from the dressing room, he clapped in delight. He snatched a multi-colored shawl in russet, gold, berry, and green off a mannequin and placed it around her shoulders. The beautifully abstract design reminded Sam of falling leaves. She fingered the material, soft, yet surprisingly warm.

"Cashmere and silk," the clerk confided. Sam lifted it to her face, caught a glimpse of the price tag, and gasped. The clerk immediately offered her a thirty-five percent discount off her entire order. "You'll have these clothes forever," he said with a knowing nod.

Sam changed back into her uniform. She felt a little like Cinderella, at least until she reached for her wallet. She couldn't remember the last time she'd treated herself. Justin seemed pleased with his handiwork.

"Your studs work well," he said as he lovingly packed her items. "Maybe add a single drop earring on the other side. You will look fabulous, especially if you let your hair down. I hope you plan to let your hair down, Lieutenant," he added, amused at his little joke.

"Not this time," she replied with a laugh. "Tomorrow is a working night."

Chapter 12

Sam picked her way over a section of South Talbot Street that had been "cobbled" to make it seem quaint. She was trying not to grab Terry's arm. The uneven surface made walking difficult, especially in unfamiliar shoes. She wanted to kick them off, wash her face, and slip into sweat clothes.

At least the weather had cooperated, bringing relatively balmy temperatures for November and a clear sky. Just right for bare legs under a dress that ended above the knee. The shawl helped.

She stumbled, let loose with a mild expletive. "These shoes are not made for walking," she grumbled. "I haven't dressed like this for a decade, at least. Don't women wear pants to these kinds of events?"

"Not if they look like you do," Terry told her. "Which is not only appropriate, but hot."

Sam made a sound that came out between a snort and a giggle. She clapped a hand to her mouth, cleared her throat, smiled. "I need to work on how I accept compliments. Thank you." She pecked him on the cheek.

"Hey, I need to work on how I give them," he replied, taking her hand. "Because what I want to say is you look absolutely beautiful, Sam Tate. And while we've stopped, will you tell me what's really bothering you?"

"You got me, Terry. I feel like I ought to be in the office, at my computer, not hobnobbing with the rich and powerful. Weller is—"

"A pain in the ass. I know."

"He's convinced Arley's death is drug-related. So is Donahue."

"You think it's tied to Fitchett's treasure hunt."

"I do," Sam replied.

"Think of tonight as undercover work. You're there to study the locals and see if you can come up with more suspects. Even better, you'll have free alcohol and my company. Donahue will be there, won't he? Can't wait to meet him."

"Don't cause me any headaches, Sloan. The local cops aren't too keen on the FBI."

"They never are."

They entered the pocket-sized lobby of JT Galleries to the sound of thumping music and animated chatter. Sam noted with relief that nearly every woman there wore black, many in dresses like hers. The men favored suits or jackets without ties. Waiters in soft-soled shoes moved unobtrusively among the crowd with flutes of champagne or hors d'œuvres.

Sam had done some research. The gallery, named after the owner, Jackie Templeton, collected and sold what its website called "contemporary naturalistic American art." Jackie, or JT, as she liked to be called, was a recent D.C. transplant who'd leveraged a lucrative career in real estate with a passion for art. Her social standing had merited a spread in the *Washington Post* Style section.

According to the article, JT was seeking a quieter lifestyle. She'd put her D.C. business and personal properties up for sale and had purchased two buildings in St. Michaels, one of which housed the new gallery.

The first floor consisted of a decent-sized space for a permanent collection. Behind that was a roped-off room for special exhibits. Upstairs was given over to office space.

Sam had wondered how Bonnet, up until now an obscure woodworker, managed a featured spot in the new space. A small sign credited funding to a generous donation from the Phoca Foundation. The tagline said, "dedicated to preserving America's natural coastline."

Sam turned away and typed "Phoca Foundation" into her phone. Ah, now it made sense. The group had been founded by Wallace's father, James, and named for Phoca vitulina, the common seal. The elder Bonnet had been a Navy SEAL. She showed Terry.

"Clever," Terry remarked. "It's nice to know the rich and powerful have a sense of whimsy. They also seem to be immune to accusations of nepotism, even in the art world. But I thought you heard the son was a struggling artist."

"That may be a story he encourages."

"Of course. What grown man wants to appear to be taking money from his *pater familias*? Wonder what changed?"

"Maybe someone's convinced James that this is his son's moment," Sam said.

The main space was predictably understated. White walls and bamboo floors provided a discreet backdrop to the artwork on the walls. Sam glanced at the paintings without really looking at them.

"See anything you like?" Terry whispered.

"Give me time," Sam replied. The truth was, she had no idea what she liked. Certain things "spoke" to her. A snatch of a tune, a remembered passage from a favorite book, a painting or a poem that caused her breath to catch in her throat because it so artfully captured joy or wonder, pain or fear. She was here to work, though, not advance her art education.

She looked around, recognized a few faces. Jake and Lucy. The mayor of Easton and his wife. The sight of Martin Lloyd, dapper in a gray jacket, surprised her. As did his glamorous date, Carol Davidson, stunning in her black sheath and heels higher than anything Sam could imagine. Well, why not?

A slim vivacious woman with cobalt eyes and smooth skin held court near the center of the room. Jackie Templeton—who else would it be? — had gathered up her thick auburn hair with a glittering clip. She'd dressed to be noticed in fitted black pants and an extravagantly embroidered green jacket that deserved its own exhibit. Four-inch heels put her close to six feet tall. She held herself with a sort of amused resignation, as if she'd decided to accept the burden of her beauty.

Watching the little tableau was Charles Fox. He leaned heavily on the bar and scowled at the crowd. He looked ready to throw a punch but limited himself to throwing back whiskey shots. Sam wondered what had ruffled his feathers.

"There's the real power in the room," Terry whispered. Sam turned to follow his gaze. She took in a tall, square-jawed, broad-shouldered figure with the bearing of a former military man. She recognized James Bonnet from images she'd seen online. He was flanked by two companions, a man and a woman. Sam guessed the petite woman with the glistening black hair was his wife, Wendy Liu. She was breathtaking in a knee-length dress best described as dark ruby. She hardly looked old enough to be Wallace's mother, yet according to the family bio, she and James had been married forty-one years.

The man on Bonnet's other side commanded a different kind of attention. He was perhaps sixty and radiated authority, even more than Bonnet. His indoor tan covered a naturally fair complexion and highlighted his strengths: a firm chin, a strong nose, an angled jaw with a whisper of a shadow, a snowy smile. He had a full head of dark hair, thick and slicked back. A touch of silver at the temples added gravitas. Tinted eyewear gave him a West Coast vibe and contrasted with his conservatively expensive suit. Probably led with a firm handshake and that blazing smile.

Something about him seemed familiar. Sam tugged on Terry's arm. "Do you recognize that man?" she asked. "Is he an actor?"

Terry laughed. "Close enough. Try aspiring politician. His name is Sean Parker. He's running for a senate seat in Maryland. He's attracted a fair amount of attention, not to mention some deep-pocket donors. Which is to his advantage, since his campaign promises to be the most expensive yet."

Sam looked back and forth between Sean Parker and James Bonnet. "Maybe the would-be senator from Maryland is getting help from a Virginia funder."

"No doubt. Bonnet's been known to involve himself in politics." Terry shrugged.

"Sean Parker," Sam murmured. The name meant nothing. The face was another matter. She risked a longer look. He was a type, she decided, common to books and movies. The CEO. The general. The statesman. She couldn't explain why her stomach tightened the longer she looked at him. Maybe she just didn't trust politicians.

She scanned the room and located a group of young guests gathered around a striking man with upturned eyes and brown hair that just skimmed the collar of his well-worn jacket. A light beard lent him a rakish air, while a slightly crooked nose barely broke the perfect symmetry of his face. Wallace Bonnet had clearly inherited the best attributes of each of his parents.

"Back soon," Sam whispered to Terry.

She moved along the edges of the room, made her way to the exhibit room, and ducked under the velvet rope across the entrance. No one had remarked on her detour. Good.

On the walls hung a half dozen or so sketches of water fowl, both hens and drakes, supplemented by carvings of ducks set on stands of varying heights. These were the folk-art decoys about which Charles Fox spoke so disdainfully. To Sam they seemed like superior examples of the craft. They might even fool a real water bird.

At the center of the modest exhibit, a different sort of fowl rested on a high stand, enclosed in glass and lit by a single beam. The bird rested in an outstretched palm, likely belonging to a woman. A single blue piece of glass about an inch in diameter represented the eye. No, not glass, something far richer. The wood, reddish brown and darker in spots, had been polished to a high sheen. Even more interesting, the carving gave the impression of being well-preserved rather than new.

Wallace Bonnet had brought Bird in Hand to life.

As she moved closer, Sam took note of a crisscross of faint red lines. A security system. For a Wallace Bonnet carving?

"Can I help you, miss?"

Sam jumped back at the sight of the uniformed guard. Had he been standing in the shadows all along?

"She's with me," replied a lighter, male voice.

Sam turned to face Wallace Bonnet. His eyes glittered in the dim light and she thought of the sky at twilight.

"Okay, Mr. Bonnet." The guard retreated to the corner.

Bonnet looked amused. "Were you so curious you couldn't wait for JT to formally open the exhibit, Lieutenant? Or are you conducting some sort of investigation?"

She hoped he couldn't see her blush. "I guess introductions aren't needed," she said.

"It's a small community and you're not exactly an unknown quantity. Although you don't look anything like the hard-boiled, killer-catching law officer we might have expected. At any rate, pleased to meet you."

The hand he offered was rough and calloused, a working man's hand. She pulled away, although she was tempted to hold on a little longer than necessary. He still held her with his captivating gaze. It was all she could do not to drop her eyes.

"What do you think?" Bonnet inclined his head towards the piece.

"Are you referring to the work itself or the security protecting it?"

He laughed. "Spoken like a true detective. The cameras, the alarms, and the gentleman in the corner? Those are JT's idea. I'd like you to review the work, if you don't mind."

"It's striking," she said. "Otherworldly, but at the same time remarkably life-like. A bird at rest yet restless, poised as if it might fly away. The wood is superior. Sapele?"

"Similar but far more versatile."

"And the eye. That's not glass or even crystal."

"Excuse me?" Bonnet leaned in to study the piece he'd created. A shadow crossed his face. "No, it's not," he said, his voice flat.

Sam filed away his reaction for consideration. "I'm curious as to what inspired you to create this particular piece," she said.

He relaxed. "That's easy," he began. "A friend shared a story about a beautiful old wood carving that survived a shipwreck and was seized by pirates who hid it somewhere around here. He even showed me what he claimed was a copy of the original sketch. I found the story fanciful, but he was absolutely sold on the idea of its truth. Then again, adults often embrace fantasy as thoroughly as children."

"You knew Arley Fitchett?"

Bonnet's laugh was as sharp as a tack. "Everybody knew Arley Fitchett, Lieutenant," he replied. "I might have been better acquainted with him than many. We went to sea for three months."

Sam felt her mouth drop open.

Bonnet's smile was tight. "I'm sure it sounds glamorous. It was anything but. This was, oh, five years ago. I was short on cash, and he got me a position with an expedition financed by some wealthy dilettante. Hard work, but we had fun. After that, we'd meet for drinks. Say, did you ever find the good-luck talisman he carried in his pocket?"

Sam had an *ah-ha* moment. "An old Spanish coin?"

"That's the one. Not worth much, I gather, but he said it reminded him that the world was full of treasure large and small. He was a dreamer, Arley was." Bonnet's blue eyes grew dark. "He didn't deserve what happened to him. I hope you find whoever did this and nail them to the wall. I'll help however I can."

She felt as if she was being pulled toward him by some invisible rope. She wanted to slap herself. Instead, she stood straighter, squared her shoulders, ever the consummate professional.

"I'd like to talk further with you about Arley Fitchett. Could you stop by the sheriff's office in Easton tomorrow?"

"I'm afraid I'm tied up the entire day tomorrow. Saturday is much better. Why don't we have dinner in St. Michaels? I'll tell you everything I can recall about Arley. You tell me what you think of our little burg. You don't bring an escort, either professional or personal. I don't bite. Besides, it wouldn't be nearly as much fun."

He stopped to listen. "Gotta go. JT is bringing the crowd to heel. I'll text you with the particulars. I can pick you up or we can meet at the restaurant. Whatever makes you comfortable." He grinned and left the room.

Sam slid out just afterwards. She snagged a glass of wine from a passing waiter.

"There you are," Terry said. He peered at her. "Are you all right?"

"Never better," she said. She resisted the urge to gulp her drink, her mind racing. Had she just been asked on a dinner date by a "person of interest" in a murder investigation? And did she say yes?

"Ladies and gentleman." JT clinked a glass and brought the room to order. "Thank you so much for coming. And thank you to the Phoca Foundation for underwriting this event. St. Michaels boasts a growing artistic community. I look forward to lending my support. Creativity is well served when culture and nature combine."

"Or when money and influence combine," Terry whispered.

"Everything you see here," JT continued, "was created by an artist with ties to the Eastern Shore. I've been fortunate to gather up some of the best work. This is a gallery, by the way, not a museum. Everything is for sale."

Appreciative laughter from the well-heeled crowd.

"I'm particularly excited about our featured artist, Wallace Bonnet. I've asked him to speak, but he's declined. Of course, his work will speak for him—"

"Or you will," someone called out. More laughter

"You're right," JT replied. "Wallace Bonnet has been classified as a folk artist. That designation has meant his work has been, in my view, undervalued. No more, my friends. Take a look; I'm sure you'll agree." She nodded at two assistants, who began to shepherd the group into the smaller room.

"She didn't say much about the generous funder," Sam observed.

Terry gave her a side-eye. "And you didn't mention that you slipped off for a preview. Don't look so surprised. You're not the only seasoned investigator. In fact, while I'm observing, I'd say our hostess seems quite interested in you."

Sam glanced up to see JT hanging back to survey her guests. She was looking in their direction. Terry turned around to grab a glass. JT continued to stare. At Sam. Then, with an icy smile, she broke contact. But not before Sam saw the challenge in her deep blue gaze.

Chapter 13

The smell was what put her on high alert. She'd just exited Terry's car—by pre-arrangement, he'd dropped her off at the path to her house—when it hit her. Cigar smoke, coming from the direction of her cottage.

It's not that she minded the odor. Some of her colleagues back when she was a Nashville detective liked to light up after a hard day. One of her boyfriends had enjoyed a celebratory cigar now and again. Her dad used to smoke on special occasions. Out in the back yard and away from the house, per her mother's orders. Cigar smoke generally had positive associations.

Not, however, when it came from her front porch at 10:30 at night.

She crept as close as she dared, well outside the circle of light. She could just make out a figure in her rocking chair. A man who smoked as if he had all the time in the world and every right to be on her front porch.

She kicked off her shoes and cut a wide berth around to the side of the house. A second set of steps led to the tiny kitchen. She reached underneath the lowest step and carefully withdrew a pistol she kept hidden for just such moments, though she hadn't really been expecting those moments to come up on her so soon into her tenure.

Gun in hand, she circled back to the porch, trying to still her breath and quiet her racing heart.

"You don't have to hide in the shadows, Lieutenant Tate." The voice was deep, the tone affable. "It's your home, after all. I'm just relaxing, listening to the sounds of nature. It's nice out here in the quiet. By the way, you might want to pick your shoes out of the wet grass where you kicked them off. No sense in ruining a perfectly good pair."

Sam ignored this last suggestion. She crept up the front steps at an angle, arms extended to approach the man in the rocking chair from behind his left shoulder. She kept herself from shivering, although her bare feet and little black dress were no match for the wind off the water, even with the shawl. She kept her weapon up and circled her uninvited guest until she was standing in front of him, gun pointed at his chest.

The warm overhead porch light flattered the good-looking man. He wore a warm wool coat, leather gloves, and boots. She took in his light brown hair, his clean-shaven, open face. The sprinkle of freckles across the nose gave him a boyish appearance, although he might have been in his forties. Friendly hazel eyes, an easy smile he seemed to know how to employ. He looked like the high school track star or the boy next door all grown up.

"You seem to have just the one chair," he continued. "May I offer you mine?" He made as if to rise.

"You may stay where you are," she ordered. "I don't consider unexpected late-night visits from strangers to be social calls. Especially strangers who know my name and where I live. You can start by telling me who you are and why you're smoking on my porch."

"How inconsiderate of me. May I put this out?" The stranger carefully cut the stogie just below the ash line and wrapped it, then laid it down. "Cigars are my indulgence," he explained. "We all have at least one, don't we?"

He folded his gloved hands in his lap, settled into the chair. "To begin, my name is Thomas Ramírez. Or Tomás. I answer to either. I'd stand up and shake hands, but it seems safer to stay as I am." He inclined his head to her weapon. "I work for a large organization with business concerns up and down the east coast as well as—"

"You work for the Sinaloa cartel," Sam interrupted.

He raised an eyebrow. "You like to jump to conclusions, don't you?"

"Really?" Sam shot back. "I suppose you could be working for some corporate developer. Or maybe the CIA, except your salary wouldn't cover the cost of your coat."

"Hah. A sense of humor to complement your intelligence."

"I'm cold and tired, Mr. Ramírez. I'm also short on patience and holding a gun. And you're trespassing. Tell me, have you brought friends with you?"

She risked a quick glance over her shoulder. She hadn't seen a car, but that didn't mean one wasn't hidden in the dark. She wasn't sure what the hell she'd do if she were outnumbered. Surrender? Take a stand? She tried to imagine the headline in the local paper. Shootout at water's edge. Organized crime claims another victim. Dressed to die for. The reporters at the local paper could get very creative.

He held up his hands. "I came alone and in peace, Lieutenant Tate. Would you at least lower your weapon or point it elsewhere? You're making me nervous."

"Somehow I doubt it," Sam replied, but she dropped her arms fractionally. "Why are you here, Mr. Ramírez? Surely you haven't come to deliver a warning to Talbot Country's head of Criminal Command? That seems pretty bold, even for cartel management."

Ramírez looked pained. "My organization doesn't operate that way, Lieutenant. We are mostly honorable men and women, in keeping with the times." He made the group sound like an invitation-only club. "I waited on your porch so that I might offer information you may find useful as you investigate the unfortunate death of Arley Fitchett."

"And what might that be?"

"To begin with, the cartel you refer to had nothing to do with his demise." He watched for her reaction.

She gave a slight nod, nothing more. "Are you saying Arley Fitchett wasn't killed over drugs?" she asked.

"I'm not in a position to make that determination, although I suspect he wasn't. You don't seem surprised, which tells me you agree with me. Unfortunately, your sheriff and your new partner would like to connect us to his death."

"How do you—?"

He waved away her protest. "Please, spare me your surprise. I'm aware because I make it my business to be aware."

The cold that dropped over Sam owed nothing to the night air. She pulled her shawl up around her shoulders with her free hand. Ramírez pretended not to notice.

"Detective Sergeant Weller is especially determined to point the finger at my employers," he went on. "Yes, we know of him. Clearly, he is embittered over the loss of his sister."

"To drugs supplied by your organization."

"Or one of our local partners, or someone else entirely separate." He wagged his finger. "No one has to use drugs, Lieutenant Tate. No one. We supply product in order to fill a need. Without the demand, we might be in another line of work."

"You make it sound as if you're providing life-saving medicine, not life-ending poison."

"There are many ways to end a life, Lieutenant. Some methods work quickly, some more slowly." He nodded at her gun, then at the empty glass she'd left on the porch railing. Was that from last night? The night before? She couldn't recall.

"Sinaloa has ways of delivering messages," Ramírez continued. "The burned hands, the garrote, the coin left in the victim's pocket, all these are the sorts of approaches you read about in the papers. Crude but effective and owing more to a vanishing way of life in the old country, where people are superstitious and perhaps more easily cowed. In this country, we are as likely to employ other methods. One can sometimes crush an opponent with a legal brief as easily as with a rock." He chuckled.

"What's your point, Mr. Ramírez?"

"Mr. Fitchett's unfortunate demise was not in any way related to Sinaloa activity. He didn't work for us or sell to us. He didn't buy, borrow, or steal from us or any of our partners or subsidiaries. Do you understand what I'm saying? Fitchett was a treasure hunter, a man with a passion for his avocation. Perhaps his latest venture caught the attention of someone with similar interests or desires. Greed and envy underpin many crimes, as I'm sure you understand."

Ramírez shifted in his chair. Sam gripped her gun more tightly.

"Maybe Fitchett took out a loan he couldn't repay. There are certain money-lending entities that operate just outside the law. I am not one to point a finger, but Bratva has a sizable presence in Baltimore and an unpleasant response to tardy payments." That smile again. "Not all criminals come from south of the border."

"I don't follow unsubstantiated rumors, Mr. Ramírez. I follow the evidence."

"Then follow it," he snapped. "I'm not saying the Russian mob is responsible for Arley Fitchett's death, Lieutenant Tate. I'm saying we are not. We are being set up. As are you, and not very well. The garrote, the drugs planted at his home, these are like something out of a movie. And mark my words." He raised a finger as if delivering a lecture. "It's not just Frank Weller and his personal vendetta who'd like Sinaloa to take the fall. You might find many people willing and eager to exploit Mr. Fitchett's death for professional or political gain. To see their names in the paper or obtain much-needed resources."

Was he talking about someone with the Maryland State Police? Or with her own department?

"Don't fall into the trap of thinking along those lines," Ramírez continued. "It would be a mistake."

She stood straighter, her face hot. "Is that a threat, Mr. Ramírez?"

"Not at all, Lieutenant. It's a piece of advice. Don't get distracted. What is it your FBI friend always counsels his students? Go with your gut." He rose in one swift movement. Sam stepped back and raised her gun without thinking.

Ramírez collected his things from the table and pocketed them. "We're enormously successful at what we do, Lieutenant," he said. "That is a fact. People die in our line of work. That is also a fact. But we do not kill thoughtlessly or carelessly. Arley Fitchett's blood is not on our hands. Find out who wants you to believe otherwise and you will find the real killer."

He smiled again. "I've kept you long enough. It was a pleasure to chat with you. Sleep well." He stepped off the porch and vanished into the darkness.

She listened for voices or footfalls or the sound of an engine starting or a boat slapping the water. She heard nothing except the whisper of wind in the marsh grass and the ragged sound of her own breathing.

She didn't sleep that night. Twice she swept the cottage perimeter after her visitor left. She turned on all the lights inside and searched each room. She changed her dress for sweatpants and a sweater and grabbed a spare comforter from her closet. She made coffee, took a cup into the living room, turned out all the lights, and sat vigil until the thrushes stirred, still well before dawn.

Dear Teresa,

We have arrived at the British Crown Colony of Bermuda, thanks to a fortuitous breeze that advanced our journey most precipitously. Here we shall remain for a week, a prospect I anticipate with relief. I am not as enamored of sea travel as others may be, viewing it chiefly as a means to an end.

The men, used to the privation of a long voyage, remained disciplined as we made our way into port, always with an eye out for barriers both human and natural. I expect they will become very different sorts once out from under the captain's supervision.

Bermuda appears a mélange of vivid colors, much like a child's drawing. The abundance of natural beauty is echoed in the surroundings, in the doors of the houses, the clothing, even the pottery. Men come to trade from all over the world, lending the port an exotic air.

We entered the port at St. George, the capital, without incident. The docks are bustling, as expected. Ships from many countries stop here, particularly in the spring. The level of activity is far greater than that which we encountered in the Canary Islands. One cannot help but be diverted by the astonishing variety of people and vessels.

I am staying at the Governor's home, per arrangement by the royal cousins. He seems a decent fellow and his house more than adequate, particularly after so long at sea. Bell had been invited to stay at Longford House as a guest of Doctor Roger Wilson, now regrettably deceased. His widow has insisted the invitation stand. The idea of an unmarried man and woman residing under the same roof would cause quite the stir in London. However, I am under the impression that acceptable practices enjoy some latitude here, and so our Doctor Bell has accepted.

Wilson was the island's first resident physician and was considered quite successful. I am given to understand his house surpasses the Governor's residence in elegance and that the Widow Wilson is herself quite comely. I cannot but wonder if the good Dr. Bell might be inclined to consider ending his voyage at this point. I should not blame him, though I should sorely miss his company.

The weather I have found surprisingly temperate. The sun blazes in a mostly cloudless blue sky, quite a change from London's oft-present gloom. I was advised to shed my coat but keep my hat on, providing I can prevent the constant breezes from snatching it off my head

To view people of different origins and stations going about their business in the port and in the town, one would not recognize the turmoil that roils beneath the pleasant affect this island presents. Captain Digg assures me it is very real. Piracy remains a plague. Although our King issued a royal proclamation granting pardons to those agreeing to leave such a life, not all have accepted his most generous offer. I am told Edward Teach, the fearsome pirate known as Blackbeard, has grown more grandiose in both ambition and execution. He is now joined by a former squire from an island to the south, a man named Bonnet. They are said to have designs on the American Colonies and on this very Island.

I am told that the slaves in Bermuda are clamoring to join pirate crews and are welcomed as long as they are able-bodied. I don't know how one parses various circumstances surrounding the enslavement of others; you and I agree it is all barbaric. However, I have heard that conditions here are exceptionally bad for the unfortunates caught in its cruel grip. No wonder men seek a different life aboard a ship, even one that relies on blatantly criminal endeavors, for the opportunity to work and breathe free. Blackbeard's crew is said to consist of a great number of Africans, including his second in command.

I do not mean to wax rhapsodic about men who make their living by stealing from others, dear Teresa. These are wicked people who break the law. Yet they may at times demonstrate a greater embrace of humanity than do those who make and uphold many other laws.

Rest assured, I am not about to launch a revolution nor cast off my duties in order to sail the world in the company of these blackguards. The precious cargo remains my primary concern. Having made safe passage across the ocean, it rests secure within its cage and stored in my room. Nothing shall prevent me from seeing this little bird settled with its intended owner, I promise you.

Until I write again,

William

Chapter 14

"No offense, Lieutenant, but you look like crap."

Gordy had entered her office to find her clutching the steaming mug of coffee in front of her as if it might get away. Her shirt and slacks were pressed. She'd even managed to wrestle her tousled hair into a bun. The circles under her eyes and her pale complexion told another story.

"Gee, Detective, none taken."

"I mean, they did serve free champagne last night, am I right?"

She laughed in spite of herself. "This punch-drunk look owes nothing to alcohol, I'm sorry to say," she told him. "It comes courtesy of an unexpected and not exactly welcome visitor." She nodded at the chair opposite her. "Close the door, and take a seat."

Sam summarized her conversation with Ramírez for Gordy. When she finished, the detective whistled. "Holy cow, that took some balls."

"His or mine?"

"Well, both. First of all, you're still here, which is damned impressive. But why the hell would anyone think showing up and threatening a senior officer on her home turf was a smart move?"

"That's just it. He didn't threaten." She responded to his skeptical look with a smile. "Okay, it came across as a little threatening. My point is, someone in that organization is apparently put out that we might attribute Arley Fitchett's death to the cartel."

"Don't take this the wrong way, Lieutenant, but I would have trouble believing anything that came from Sinaloa's so-called management."

Sam took a slug of coffee. "Damn, that's hot." She leaned forward, her fatigue momentarily forgotten. "I agree with you, Gordy. Ramírez isn't someone I trust. But it's not out of the question that cartel brass doesn't want to get caught up in a potentially high-profile murder case. Beloved local guide's body washes up on the Eastern Shore, home to expensive mansions and cute little towns with cute little stores that sell overpriced trinkets. For good measure, his throat is wire-sliced and his hands burned. It's too specific, too personal, and frankly, too out in the open." She paused. "Ramírez seems to know who Weller is."

"Frank's been pursuing a lot of drug-related cases over here in the last few years," Gordy said.

"Ramírez suggested Weller *wants* Arley's death to be a drug hit."

"It's no secret Weller has a hard-on for the cartel."

She nodded. "Drug trafficking is on the rise on the Eastern Shore."

"So are drug-related homicides," Gordy added. He regarded his boss. "But you don't think this was drug-related."

"I don't. Think about it. Fitchett goes to all the trouble to create a hideaway in the back of his shed and leaves his drug paraphernalia in a kitchen cabinet? Nothing indicates he was selling. And from everything I've been hearing about Arley, he wasn't using drugs, never mind past history."

"He wasn't using drugs." Gordy shook his head for emphasis. "You won't find anyone around here who says anything else."

"Could he have borrowed money from the cartel?"

"If Sinaloa is in the money business, it's laundering, not lending." Gordy paused. "Even if this Ramírez character has a vested interest in getting us to look away from his group, I think he's telling the truth about Fitchett and the cartel."

Sam rubbed the spot between her eyebrows. "I need to get Frank Weller on board. McCready's doing a deep dive into Arley's financial history with Shana's help. I want you to go back to the house again. Take Tyler Caine with you this time."

"Seriously?"

"Yes. Fresh set of eyes, good politics, the whole package. You know I'm right."

Gordy nodded, his lips compressed.

"Meanwhile, I want to have another chat with Charles Fox," she continued. "He seemed very agitated at the opening last night. I suppose I'll ask Weller, if he's willing to come. Jackie Templeton might be someone to talk with as well. No idea if she knew Arley, but she must know something about Bird in Hand, since her central exhibit revolves around it."

"What about Bonnet? It's his baby. And he had dealings with Fitchett."

"We're meeting tomorrow."

"Tomorrow? You're going to ask Weller to work on a Saturday?"

Sam shifted in her chair. "Um, no. I think this will end up being pretty late in the day. Probably better to keep it solo."

Gordy gave her a side eye. "Date night?"

"What? No!" Sam protested. "It's more like—" They were interrupted by a firm knock on the door. More like a rapping that made Sam think of a schoolteacher.

"Excuse me, Lieutenant Tate." Betty Claiborne stood at the entrance. "You have a visitor. A Mr. Hart, the president of the Maryland Free-State Treasure Club."

Sam rose. "What? Today? Damn it, we've been trying to reach him for the past two weeks. And who told you to come get me? That's not your job. Where's Rose?" She stopped, took in a lungful of air, and let it out before she continued. "Sorry to be so cranky."

"Don't worry about it, Lieutenant. We all have those days. As for Rose, she's making Mr. Hart comfortable in the hallway." Betty looked as if she might burst out laughing.

"Give me a minute. Detective Gordy, go forth and find me something." She gave him a double thumbs up. "Betty, please tell Rose she can, ah, escort Mr. Hart to my office."

Several long minutes later, Rose poked her head into Sam's office. "Mr. Hart is here," she announced. She looked flushed, as if she'd sprinted to the door. Her salt and pepper hair stuck to her damp forehead. Behind her, Sam caught a glimpse of several other women. Had they all decided to accompany poor Mr. Hart?

"I told you, Rose. You can call me Ben. Very nice to meet you, by the way. And the rest of you as well." The owner of the strong, confident voice entered, closed the door with a self-deprecating smile, and shrugged. Sam struggled to keep a straight face.

If she'd had to describe the leader of a group of metal-detecting enthusiasts, she'd have imagined a middle-aged man, either hefty or scrawny but out of shape. Likely round-shouldered after spending so many weekends hunched at a computer or bent over a high-tech metal detector. Obsessive and knowledgeable about his hobby and his administrative responsibilities but not about much else. A loner, someone who might otherwise spend too much time in front of a screen.

Benjamin Hart smashed her stereotype to smithereens. The young man who walked into her office was a real-life Adonis. Sam's expert eye put him at six feet and 185 pounds, nearly all of it muscle. His wide shoulders tapered to a narrow waist. His navy sweater failed to conceal his six-pack abs. He was in his mid-twenties, with an outdoor tan, a disarming smile, and a shock of sun-kissed blond hair that flopped over one brown eye.

All in all, Ben Hart looked more like a lifeguard or an extreme sports enthusiast than a treasure hobbyist. No wonder the department was swooning. While Sam had long ago discovered she was immune to the charms of a particular type, she was nevertheless impressed. She was also annoyed that he chose to show up today of all days.

"Ben Hart." He stuck out his hand. "I'm happy to meet you."

She gave him a handshake that made him wince. "Seems like you've made quite the impression on the staff, Mr. Hart," she said. "I don't understand, though, why you managed to be unavailable for two weeks and then decided to drop in today."

"I apologize, Lieutenant. I was completely unplugged until last night. We were trekking in Nepal, if you can believe it."

I can believe it, Sam wanted to reply.

"Anyway, when I got back and saw all the messages, and then heard the news about poor Arley Fitchett—well, I caught a couple of zzz's, called my mother, and came right across the bridge from Annapolis."

Sam felt some of her irritation ease. "Mr. Hart—"

"Call me Ben."

"Ben, please sit." She gestured at the chair across from hers. "I assume you got something to drink out there?"

He nodded. "I was well taken care of."

"Good. Ben, we're trying to collect information on Arley Fitchett, anything that will help us understand what he was up to and why anyone might want to kill him."

"Is it true he was—?" Ben used both hands to pull an imaginary rope or wire and made a choking sound. "And his hands? God." He shuddered.

"What exactly does the Maryland Free-State Treasure Club do?"

Ben leaned forward, his eyes bright. "You could call us dedicated hobbyists, although that doesn't do us justice. We use the latest technology to hunt for objects that have been lost. Metal, obviously. Mostly old coins and jewelry and such. It takes patience, focus, and skill. We have workshops for weekenders and school kids. I've noticed a lot more women recently."

I'll bet you have, she thought and immediately felt guilty. What did she have against this nice young man who couldn't help it if he looked like a demi-god?

"We even have a program for troubled adolescents," Hart went on. "One kid found a piece of a bomber plane from World War II. You wouldn't believe how excited he got. Oh, and we've gained a reputation as the go-to group for lost wedding bands."

"You sound like a civic-minded kind of organization. How did Arley Fitchett fit in? He was a member, right?"

"Honorary member. Arley came to a couple of meetings to talk about his experiences. Last time was, oh, June. Just before we took our summer break. He was a hit with the detectorists, I can tell you."

"Detectorists?"

"That's how we refer to ourselves." He looked almost apologetic.

"What made Mr. Fitchett so popular?"

"Most of us do this because we like to use nifty tools and make like we're explorers. Every now and then, someone turns up an antique spoon or a Civil War coin or even an arrowhead. No one expects to actually locate buried treasure, but we always appreciate the chance to hear about the work from a professional. I mean, Arley had been with crews that located spectacular riches all over the world. He was the real deal."

"Did he ever talk about more localized treasure hunting? Say, for a specific antique that may have been lost in the area?"

Ben laughed. "You're talking about Bird in Hand. Yeah, that's a fairly durable legend. Look, Arley was a guide whose schtick included a fair amount of folklore. Everyone who lives in the area knows the stories about pirates and buried treasure, Lieutenant. No one believes them."

Sam pressed on. "Did anyone at these presentations seem especially interested in Arley's stories about local treasure?"

"Nothing out of the ordinary."

"How about you? Did you spend some time talking to Mr. Fitchett about his projects?"

"Me? Not really. I think we had a drink once."

"More than once, according to the bartender at Hunter's Tavern."

"It's possible. That was Arley's favorite hangout."

Sam looked down at the blank pad in front of her. "Dinner at the Purser's Pub in St. Michaels must have been a nice change. Was that his idea or yours? Who treated?"

Hart, who had been slouching in his chair, sat straight up, his eyes wide, his body tense. "Hold on, are you having me followed?"

"No one's been following you, Ben. We've been tracing Arley's movements over the last few months. Who he called, who he saw. Who he worked with. Who he drank with. What he talked about. Your telephone number showed up. Your name and face also showed up. I'm just trying to understand how well you knew Arley Fitchett."

"Everybody knew Arley Fitchett, Lieutenant. He liked to drink, and he liked to talk. Maybe he was after something close to home, or maybe he was just spinning a story. I have no idea."

Hart stood up abruptly. "If you don't need me for anything else, I'd like to get reacquainted with my real life. You don't have to tell me not to leave the area. I just got back, and I have a shitload of work to do."

Sam rose from her chair. "Thanks for your time, Mr. Hart." She offered a hand Hart ignored as he stomped out.

After he left, Sam engaged in a round of mental butt-kicking. She didn't manage that well. She wanted to ask him about rumors of a rare antique made of wood, about club members who pursued different kinds of exploring, about members wealthy enough to finance a particular kind of hunt, about old letters that were a means to an end. Instead, she'd spooked him, even though she hadn't tagged him as a person of interest, since he'd been climbing mountains halfway around the world.

Yet something about Mr. Hart struck her as too facile. She couldn't cross him off her list, not yet. Which put her where she'd been two weeks earlier. At square one.

Chapter 15

A strong wind stirred the bay on Sunday afternoon, tossing graphite waves onshore. Heavy lead clouds rode low in the steel sky. Nickel, lava, fossil, flint, iron, smoke, slate. Fifty shades of gray, any one of which could describe her foul mood.

Wallace Bonnet was a no-show Saturday. She'd prepared for the dinner (*interview with a meal*, she kept reminding herself) with the fluttery anticipation of a high school girl getting ready for a date, or maybe a thirty-something woman stepping out on her sometimes boyfriend.

No, that wasn't it. She felt on the verge of a breakthrough. Bonnet knew something about Fitchett's hunt and maybe his death. She couldn't believe he just happened to create a replica of the treasure Fitchett (and who knows how many others) sought. What was going on beneath the man's self-contained affect? Jealousy, hunger, desire? He didn't seem the kind to want or need the attention bestowed on him. Maybe he'd perfected the art of bemused indifference. She aimed to learn more over the course of an evening of food and drink, if that's what it took.

The text came in at 7pm. "Quasi-emergency," it read. "Can't make dinner. Rain check?" followed by an emoji of an umbrella and a bird. Was that meant to be provocative? Sam didn't know or care.

She fixed herself an omelet and poured herself a double shot of George Dickel Barrel Select. It had been another gift from her staff back in Tennessee. The memory of the farewell party tightened her gut. She'd put in a lot of work to fit in. Then, just as she'd begun to feel comfortable in her position, everything changed.

Terry seemed to get busier with each passing week. In addition to studies and field assignments, he was now in Florida for a few days to provide support on an old case. Sam admired his determination, and she didn't begrudge him his opportunity to advance. She just wished she had her own ladder to climb. She didn't want to be the new kid on the block, one who wasn't living up to her reputation as a crime-busting homicide detective.

Sunday morning, she drove up to Delaware to see her mother. Colleen Russo had lapsed back into silence following her two-word command or plea to "find him." She sat in her usual spot close to the window, a slight smile on her face and her abundant hair brushed and tied with a ribbon. She looked like a cooperative child, one with a hidden life or a secret.

On the way back, Sam drove by Wallace Bonnet's house. He'd made it sound like they occupied similar properties: cozy, modest, private. Except the two homes were about as similar as a packhorse and a thoroughbred.

Sam's cottage could fairly be described as ramshackle. The floors creaked, the porch sagged, the roof leaked, and the furnace grumbled. Her view of the Chesapeake was oblique, off to one side and just beyond the marshy tributary that the rental agency described as bay front property. Only a dedicated gardener, patient and without a full-time job, could have tackled the riot of vegetation that surrounded the structure.

Bonnet's place looked as if it were posing for *Architectural Digest*. Though small by millionaire standards, maybe 2500 square feet, it had been ingeniously redesigned. The original cottage, a white shingled affair, had been expanded to the back and on one side to create an L shape that maximized space and privacy. The landscaping was English garden-style, likely abundant in spring and summer, now neatly bundled, mulched, and covered. A small picket fence separated the property from a well-tended beach that was actually on the Chesapeake, so that the owner had a direct view of the birds, the boats, and the water.

She thought about parking, walking up to the door, and presenting herself. She sent a text and waited a minute for a reply that never came. Then she headed back to her own abode, which looked close and cramped and impossibly rundown. The bottle of high-end bourbon beckoned. Not a good idea on an empty stomach.

Better to head into St. Michaels. Sunday nights this time of year, the streets were almost deserted. At least she knew the Blackthorn Irish Pub would be open. Maybe she'd have stew or crab cakes and a stout to ease her loneliness.

She pushed open the door to loud music, laughter, and warmth. She nodded at the bartender, ordered her beer, and sat down to peruse the menu. She was hungry, a good sign.

The bartender put down her drink and pointed his chin over her shoulder. "Seems like your friends are signaling you," he said.

"Friends?" she repeated and turned. Carol Davidson and Martin Lloyd waved her over to their table, tucked into the corner.

Well, hello. She picked up her beer, lifted it above her head, and pushed through the boisterous crowd.

"Lieutenant, hi," Carol said. Then, almost shyly, "You remember Investigator Lloyd, don't you?"

Lloyd half rose to pull out a chair. "Thanks for joining us," he said. "We were just about to order."

After they snagged a cheerful waitress and put in their orders, Sam settled back in her chair. "Lively here," she noted.

"And warm," Carol said. She lifted her glass. "This time of year, I switch to red wine."

"I guess it's the damp that gets to me. Still getting used to it."

"You're experiencing our subtropical climate," Lloyd said. "Hot, humid summers and wet, rainy winters. An occasional snowstorm, complete with squalls."

"At least I'm familiar with hot, humid summers. The less adjusting I have to do, the better."

"Yeah, I wondered about that." Lloyd looked at her, his brown eyes assessing.

Please don't ask me what it's like to go from being a sheriff to working for a sheriff, Sam pleaded silently.

"I'd have to believe that life on the Eastern Shore isn't actually all that different from what you experienced in your part of Tennessee. Emphasis on community, on what some would call small-town values, and others would label as conservative or out of touch."

"People seem very friendly in Talbot County," Sam said carefully. "Easton isn't a small town, not like Byrdstown. It's got four times the population of all of Pickett County. And you all are closer to major cities than we were back in our part of Tennessee."

"The Eastern Shore developed very differently from the rest of the state," Carol said. "You may not realize just how isolated it was before the Bay Bridge was built in the nineteen-fifties. In fact, there've been three or four attempts to split off and form a new state."

"No kidding."

"People here identify more with Virginia than with Western Maryland," Carol went on. "A lot of them actually consider themselves southerners."

"That explains the dialect. More like I'm down in the Carolinas." She turned to Lloyd. "What about you? You sound like an easterner."

Lloyd laughed. "The effect of a liberal arts education at a small college in New Hampshire. I assure you, though, I am native to the area. The Lloyds were one of a group of prominent original Eastern Shore families, along with the Goldsboroughs and the Hollydays."

"What about Templeton? Is that a name with a significant regional history?

"You're talking about Jackie Templeton?"

"Well, she made a point about her deep connection to the region at the gallery opening."

Lloyd took a draught of his beer. "Templeton is a name with some history in these parts. Who knows with JT, though? I met her last year at one of her D.C. galleries. When she found out I lived across the bridge, she attached herself to me like a barnacle. Wanted to know a lot about the area. She mentioned 'retiring' to the Eastern Shore. People do that, but JT doesn't seem the type. She's always got an angle. I can't help but wonder if she's here to look for her roots or rip everything out and plant her own version of an idealized life."

Sam found his assessment interesting but wasn't ready to comment on it. "If you don't mind my asking, how did you become a County Forensic Investigator?"

Lloyd took a sip of his stout. "I started in pre-med. I trained as an EMT and worked in some pretty rough neighborhoods in Baltimore. It got to be a little much." He looked pained. "So, I came back to the place where I grew up and registered as an on-call county forensic investigator."

"And what do you do when you're not investigating homicides? There aren't too many of them, at least I hope not. The fewer the better."

Lloyd chuckled. "Can't argue with that. You're right, though. This isn't a full-time job. I teach biology at Wor-Wic Community College."

"He's also pursuing his PhD in marine biology at University of Maryland," Carol said with a note of pride. "I like to tease him that he prefers plants and animals to people. Even dead ones."

"I feel the same way," Sam cracked, earning a hearty laugh from her dinner companions.

There followed a brief period of silence. To cover any awkwardness, Sam asked, "Are you as much of a regional history buff as Carol?"

To her relief, Lloyd nodded, almost eagerly. "I'm not sure I match the enthusiasm she shares with her brother," he said, "but there's a lot of fascinating folklore to go with the equally compelling history."

"Like what?" Sam was genuinely curious.

"Oh, sunken ships and buried treasure," Lloyd said with a wink. "Ever heard of Captain Kidd? He was rumored to have hidden his loot up and down the eastern seaboard in the late 1600s, particularly on the lawns of the bigger mansions on both sides of the Chesapeake. Treasure hunters are still poking around on the smaller islands and along the lesser estuaries. Makes for a fun birthday party."

"What about Blackbeard?" Sam asked.

"I'm not sure. I seem to recall Blackbeard did all his dirty work in North Carolina and Virginia, although, hang on. Carol, wasn't there some story circulating once upon a time about a missing piece of art pilfered from a sinking ship or some such nonsense?"

Carol took a gulp of wine. "Might have been," she said, watching her glass.

Lloyd went on, "Believe it or not, there are a lot of ships lying at the bottom of the Chesapeake Bay or its tributaries. I mean, a lot, something like eighteen hundred. And those are the ones that have been discovered." He looked back and forth between Carol and Sam. "Is there a reason we're talking about missing treasures of the Chesapeake Bay? A reason related to an apparent homicide I was called to investigate not two weeks ago?"

"Oh, look," Sam said. "Our food has arrived. I don't know about you, but I'm famished."

"Do you know what I've been dying to ask you, Lieutenant?" Carol ventured as they dug into their food. "What was it like to be a lead on the Wedding Crasher case? How did you work it out with all those agencies involved? What were some of the breaks in the case? Which agency supplied the crime scene investigators? What was it like to work with the FBI? I hear they can be pretty annoying. Oh, I forgot." She giggled. "I guess you didn't mind that part."

Sam shared in the laughter. "I did work with some good people, including but not limited to Terry Sloan." She recalled for them some of the less painful and more interesting aspects of the case, grateful that Carol had shifted the conversation. Lloyd looked properly engaged.

Two hours later, filled with good food and goodwill, she headed to her car. A double ping told her she had two text messages. Terry wrote, "Call when ur in bed. I'll sing u to sleep."

The other text was from JT. "A little birdie said you wanted to speak to me," it read. "Pls drop by gallery early a.m. Free coffee, free gossip. JT"

Sam began the ride home pleased with herself. As soon as she pulled into her driveway, her elation evaporated. She exited the car and made her way carefully up the steps. All clear.

She walked inside and poured a bourbon she didn't need. Damn it, her home was supposed to be her refuge. Now it felt unfamiliar, just another place where she couldn't let down her guard. She hated that. Hated Ramírez, the cartel, the gunman who put her mother in a position to need her daughter close at hand.

Most of all, she hated foolish men with foolish dreams that got them killed.

Chapter 16

The small lobby of JT Galleries was flooded with light at 8am. The young woman who answered the door was rangy, red-headed, and blue-eyed. She bore an uncanny resemblance to her boss.

"Hi," she said with a cheery smile. "I'm Amy Reed. You must be Lieutenant Tate. Come in. I'll fetch JT."

Sam took the opportunity to look at the artwork, something she hadn't been able to do at the opening. Landscapes and portraits dominated the permanent collection. A few featured close-up studies—a leaf, an insect, a window—and at least one seemed to be set underwater. She found the work soothing rather than inspiring. There were worse things to derive from art than a sense of comfort and familiarity.

She imagined Weller making some smart-ass remark about the art. She'd texted him about doing the interview together before their group meeting, scheduled for 9am.

To her surprise, he'd postponed the meeting by one day. "Big case," he'd texted back. She didn't believe him for a minute. At least Gordy and Tyler Caine had a more fruitful exchange. They were set to return to Fitchett's house in the afternoon.

She was brought out of her reverie by an unmistakable trill. "Lieutenant Tate, how good to see you."

Jackie Templeton appeared in black slacks and a fitted tunic sweater in fuchsia, which she'd adorned with a single gold strand that complimented her tasteful earrings. Tortoiseshell reading glasses perched on her head. Her makeup was understated and skillfully applied. She'd pulled her hair into a messy pony tail. She came across less as proprietor and more as entrepreneur. Still chic, still stunning. Even the small scar over her right eye, which Sam hadn't noticed at the event, added to her appeal.

"Thank you for seeing me so early in the morning, Ms. Templeton," Sam said.

"JT, please. It's no bother. I'm up with the birds. Did anyone get you coffee? Hold on." She entered three digits on her phone and spoke quietly. Within thirty seconds, Sam held a steaming mug of coffee, courtesy of the same young woman. The velvety aroma made her want to sink cross-legged to the floor and hold the hot cup with both hands. She settled for a deep inhale and a careful sip.

"Delicious, yes? Kona. The money people who I expect to visit us out here are entitled to a decent cup of joe." She chuckled.

Sam nodded, took another sip, and tried not to groan with pleasure.

"I'm glad we could connect," JT continued. "I'm headed back to Washington this afternoon for a few days. I still have business there." She swept her arm in a wide arc. "What do you think? Does the space still hold its appeal by the harsh light of day?"

"It really honors the artwork," Sam surprised herself by saying.

JT nodded her approval "I love the architect. He's also renovating the old building across the street. We do have to comply with some preservation requirements, but those are minimal, all things considered."

"Do you think the gallery will be—" Sam almost said, "self-supporting"— "open full-time?"

JT smiled. "I think we'll split the difference. Open Thursday through Sunday, that sort of thing. More during the holidays and in the summer. St. Michaels has really taken off as a tourist destination, you know."

"How's your living space coming along? Are you ready to move in?"

JT sighed. "I'd like to get in before spring, but I'll have to readjust the schedule. Actually, that's for the best. I have my eye on another place in town, a retail space that looks like a good investment. Even if I don't sell my D.C. properties until the cherry blossoms are out, I should be able to realize maximum profit." She spoke with the self-assuredness of someone used to dealing with investments, schedules, and maximized profits.

"As delightful as it is to see you, Lieutenant Tate," she continued, "I don't think you came to talk about my living quarters or to admire my workspace. As I understand it, you'd like me to help you with your investigation into that poor man's death. Arley Fitchett. What a name! I didn't know him, although I understand nearly everyone else in town did."

"I'm more interested in what you can tell me about Wallace Bonnet."

"Really?" She arched an eyebrow. "Is he what the police call a person of interest?"

Sam didn't answer.

JT shrugged. "If we're going to gossip about my star artist, let's step into the room that features his work, shall we?"

Bonnet's signature piece stood in the center of the room, nestled within its square glass shell, oblivious to the mix of display and security lighting around it. The blue eye seemed even deeper and more faceted than it had the other evening. Sam found herself staring.

"I'm happy to let you study the piece, Lieutenant, but I'm sure we both have busy schedules. Let's have your questions, shall we?"

Sam ignored the superior tone and pulled out a notepad. Old-fashioned, but jotting ideas on paper helped her to order her thoughts and quell her impulse to give voice to some of them.

"Were you aware that the victim, Arley Fitchett, was hunting for a carving that looks very much like Mr. Bonnet's piece?" she began. "Was that your idea or Mr. Bonnet's?"

JT's laugh was low and smoky. "Well, it's quite the story, isn't it?" she replied. "A young man on his way to the New World carries a priceless gift from his royal cousin. The ship goes missing just before it reaches its final destination. Did it sink in a storm at the mouth of the Chesapeake? Did it get waylaid by pirates? What happened to the treasure?"

"You seem to know quite a bit about it."

"The story of Bird in Hand is part of a collection of fables about buried or hidden treasure in and around the Chesapeake Bay area. It doesn't hurt that our shallow piece of liquid real estate is home to so many shipwrecks."

"I'd heard as much," Sam said.

"Yes, well, it seems something is dredged up every other day. A piece of a ship's mast. A lone coin. Suddenly all sorts of silly little clubs and ad hoc groups descend with shovels and metal detectors, ready to dig up the shoreline on both sides of the bay. Local officials and property owners raise holy hell and the interlopers depart. Nothing ever comes of it. Here today, gone tomorrow." She slapped her hands as if wiping them clean.

"But here we have a new spin on an old story. A popular tracker of artifacts claims to have very specific information that can pinpoint the fate of the infamous antique. He may have been less than discreet in what he shared and with whom. Perhaps he became too entangled with the wrong sorts of people. And he ends up dead, murdered in a most gruesome manner. Why? By whom? Did he have information on the missing piece? Did he find it? Did someone else?"

"You didn't answer my question, JT. Whose idea was it to create artwork that mimicked, for lack of a better word, the antique of the legend, right down to the aging? And who decided to exhibit the piece behind glass and protected by a guard and an impressive amount of security? Almost as if it were worth far more than work by a featured artist whose professional reputation has been middling at best. Maybe a better question is why?"

JT's cobalt eyes closed briefly, a single blink. "The original idea belonged to Wallace. He was quite enamored of Arley's stories, inspired by them. And he is far more skilled than others believe him to be, especially the critics." Her comments were tinged with almost proprietary pride.

Sam was so close to the piece she could almost touch it, almost smell the wood. "Skilled at what, though?" she asked. "Representation or restoration?"

She expected a laugh or a protestation, but when she glanced up, she saw only a sly smile on the gallery owner's face.

"You're quite the clever one, aren't you?" JT said. "I suppose it must be one or the other, mustn't it?"

"You're not suggesting—?"

"That you are looking at a three-hundred-year-old antiquity and that my artist is in on the joke? Can you imagine anything more absurd?" The smile stayed.

"Yet there's an attempt to create a certain impression."

"Well, you're seeing it in a different context than others might. And, as they say, beauty is in the eye of the beholder." She laughed lightly. "You must realize the story of Arley Fitchett's unfortunate quest and even more unfortunate ending is catnip for the media. I was already approached by the *Washington Post* to comment on the rumor that the poor man was murdered over pirate treasure."

Sam gritted her teeth. "What did you say?"

"What could I say? People are attached to their beliefs. Sometimes those beliefs prove dangerous. I think that sounded adequately provocative without giving too much away. I hope they quote me."

She and Donahue had been contacted by the local papers, of course, as well as by the *Baltimore Sun*, the *Post*, and at least one wire service. They'd offered little while giving specific instructions to the department about keeping mum. That didn't mean she could account for everyone who worked in the department.

Then there was the civilian population. Arley had shared confidences with a number of people. The body had been discovered by an anonymous fisherman, but he might have told someone. Not a lot could be kept secret.

Sam tamped down her frustration. "Can you help me understand why you're playing coy with a piece of art whose provenance could be easily authenticated? As you pointed out, who would believe the story?"

"Which one?"

The question confused Sam. "I don't follow."

"There are two stories, Lieutenant. One involves Bird in Hand. I can't begin to say which parts of it are true, if any, but if the belief in buried treasure encourages tourism, I'm all for it. I know that runs against the grain. Most people who move out here claim to seek solitude. Really, though, they're simply trying to refashion their city lives of wealth and privilege in a slightly less toxic environment. Fine by me. As far as I'm concerned, we could all stand to have a few more people and a lot more money invested in this area."

"What's the other story?"

"Arley Fitchett's death, of course. What could he have possibly known? Who would care? Even if these long-lost letters which conveniently turned up add to the historical record, so what?" She watched Sam's face. "Don't look so irritated, Lieutenant. I learned about the letters from Charles Fox. He often trades discretion for self-aggrandizement. I suspect he wanted to be part of the fuss surrounding the Arley Fitchett murder and indeed he is. Convenient, isn't it?"

Sam stared at JT. "You think Charles Fox has something to do with Fitchett's death?"

"Oh, my, no," JT guffawed. "The idea is preposterous. He hasn't the balls. I think he hoped these dubious letters would burnish his reputation as a local historian and would-be art appraiser. Although he seems to know little about history and even less about art."

"Do you think the letters are fake?"

"Does it even matter? The story has taken on a life of its own. Lost letters from a doomed young emissary. A priceless treasure that disappeared three hundred years ago. An intrepid fortune hunter cut down in his attempts to locate it. Who knows how many people are willing to prod, poke, and maybe even kill to get their hands on this elusive prize? Motivated by desire, greed, perhaps even jealousy. The allure of possessing what one does not possess."

JT walked over to the piece that sat in the center of the room and looked at it lovingly. "Wallace's exquisite piece is provocative in its own right. One could argue about whether it serves as commentary or inspiration, whether it replicates, renews, or restores. Not that I'm claiming to be exhibiting a missing antiquity at the center of a murder investigation."

Her laugh was light, almost a giggle. "I will say that this piece does far more to capture the heart and soul of the Eastern Shore than Fox's unread books and papers ever will. What more could you ask for?"

Fewer suspects, Sam decided.

Chapter 17

Another seafaring dream. This time, the entire wedding party from her brother's ill-fated ceremony huddled together on a plank, shivering in the wind. High waves soaked them to the skin and threatened to knock them into the churning waters below.

The pirate was dressed in a tailored gray jacket, his wild beard combed, his unkempt hair slicked back, his eyes hidden by tinted glasses. In his hand was not a weapon but a piece of paper.

"Give me what I want," he yelled and pointed to the little girl in the pink dress.

"I can't," she responded and the adult Sam said, "I won't." Then she woke up.

She was in by seven. Five days since JT's opening, three since Wallace stood her up. No, since he didn't appear. It wasn't a date. Still, she was miffed he hadn't contacted her since. Professional courtesy at the very least.

Three weeks had passed since the discovery of Arley Fitchett's body. That was the worst marker of all. The majority of homicides were solved within a week. Sam knew the percentages had altered for the worse in recent years, especially with the growing mistrust of the police. She didn't care. She didn't want her first major case on the job to turn into a cold case.

She considered her options. She was just beginning to form a theory about Arley Fitchett's death she wanted to run by Gordy before she tried it out on the larger group that included Weller and his minions, scheduled to meet at 9:30.

A half hour before the meeting, she got a text from the detective sergeant that read, "Wrk in Baltimore. Pls reschedule for mid-late afternoon."

"Asshole," she said to the phone and slammed it down on her desk for good measure.

Gordy popped his head into the office and immediately sensed trouble. He looked at the cellphone, then at his boss. "Bad news?" he asked. "You look like you're ready to spit nails."

"More like split open someone's head," Sam retorted. "Weller wants us to delay our little get-together until this afternoon. His message was about as terse as it gets."

"Do you think he's working another case? Or another angle to our case?"

Sam put her hands to her head. "I have no idea. I don't like the idea we might be cut out of the loop or treated like hicks who can't run a proper investigation."

"Won't be the first time."

Sam resisted the temptation to pick up her poor phone and throw it against the wall. "It's gonna be the last, I can tell you that," she said.

"Let me get hold of Tyler Caine," Gordy suggested. "If Weller doesn't have him tied up, maybe he can go back to the house with me this morning. Or I'll take Carol. Oh, by the way," he added nonchalantly, "she mentioned she and her friend had dinner with you last night."

Sam cocked her head. "Her friend? I think he's a little more than that."

Gordy shrugged. "I guess."

Now it was Sam's turn to notice micro-changes in Gordy's disposition. He seemed to stiffen, grow tighter. "What's up, Gordy?" she asked. "You don't approve of your younger sister's suitor?"

He looked embarrassed. "I don't know what it is."

"Then either work it out or talk it out. Big brothers are—" she stumbled over her words, shook her head. "You always want to be a protector, and that's fine. You just don't want to create any hard feelings."

"I get it," Gordy said. "It's more ... never mind, you're right."

Time to change the subject, she told herself. "You did a couple of interviews with people who worked with Arley, right?"

"I did."

"Get those notes to Pat McCready. He took some of the phone interviews. I want to put together a fuller picture of Arley Fitchett. Who he was, what he did in his spare time."

"Will do."

Sam looked off, then nodded to herself.

"Never mind about bringing Tyler Caine out to Arley's house, Gordy. I think Weller has his team tied up. Besides, Carol's a more than capable partner. Spend as much time there as you need. I know it may feel like you're going over old ground, so to speak."

"What are we looking for?"

"Any evidence Arley was a drug user or, conversely—"

"A treasure map?"

Sam gave a slight smile. "We should be so lucky."

* * *

Frank Weller showed up at quarter to five. He brought Sarah Pollack and Tyler Caine. Pollack seemed to have something on her mind. Caine sat down and busied himself with his notes. As for Weller, he looked like the kid in the class who can't wait to say, "I told you so."

"Sorry we're a little late," he said. "Bridge traffic was a bitch, as usual."

Sam took her place at the end of the table. "I thought we'd begin by—"

Weller couldn't contain himself. "We were in Baltimore representing MSP on a newly-formed strike force created to combat drugs in the state."

"I heard about that," Gordy said. "You're part of a multi-agency effort that targets everybody from street dealers on up, right?"

"It's quite a show," Pollack replied. "BPD, of course, along with our team, DEA, the Bureau of Alcohol, Tobacco, Firearms and Explosives, the FBI, Homeland Security Investigations, and the U.S. Marshals Service." She shook her head. "Never thought I'd see the day."

"Maybe we could discuss your day after the meeting," Sam said. She had to work at sounding measured instead of testy.

"I think you'll find this relevant, Lieutenant," Weller continued. "While we were all trading war stories, Pollack and I came upon some interesting information. Seems there's a local guy, mid-level dealer, who thinks he's a player. He buys and distributes mostly fentanyl and heroin from Sinaloa."

Weller leaned in as if confiding a secret. "Apparently, this guy favors a violent approach to problem-solving. Kind of showy. Maybe he thinks it'll ingratiate him with the big guys. Turns out he has a particular way he deals with cheaters or snitches or crank heads or maybe just people he doesn't like."

"Let me guess," Gordy interjected. "He uses a wire on them, or maybe a blowtorch for fun."

"Give the man a gold star," Weller crowed. "Yeah, gruesome and effective. BPD found three bodies just last month. Anne Arundel County Sheriff's Office found another one just across the bridge from you all. Coincidence, wouldn't you say? Anyway, here's all the information. Sorry I didn't have time to make copies." He slid a fat file towards Sam, his expression almost smug.

She felt her temperature rising. She clenched and released her hands under the table, then brought them up and folded them in front of her. "Were any of these murders reported in the media?" she asked. "I mean, with specifics?"

"All of 'em," Pollack said. "*The Baltimore Sun* had a story and local affiliates covered the county killing. There might have been something on the evening news in D.C." She caught Weller's glare and bit her lip.

"So," Sam went on, "these deaths are played up, at least locally, because of the way in which the victims were murdered and because they may be tied to the cartel. These stories came out days, maybe even weeks before Arley Fitchett was killed. That's certainly a coincidence. We all know how media stories often provide not only information but also inspiration for bad actors."

Weller gathered himself like a thundercloud. "Do you have something against solving this case, Lieutenant Tate? Or maybe you've got a problem seeing it as part of a larger investigation." One you can't control, he seemed to suggest.

Sam was squeezing her hands so tightly she thought she'd cut off circulation. She flattened them on the table, narrowed her eyes, and spoke in a low voice.

"I don't have a vested interest in the outcome of this case, Detective Sergeant Weller. I don't have any scores to settle, and I don't have anything to prove. I want justice for Arley Fitchett. I didn't know him, but people around here knew him. They liked him. They respected him. A lot of them will swear that he wasn't in any way connected with drugs." She pushed a folder at him

"What is this?" Weller demanded.

"Interviews with people who knew Fitchett. Including his doctor, who is willing to swear Arley never showed evidence of using anything except tobacco, which he was trying to quit, and perhaps a little more alcohol than strictly advisable. And sources at the DEA and the FBI who will swear he wasn't an informant. Meanwhile, this—" she leaned across the table and placed a second folder in front of him— "contains detailed notes on names we consider people of interest. People who shared Fitchett's fixation with the artifact he was looking for."

She locked eyes with Weller. "I'm well aware of the problem with drug trafficking in our area, Detective Sergeant. It must have seemed—" she almost said "convenient" but stepped back— "logical to chalk Mr. Fitchett's death up to the cartel's local presence. We believe, though, that his death was about something else. Something both more local and more personal."

"A treasure hunt," Weller scoffed.

"A failed treasure hunt," she replied. "Which leaves us—"

McCready jumped up at the sound of shouting. He reached for the door and nearly collided with Rose.

"Two 9-1-1 calls, Lieutenant, just a few minutes apart. One to report a loud fight over at Wallace Bonnet's place, the second to report a fire. Same neighbor. Police and firefighters from St. Michaels are on the way and Fire and Rescue's been alerted. I figured you'd want to know, given everything that's going on."

Sam sprang to her feet. "Gordy, with me. Pat, Carol, grab a couple of deputies and follow. Now!"

She ignored Frank Weller's open mouth and rushed out the door.

Chapter 18

Gordy covered the eight miles of backroads in under ten minutes. He tore up the driveway and parked behind a St. Michaels fire truck close to the art studio. A half dozen men and women surrounded the structure. All were volunteers, members of the collective known as Talbot County Fire and Rescue Association.

"Any signs of life?" Sam asked a firefighter with enough equipment to bring most people to their knees.

"Don't know," he replied. "As soon as we clear—shit!" He turned and yelled at the others. "Back away now! Evacuate!"

"Evacuate!" the call echoed through the ranks as firefighters scrambled away from the smoking structure.

The flames came roaring out of the little building like a beast who'd been aroused from sleep. Sam was thrown onto the hard ground, along with several others standing closest to her. Her left arm was engulfed in flames. Gordy ran over and pulled off her jacket. He beat the flames into submission, then dragged her further away.

The fire expanded three-fold. The blaze leapt to the cottage, propelled by oxygen and enticed by the dry logs stacked by the back entrance. An Easton pumper and a truck arrived and disgorged a dozen more firefighters who split between the two structures.

"Is everyone okay?" Sam asked, struggling to stand. "Where's the firefighter I was talking to?"

Gordy looked around. He kept his hand at her back. "He's sitting up. Seems to have a nasty gash, but he's got an EMT by his side. Speaking of which, you need to get that arm looked at." He stuck a hand in the air. "Hey, need an assist!"

"I'm fine," Sam insisted, even though her arm hurt like hell. She was surrounded. Carol Davidson and Pat McCready, looking frightened, stood next to two men, one broad and balding, the other thin and white-haired. Joe Constanza, chief of the St. Michaels seven-man police department, and Jim Phillips, its fire chief. Pushing his way to the front was a fresh-faced kid with a backpack and a patch that said "medic."

"Dress it and wrap it to go," she ordered the young man. "See, everyone, I'm getting help. Gordy, I'll need my jacket back, assuming it's not too singed." She forced a smile.

The EMT worked quickly while Sam swigged from a water bottle. She took two of the extra-strength Tylenol he offered, then stood with Gordy's help. She felt momentarily dizzy, but it passed.

The conflagration was well on the way to devouring the studio and, Sam supposed, Wallace Bonnet's work. *But please, not Wallace*, she thought. The lump that formed in her throat surprised her.

"Getting hit by a backdraft is no joke," Phillips said, his voice tinged with concern. "You should get that arm checked out."

"I promise." She moved, winced, stopped moving. "Can you tell me what you know so far, Chief Phillips?"

"A neighbor called in the fire about 4:45pm. "We were all here within minutes. We figured it for something small and containable. We were wrong."

"9-1-1 got a complaint about an altercation coming from this address around the same time," Constanza said. "It all goes over the same system. You think the two are related?"

Rather than answer, Sam said, "We'll need to determine if this was accident or arson."

"We've notified the state fire marshal's office," Phillips said. "They're sending the experts."

DSFMs, deputy state fire marshals, were certified fire investigators as well as sworn police officers. The office of the State Fire Marshal was an agency of the Maryland State Police.

"Probably Landau and Abrams." Weller came striding up, Sarah Pollack and Tyler Caine on his heels. So, he'd decided to show up. She wasn't surprised he might know the investigators. MSP seemed to be one big happy family.

"Got a body," someone called out. "In the studio."

"That should complicate things," Costanza said.

Phillips added, "Guess we'll let Sheriff Donahue sort out who's in charge of what. Where is he, anyway?"

Sam ignored the sick feeling in the pit of her stomach. "He's stuck on the bridge," she said. "That means right now you've got me." She emphasized the last word.

Weller raised an eyebrow but kept his counsel.

"You've also got me, for what it's worth." The low voice, curiously soothing, belonged to Martin Lloyd. "I picked up the 9-1-1, thought I might be needed."

There was little he or anyone could do until the firefighters brought at least part of the blaze under control. It took more than an hour. By that time, a third firetruck had shown up, and so had a number of gawkers and at least one local news crew. Deputies from St. Michaels, Easton, and Talbot County departments controlled the swelling crowd.

Sam sat on the bumper of the car, watching the volunteers wrestle with the inferno and trying not to notice her throbbing arm.

When Jake Donahue finally arrived, she filled him in. He said nothing but stood, arms folded and face unreadable. Weller watched him like a hawk.

"Coming out!" one of the firefighters yelled. Two men, silhouetted against an orange backdrop, carried a body clear of the burning structure and set it on the ground.

They formed a semi-circle around the soot-blackened form, which lay curled in a fetal position, hands clutching a towel to the face.

"We found him next to the door," one of the firefighters said. "Some surface damage but otherwise intact."

McCready looked pale.

"Breathe, Deputy," Sam whispered.

"May I?" Lloyd inquired politely. He pulled latex gloves and a mask out of his bag. He also retrieved a soft brush, which he used to work around the head.

"That's Charles Fox," Gordy stated. "What was he doing here?"

Charles Fox. Sam realized she'd been holding her breath. She exhaled with relief, followed almost immediately by guilt. No one deserved this death.

"Where's the homeowner?" Donahue asked. "Bonnet?"

Another firefighter exited the building and waved them over. She issued her report to Phillips, who came back to the waiting assemblage.

"Here's what Halloran saw. It's all got to be confirmed by the investigators, but she's got a lot of professional experience. First, the window glass is clear, which indicates a very hot fire, not a smoldering one caused by, say, a cigarette or a single electrical outlet. There's also a lot of ash, another indication of a fast-burning fire. Third, and a couple of others confirmed this, it appears the fire burned *down*."

No one asked what that meant. Fire almost always burns upward unless a liquid accelerant has been poured on the floor. The fire will follow the catalyst down to whatever has soaked into the wood and any concrete beneath.

Lloyd remained crouched by the body. He looked up at the group and cleared his throat. "For what it's worth, the victim appears to have sustained a blow to the back of the head."

"From a fall?" Gordy asked.

Lloyd shook his head slowly. "I don't believe so. I thought maybe he'd been hit by falling debris, but the angle of the wound suggests a deliberate movement."

"Someone hit him," Sam said.

Lloyd bent closer, holding tweezers he'd pulled from his bag. "There are splinters in his hair and nowhere else. But there wasn't enough force behind the blow to kill him."

"Cause of death?" she asked.

"Preliminary, as always. He's got soot in his airways. The bright red skin suggests carbon monoxide poisoning. Severe burns on his legs would have sent him into shock. If he had any preexisting conditions, such as heart or pulmonary issues, he could have suffered an attack."

"And if someone incapacitated him ..."

"Then we have a potential homicide, likely followed by arson," Donahue finished for Sam. He kept his head down and his arms folded, staring at a spot beyond Fox's lifeless body.

They all looked up at the sound of the car emblazoned with the Maryland state seal that came screeching to a halt. Two men in blue shirts with yellow writing jumped out and ran over, hard hats in hand. Landau and Abrams. Sam saw Weller make a beeline for the men, but Jim Phillips got there first and brought them over to Donahue.

More handshakes. Donahue cleared his throat. "Okay, here's how it's going to play out," he announced. "This area is, for all intents and purposes, a crime scene. We will be investigating one or possibly two crimes. As these took place in Talbot County, the Sheriff's Office will lead the investigation under the direction of the Criminal Commander, Lieutenant Sam Tate."

Sam tried not to look grateful. She bobbed her head in affirmation.

"Sheriff," Weller spoke up, "State Police are happy to—"

"I'm not done. No one has any problem asking for assistance as needed, Detective Sergeant. MSP clearly has the resources. But someone has to lead. Right now, that's my office. Our office."

He looked first at Sam, then at Weller. "We need your input, Frank. But right now, this is Tate's case. She will make the calls and the decisions, reporting back to me, of course."

Again, Sam nodded. "Sheriff, we'll want to put out an APB on Wallace Bonnet. We can keep it general, just list Bonnet as a person of interest."

Donahue rubbed his head. "That won't sit well with the father. Never mind. Do it." Sam looked at Gordy, who immediately got on the phone.

"I'm going to need to head back to Easton to make calls and manage the inevitable political and media shitstorm I expect will result," Donahue continued. He turned to leave, then gestured over his shoulder.

"Lieutenant, a word."

Sam hustled to his side. His face looked drawn, almost garish in the mix of the fire's neon salamander glow and the searing white lights from the trucks. "I assume you think this is related to Fitchett's death," he said.

"I do, sir. We had a short list, people who all seemed interested in the same elusive antiquity. Now two are dead and one is missing even as his home burns down. I don't believe in coincidences."

"I don't, either. Let's assume the drug angle is off the table. The media's gonna be all over this, Tate. Pirates and hidden treasure and the missing son of a rich and powerful man."

"That won't please Detective Sergeant Weller."

Donahue sighed. "Go easy on him, Lieutenant. For one thing, we still may need some assistance from MSP. As for Frank, he comes across as gruff, but he's a damned fine investigator and thoroughly trustworthy. He may be willing to admit he's misjudged a situation without being reminded."

But does he take direction? she wondered. Out loud, she said, "I read you, sir."

He turned to head towards his car. Sam was already making a mental list of the steps she needed to take, all the while wondering what the hell had happened to Wallace Bonnet.

"Sheriff, Lieutenant, hold up." Constanza, practically at a run, came at them. He stopped to catch his breath. "Just got a call about a retail break-in in town. Hit and run, in and out. We're about to send a deputy—they're all out here— over to take a statement. Except—"

"Ask the dispatcher to request someone from our office, if your deputy wants backup, Joe." Donahue tried not to sound annoyed. "You don't need either of us."

"Except for one thing. The break-in was at that fancy new art place. JT Galleries."

Sam and her boss snapped to attention, all fatigue forgotten.

"Who reported it?" Sam asked.

"The owner. Jackie Templeton. She asked specifically for you, Lieutenant."

"Did she say what was taken?"

"I'm not sure. The dispatcher says she was going on about a bird."

Sam's phone buzzed. The text read: "The bastard stole Bird in Hand. After all I've done 4 him. Get here ASAP. JT." She showed it to Donahue.

"Presumptuous," he remarked, "but it may bear looking into. This scene takes priority, obviously."

"I'll handle it, Sheriff," she said, but he was already headed to his car.

She shivered in the freezing mist that settled on her shoulders and punched through her down jacket. Her arm hurt so much she wanted to rip it off and beat someone with it. She had at least one candidate. Who did JT think she was, anyway? Did she believe the police worked only for her? Was she oblivious to the the sirens, the lights, the acrid smell of smoke carried by the damp air?

"Will get there as soon as I can," she texted and pocketed the phone, ignoring the ping that immediately followed. She walked back to the small knot of officers, a look of purpose on her face. Her scene, her command, her orders.

"APB's out," Gordy offered.

"Great. Stay on top of that, okay? Also, make sure Martin Lloyd knows I want that autopsy report ASAP. I don't want to hear about the backup in the Baltimore ME's office."

"You got it." He watched her. "You going somewhere?"

"We have a situation at JT Galleries. Normally, I'd send you, but ..."

"No need to explain."

"Thanks. I won't be long."

"You want me to start a list of possible interviewees from the local community? People Bonnet knew or people who thought they knew him? Maybe we can get some assistance from Chief Constanza."

"Good idea. I want CSI Davidson to stick with the state arson investigators, pool resources, and share information. If Detective Sergeant Weller and his colleagues are willing to help on this case, I'd appreciate the extra bodies." Sam shifted her focus to Weller, who inclined his head.

"Tyler, you're with Carol. Detective Pollack, work with Detective Gordy, please. Start by scanning the crowd for anyone suspicious. Ask the local deputies if they saw anyone they thought looked hinky. I realize it's full on dark, but there's always the chance that the perp was and still is hanging around to admire his handiwork." Sam doubted it, but she had to cover all the bases.

"What about the kid?" Gordy indicated Deputy McCready, working on his own to try and keep the crowd contained.

"Use him."

Gordy raised an eyebrow, then spoke quietly. "And him?"

Frank Weller stood slightly apart, eyes hooded and arms folded, waiting for orders. Sam couldn't tell if this latest turn of events had moved the needle on his unshakable conviction that drugs played a role in Arley's death, or if he was assuming the role of inscrutable observer. She didn't much care.

Play nice, she reminded herself.

"Detective Sergeant, how would you like to take a short ride with me?"

"What, now?"

"Yes. Another crime, less serious, has just occurred. I think it may tie in with—" she moved her good arm in a circle— "all this. Detective Gordy will run point and we'll be back quickly enough to make sure people know the MSP is helping us."

A flicker of surprise brightened his eyes for an instant. "Where we going, Lieutenant?"

"We're seeing a woman about a missing bird."

She had the pleasure of seeing his unguarded look of surprise before she turned on her heel and headed for the car.

Chapter 19

On the short ride over, she brought Weller up to speed. Problem was, all she could do was extrapolate from a terse message. She could feel Weller struggle to refrain from commenting, though she caught the frown out of the corner of her eye. Just before they pulled up, his restraint splintered.

"Why are we here, Lieutenant? A veteran MSP homicide investigator and the criminal commander from county sheriff's office. I suppose burglaries fall under your purview, but still."

"You know as well as I do that Bird in Hand is the through-line running from Arley Fitchett, our first victim, to Charles Fox, found dead in a burning art studio belonging to Wallace Bonnet. Now Bonnet is missing. So is the piece he carved to look exactly like the sketch on Fitchett's wall, a piece he exhibited at Jackie Templeton's gallery." Sam took a deep breath and let it out.

"I don't see it, Tate." He'd dropped all pretense of formality, reverted to his former obstinance. "Fitchett and yeah, maybe Fox were hot on the trail of a precious treasure that they believed against all odds had survived time, elements, and a pirate attack. The perfect definition of a wild goose chase. Bonnet and Templeton were just riffing off a popular legend."

"Why did he take it?" she murmured to herself.

Weller half-turned in his seat. "Wait, you think you know who stole it?"

She shook her head. "I don't know much of anything right now. Let's see what Ms. Templeton has to say."

JT came running to unlock the front door. Her flame hair was carelessly pinned back, stray tendrils falling over her shoulder. She wore jeans and a sweatshirt smudged at the cuffs. Her feet were shoved into casual loafers. Reading glasses hung around her neck. Not a look Sam would have associated with the stylish art promoter, but perhaps she'd been pulled away from exercise or meditation or a bowl of popcorn.

"Thank God you came!" she cried, then, more quietly, "But not alone."

Was she surprised? Disappointed? Impressed? Sam couldn't tell.

"This is Detective Sergeant Frank Weller, Maryland State Police. He's partnering with me on the Fitchett homicide as well as another case that popped this evening."

JT ignored the hand Weller proffered, all her attention on Sam. "Oh my God, yes. Amy told me." Amy, the comely look-alike assistant, who materialized just then with coffee. "Was it Wallace's place that burned to the ground? And someone said there was a body? Do they know who it is?"

Sam declined the beverage service. Caffeine was the last thing she needed. She'd have to be content with inhaling the strong scent.

Weller grabbed the hot cup and downed the beverage in one gulp. The man probably had a cast-iron stomach.

"We're still sorting through the evidence." Sam wasn't about to give out details, especially to someone whose motives she didn't fully understand. "Let's focus on what's happened here. You indicated the carving of the bird resting in the hand that was on display in the other room was taken. What else is missing?"

"That's it. Just that."

Sam glanced over at Weller. He'd moved back to the entrance and was studying the ceiling. Looking for signs of a break-in and finding none.

"When did you first notice the piece was gone?" Sam asked.

JT pulled at a stray curl. "I came in to do paperwork about an hour or so ago. I normally head up to the second floor. I guess it was some sort of sixth sense that pushed me to look in the small exhibit room. I texted you immediately." The statement carried an undertone of aggression.

"Did you contact the insurance company yet?" Sam asked. "You do have insurance?"

"Of course. I thought I'd start with the police. That's best, isn't it?" JT covered her hesitation with an expression that suggested she wanted to cooperate.

Weller returned to stand next to Sam. "Nothing seems disturbed. Do you have security, Ms. Templeton, outside of the small room in the back? Cameras, motion detectors, recorders, anything like that?"

JT broke eye contact, just for a second. Then she looked up with a rueful smile. "I have a coded alarm system but no video surveillance. My clients value their privacy, and it's a bit intrusive."

It's also expensive, Sam thought. "What about other points of entry?" she inquired. "A backdoor, rooftop access?"

"We have a small fire door in back. It's a key entry, but it's always locked."

Sam shot a glance at Weller and saw the skepticism in his eyes.

"Why don't we see where the crime took place?" Weller moved before he'd finished the sentence and made a beeline for the back room.

"Before we go in, I should explain—" JT began, but the homicide detective had ducked under the velvet rope. She practically bounded after him.

"Mind telling me what's going on, Ms. Templeton?"

Frank Weller kept his voice low, almost pleasant. His expression gave no hint of the anger Sam sensed beneath his words. He was a volcano ready to explode. She didn't blame him.

The carved bird in the human hand sat inside its transparent prison, its single eye winking in the spotlight. Nothing was out of place, no smashed glass or broken wires or even an interruption of the crossing red beams.

Several expressions flitted across the gallery owner's face: chagrin, guilt, embarrassment, all quickly replaced with defiance.

Sam felt a headache coming on. Did this woman drag them away from a major crime scene for her amusement?

"This is not what it looks like," JT began, then stopped. "That is to say, this situation is not a prank. That—thing—is not the piece that was here this morning or last week. It's not the piece Wallace made for the exhibit. It is not Bird in Hand. Do you understand what I'm saying? It's a fake, junk, a grade school art project. Can't you see that?"

Sam held up a hand to stave off Weller's undoubtedly impolite reply and stepped forward.

"Wait, I'll—" JT moved towards a pad on the far wall. Too late. The red beams hit Sam like so many knife cuts as she strode over to the carving and lifted the glass box. Nothing happened, no screeching sirens, flashing lights, locking doors, or mechanical voice that issued a warning.

Weller walked up and waved his hand through the lights just before JT punched in the code that shut them down. "Fake security for a fake bird," he growled. "Oh, this just gets better and better."

Sam stared at the carving. It looked unfinished. All the elements were in place, but they lacked any finesse. Detailing was almost completely absent. The materials were inferior, the wood cheap and unevenly stained, the eye lifeless, like a used marble. Seen up close, the piece didn't even measure up to Bonnet's more workmanlike decoys.

"Wallace's piece was not fake," JT declared. "It was an original."

"What does your insurance cover, Ms. Templeton?" Weller asked.

"It's fairly basic at this point. I intended to increase the coverage as soon as I'd made a sale."

"And was Bird in Hand—the one you originally had here— separately insured?"

"Separately?"

"That's what I asked, Ms. Templeton."

"Oh, well." JT stumbled in her response. "Wallace and I were going back and forth about all of that."

"Why the pretend protection? The lights, the guard?"

JT compressed her lips and crossed her arms, the very image of defensiveness.

"The security added to the impression of value. Not that Wallace's piece needed the help. It's a masterpiece that brought to life not just the bird but the entire legend of the lost piece of art. A one-of-a-kind piece that looked as if it could have been a royal commission bound for the new world."

Sam shot JT a disbelieving look. "We already had this discussion, JT," she said. "Even if you present it as a sort of 'is it or isn't it' tease, you're still dangerously close to fraud."

"I haven't once claimed that what I showed at the gallery was anything other than Wallace Bonnet's work," JT snapped. "I cater to the whims of particular clients for particular pieces. If one of them wants to offer top dollar, if he wants to pretend to his friends or himself that he has purchased a treasure of some sort, he is well within his rights. Wallace's creations would fetch top dollar on their own."

Weller was prowling around the room. "I'd like to see the second floor," he said.

"You can do that," JT replied, "But nothing has been disturbed."

"How many people besides you have access to the gallery?" Sam demanded. "The code to the front, maybe a key to the back?"

"It's a short list, Lieutenant. Me, Amy, Evan Carr, the young man who has worked for me a short time, the cleaning woman, perhaps one or two of my contractors."

"That's a long list," Weller observed.

"What about Wallace Bonnet?" Sam asked.

She looked startled, her blue eyes wide like a deer caught in the headlights.

"Wallace? Why would you ask that?"

"You texted, 'The bastard took it. After all I've done for him.' I'm guessing you don't mean either Evan or your contractors. Maybe you gave your star artist a way into your studio." *Or more than that*, Sam thought.

JT shook her head. "I shouldn't have said anything."

"But you did," Weller replied with his trademark impatience. "You implicated Wallace Bonnet. Which means that the same night his place burns to the ground, he makes a trip to your gallery and removes his own work. Or he takes something that never belonged to him in the first place. Which is it, Ms. Templeton?"

Dearest Teresa,

I am writing from Charles Town, where we have just docked. Our crew is filled with new faces, the deserters having been replaced by those eager to escape their misery. Captain Digg exercised some discretion, I am pleased to note. But for his offers, many of the desperate souls would have joined with the thieves who roam the seas.

Thaddeus Bell, our ship's surgeon and my steadfast traveling companion, left us in Bermuda, as I predicted. He decided to marry the widow whose acquaintance he had made but a week earlier. The brief wedding ceremony, presided over by a dyspeptic minister from the Church of England, was followed by festivities that lasted until dawn. I repaired to my room much before then and slept deeply, aided by copious amounts of rum, I must admit.

The unexpected union delayed our trip by a few days, an event that proved to be providential. Not two weeks earlier, the notorious scoundrel Blackbeard sailed into the Charles Town harbour with four ships and several hundred men. According to the residents, many still quite shaken by their ordeal, the pirates captured the pilot boat and held some eight ships in the bay awaiting departure. They prevented inward-bound ships as well, so that trade came to a halt.

Thankfully, there were no casualties, though there was property damage in the form of smashed windows and small fires. Yet little was taken from the shops and homes, or so say the town citizens.

Even more surprising, the treacherous thief negotiated a peculiar price. Not silver or gold but a chest of medicines and a quantity of food. The good people of Charles Town, exhausted from warring with the Indians who regularly threaten, acquiesced to Blackbeard's demands with something like relief.

Not a week after arriving, he and his men departed. No one knows where he is bound, except that his ships were seen heading in a northerly direction.

Once again, our pirate has surprised us. Perhaps he is not the blood-thirsty monster of legend, but a man who commands a motley group of other men, all of them outliers scrambling to survive in a harsh new world while savoring a taste of freedom.

We may never know. Like many others, I regard the pirates with a mix of trepidation and curiosity. I am well aware that they are all criminals. They have broken the law and have caused much economic and personal distress.

Yet I do not fear them, Teresa. They are not killers but vagabonds, tired and ill and much depleted in resources and in spirit. I suspect they will look for a way to arrange for a pardon, albeit on their own terms, and we shall be free of them at last.

Yours in devotion,
William

Chapter 20

Another restless night during which Sam imagined she was trapped between a wall of fire and wall of water. She wasn't alone but surrounded by dozens of people who kept reminding her she was sworn to protect them. Fat chance of that.

She woke to see her left arm lying heavy on the bed. The bulky bandages reminded her how badly she'd been burned. She didn't need to be reminded how much it still hurt.

Her analog clock, one that had belonged to her father, read 6:15. Four hours wasn't nearly enough sleep. Especially the way she slept.

She should have headed to the critical care center instead of rushing over to see JT. She'd hoped she could tie whatever happened at the gallery to the fire and homicide at Bonnet's home. Instead, the visit only produced more questions. JT was holding something back; that much was clear.

By the time Sam and Weller left, her arm was killing her, and he was on his last nerve.

"Talk about back-peddling," he'd fumed. "Ms. Templeton suddenly can't be sure who took the piece or how valuable it was or even if she wants the place swept for evidence. I'd like to arrest her for wasting our time."

"She's protecting someone," Sam suggested. "Probably Bonnet."

"Protecting him from what? Overvaluing his own art? Breaking his contract?"

"The piece I saw at the opening wasn't ordinary by any stretch of the imagination. The real question is, what makes it so valuable that he'd risk stealing it?"

"No, it isn't," Weller retorted. "The real question is, what does any of this have to do with our arson slash homicide?

Unless Bonnet is behind all of it. Hell, maybe Fitchett and Fox stumbled onto the fact that he's a fraud as well as a failure. Maybe he used Fitchett for inspiration because he couldn't come up with an original idea to save his life. Maybe he got a talented friend to carve the piece. Everyone says he's a good-looking guy. Maybe he wowed Ms. Templeton with his smile, even though she suspected he's a phony. Maybe he decided to humiliate her just before he ran off."

"That's a whole lot of maybes, Frank."

"Yeah, well, maybe this whole thing has turned into a colossal cluster-fuck, Lieutenant."

"You can bail anytime, Detective Sergeant." Sam kept her eyes on the road. She didn't need to look at him. She figured the suggestion would sting.

In the forty-five minutes they'd been absent, the fires had diminished and the crowd had grown. Sam hadn't realized so many people lived in the area. Or maybe this was what passed for entertainment in the late autumn after most of the tourists had packed up and gone.

Gordy and McCready were in the thick of things, as were four other arson investigators Sam hadn't seen earlier. Gordy was listening to a bystander who, from what Sam could hear, mixed a bit of knowledge with a lot of innuendo.

She heard McCready explain to another crowd member that the investigating officers wanted to talk with people who had seen visitors to Bonnet's property in the last week or so.

"I saw her drive by," the young man said and pointed at Sam. "Does that count?"

She and Weller made their way to the lead arson investigators. Josh Abrams, his face sooty, raised a hand in greeting. "That didn't take long. Learn anything?"

"Nothing useful," Weller replied before Sam could say anything. "You?"

"The primary accelerants were gasoline and turpentine. I could see how the latter might be found in an artist's studio but not the former, not with all that wood around. Oh, and your forensic investigator determined that someone poured accelerant on your victim. Didn't quite cover him but got the legs."

"Intentional," Weller said.

"And cruel," Sam added with a shudder. "No one ought to spend his last hours on earth that way."

Shortly after, she'd gone home to dream about death and suffering, torture and cruelty. Fire and water.

She threw back the covers and shivered in the moist air that had made its way in via the old cottage's leaky seams. She loved fresh air, loved waking to the briny smell of the bay and the plaintive cries of the waterfowl. But it was late in the season now. Even with her gun by her bed, she didn't feel as if she could keep a window open.

Maybe I do need a dog, she told herself. *Or a less remote romantic partner*.

She popped two extra-strength Tylenol. Safe enough, except when washed down with bourbon, which she might have done last night. She sighed and flipped on the coffee machine. Her abbreviated yoga session didn't lessen the pain in her arm, but it loosened other muscles.

In the shower, she ventured a peak under the bandages she wasn't supposed to touch. The skin was raw and gave off an unpleasant smell, a mix of salve and burnt skin that made her recoil.

She was at her desk by eight, steaming mug of coffee at hand. She reviewed the notes left by Gordy and McCready. The near universal opinion of Wallace Bonnet was that he was a hardworking neighbor, helpful and even generous in lending his carpentry skills as the need arose. He seemed to be easy with working folks and wealthy inhabitants alike.

Just before lunch, Gordy entered with his own mug and sat opposite her.

"How's the arm?" he asked.

"You don't want to know."

"Will you at least get it looked at by a medical professional?"

"I promise." She seemed to make a lot of promises these days, including to herself, that she wasn't sure she could keep. "I was just going over your notes. It seems Wallace Bonnet is a model citizen."

"Regular Boy Scout," Gordy replied.

"Not the sort to strangle a man and burn his hands or torch another one."

"Not even the sort to break into the gallery of a benefactor and steal back his prized piece except under duress."

Sam sat back. "What are you thinking, Gordy?"

"Let me get back to you on that. I have another tidbit that may mean something or nothing."

Sam sighed. "Like everything else about this case. Shoot."

"I caught a glimpse of Ben Hart in the crowd."

She shuffled through the notes on her desk. "Is that in here?"

"You might not have gotten to it yet."

"Did you talk with him?"

"Tried to. By the time I pushed through, he'd vanished."

She sank back down. "St. Michaels is not next door to Baltimore. How did he happen to be in the area just about the time of the fire?"

"I was wondering the same thing. And while we're on the subject of Mr. Hart, Pat did a little digging. He made some interesting connections."

Pat, not Deputy McCready or "the kid." Sam suppressed a smile. "Do tell."

"Okay, let me see if I got this straight. Ben Hart is a descendant of John Hart, the provisional governor of Maryland whose picture we found on Fitchett's wall. The name also showed up in the photocopied letter as the probable recipient of the carving."

Sam steepled her fingers. "So, Ben Hart may have a stake in the discovery of Bird in Hand that goes beyond the vicarious thrill of a treasure hunt."

Gordy nodded. "Not out of the question. Family history is still more important to some people than money. Especially in parts of Maryland and Virginia."

"He may, in fact, feel as if the carving belongs to him," Sam said.

"Assuming it exists."

"There's always that. Nevertheless, I'd like to have him in again." Sam rubbed the familiar spot in the middle of her forehead. "Is it just me, or is our suspect list growing longer?"

"You could argue it's a wash, especially as at least one of our former persons of interest is now our latest victim." He hesitated. "What's next?"

"I need more information. Where do we stand with the DSFM report?"

"There's a fresh crew out there this morning, along with one of the two leads from last night. Abrams, I think. They need a couple of days, and that's rushing it. Donahue got the autopsy on Charles Fox expedited. That takes place later today. You want me to head up there?"

"Please."

"If you don't mind my asking, how does Detective Sergeant Weller fit into all this?"

Sam's cell phone chose that moment to signal her. "Speak of the devil," she said. "Weller has to stay in Baltimore, but he's sending Pollack and Caine in to, in his words, receive their assignments. He almost sounds apologetic. What do you know?" She noticed her lead detective's expression. "You look skeptical."

"Not sure I trust Weller's change of heart. He seemed ready to walk last night."

"We were all on edge. Look, can you work with Pollack?"

"Sure. You want Carol back on site with Tyler Caine?"

"Let's do that." She looked at her watch. "Damn, I need to sit down with the sheriff."

Sam found Donahue in his office. He looked like she felt, frustrated and exhausted.

"Sit," he ordered. "What do we have?"

She filled him in with the little she had.

"The Ben Hart lead is interesting, but Wallace Bonnet remains our primary suspect. No love lost between him and Fox, according to your previous reports. Hard to believe he'd set the guy on fire and burn down his own place in the process."

"What if Fox set the fire and Bonnet caught him?"

Donahue leaned forward, his fatigue momentarily forgotten. "Explain."

Sam thought a minute. "Fox claimed his interest started and ended with the old letters Fitchett was collecting. To hear him tell it, he knew nothing about Fitchett's hunt for the wood carving. In fact, he dismissed it as a fable."

"You didn't believe him," Donahue said.

"No. Something about how he looked at the sketch we showed him stayed with me. He was covetous, that's the word. Maybe he found out Fitchett was holding back as to the carving's hiding place—" she caught Donahue's doubtful look— "okay, supposed hiding place. If Fox felt betrayed by his partner, he might have decided to act. Not directly; he'd hire a killer, maybe plan to make it look like the work of a cartel assassin."

"And Bonnet?"

"Bonnet and Fitchett were friends. They might also have been partners on this venture. Bonnet has access to more money than he pretends. If Fox thought he was being played or cut out, he might have decided to threaten Bonnet by burning his workplace. Let's say Bonnet catches him, they argue, things get out of hand, Fox ends up on the floor, trapped inside, and Wallace Bonnet runs."

Even as she spun out her theory, Sam recognized the holes in it. She waited for Donahue to shoot it down. He nodded and said, "Too bad we can't ask Fox."

"We need to bring Hart in and find Bonnet." Sam jumped up, headed for the door, and stopped. "Sir, how's this playing on the outside, if you don't mind my asking?"

"You mean in the press?"

"Or Annapolis."

"What's on your mind, Lieutenant?"

In for a penny. "Early on, you suggested we might be out of our depth," she said. Yet you've essentially brought this case back to our office. What changed?"

Donahue gave a weary half-smile. "MSP has legitimate concerns about increased cartel presence in the state. Those concerns conveniently coincide with increased political pressure and that frees up state money to address the problem. Which means the agency also has a set of priorities and a blind spot where local issues are concerned. You're new, but you already have a feel for the players and the stakes involved."

She nodded slowly. "It feels personal."

"It is. Everybody knew Arley Fitchett."

Chapter 21

Over the course of the next seven days, Sam slept poorly if she slept at all. Bad dreams weren't what kept her up, though. She owed her fatigue to poor Arley Fitchett, not to mention the late Charles Fox.

Two days after Sam's conversation with Donahue, she had Benjamin Hart back in her office, looking less self-assured than he did during his first visit.

"We saw you at the scene of a suspicious fire and likely homicide," Sam began without preamble. "It's been all over the news, so don't pretend you don't know what I'm talking about. I want to know why you were there."

Hart looked stricken. "I came to St. Michaels to see Charles Fox."

"You had an appointment?"

He hung his head. "No. He wasn't in his office."

"Explain. All of it. Don't leave anything out."

Fitchett had told him about the old documents he believed led to a treasure hidden somewhere on the Eastern Shore. "When he mentioned Bird in Hand, I almost laughed," Hart recalled. "Arley was serious, though. He showed me the letters. The two originals looked, well, original. The others, who knows? I thought he was getting scammed. His contact, friend, whatever, wanted $50,000. He'd already sent $15,000. That was a lot of money for him."

Fitchett had all but demanded an introduction to any potential investors among the Maryland Free-State Treasure Club members. He'd even pushed Hart to float him a loan.

"Arley thought the carving was probably worth something to my family. That was crazy. I mean, no one cares about heirlooms anymore. A gemstone eye, sure. But an old wooden bird? Besides, what are the chances it even survived? Anyway, Fitchett came up to Baltimore in August to tell me he had a new partner, an appraiser from St. Michaels, and I'd missed a golden opportunity."

"And after he died, you decided to investigate on your own?"

Hart glanced away. "I did. There was Fox, and there was this artist who'd just made a big splash with his carvings, one of which sounded like Arley's bird. I didn't think it was a coincidence.

"Wallace Bonnet."

"Right. Anyway, I was going to try and catch Fox late in the day, but he'd already left his office. Then all the sirens started. I went to check it out. I never imagined—" His eyes widened. "Did Bonnet kill Fox? And Arley?"

Sam ignored the question. "Why didn't you come to the police? To me?"

"I find things, Lieutenant. I figured I could find out enough on my own and then bring it to you. I liked Arley. I wanted to do right by him."

Sam dismissed the chastened young man with a stern warning about the consequences of meddling in police business.

The reports that came in over the next few days were as expected. The fire marshal's office confirmed arson. A singed container found close to the studio pointed to gasoline as the primary accelerant.

Charles Fox's autopsy suggested a man in less than optimal health, under-exercised and over-fed. He had high cholesterol and blood pressure, both of which he'd treated with medicine. Would he have been able to drag or roll a heavy gas canister into the studio? Was he nimble enough to set the fire with any hope of escape? Could he have engaged in a struggle with Bonnet while the flames rose around them? Her theory about Fox as the instigator and victim of his own crime didn't hold water.

That was before she read that a tiny splinter was found embedded in the back of the victim's skull. The material looked to be white ash. No traces had been found in Bonnet's studio. He used cedar wood for his carvings or, in the case of his special carving, an African hardwood.

"You know what's made out of white ash?" Gordy said. "A baseball bat."

Sam began to consider whether Wallace Bonnet was capable of murder. What did she know about the man with the slow-to-start career and the well-connected parents? More significantly, why would he kill a man he called his friend and then kill another man and destroy his life's work? These were among the many questions she would ask him when she tracked him down.

If she tracked him down.

She contacted Frank Weller about interviewing James Bonnet. It was hard to believe the father was completely ignorant of his son's whereabouts. Weller eagerly accepted her invitation to join her. He was obviously aware that their positions might once again be reversed if she couldn't make headway with the case. He might even decide during the ride to D.C. to take a poke at her leadership skills and put in yet another none-too-subtle suggestion about MSP's suitability to lead the investigation.

* * *

The last thing an exhausted Sam wanted to see when she got home that evening was a black Escalade idling in plain sight in front of her cottage. She pulled off the path and killed the engine and the lights. She could barely make out the driver, a male figure in a cap. The visibly agitated man pacing her front porch was easier to spot. This was no cartel representative, she realized. Nonetheless, she pulled her gun from her tote bag and held it loosely at her side, safety off.

She sidled up to the car and tapped on the window. "Step out, please."

The startled driver did so. Sam quickly patted him down, then looked through the car, all the while keeping her gun trained on him.

"You don't need to do that, Lieutenant," the man on the porch called out.

"Oh, but I do, Mr. Bonnet, especially with unexpected visitors." She motioned the man to move away from the car and stay within the circle of her porch light.

James Bonnet stopped pacing and stared at her gun "We need to talk," he said. "Could you put that thing away?"

Sam looked over at the driver, who'd moved off to one side. He was holding a cigarette; his hand was shaking.

"Roberto's been with me for thirty-one years," Bonnet added. "As a driver, not a bodyguard. He doesn't carry a weapon."

"Fine." She lowered her gun. "Let me dump my stuff inside. Hope you like bourbon."

She threw her bag on the couch, tucked her gun into her waistband, and came back out with two drinks. Bonnet downed his in two gulps and launched into a rambling defense of his son.

Sam let him go on for a minute or two. Then she interrupted him to ask about Wallace's work, his friends, even his bank account.

"He's got money from his mother's side of the family, enough to keep him comfortable," Bonnet said. "She has her own source of funding. We consider his St. Michaels home to be an investment."

Sam was struck by an idea. "Does your wife have relatives abroad?"

The older man bristled. "If you think Wendy snuck our son out of the country, you're barking up the wrong tree."

About Wallace's current life his father had little to say. "Wallace has talent," he conceded. "But he's terrible at marketing himself. JT was the one who persuaded me his work might turn a profit."

The idea that the artist might have been inspired by an old fable made sense to the elder Bonnet. "It probably appealed to his whimsical side," he said.

He knew even less about his son's relationships. He'd never heard about any treasure hunting friends named Fitchett. He'd been told JT had an eye for slightly younger men. Possibly her interest was more than professional. He had no idea whether Wallace reciprocated. "She's attractive and he's an adult" was all he had to say on the subject.

An hour later, James Bonnet took off for a political function, leaving Sam with nothing but a desperate plea from a desperate father.

"Find him, Lieutenant. He's not a killer. I'm worried he might be a victim."

* * *

She went to Donahue the next day to report on her interview with Ben Hart and her surprise visit from James Bonnet.

"Close the door, Lieutenant," he said. "I've already heard from someone very high up in the governor's office. Early this morning, before I had time to finish my second cup of coffee." He exhaled. "Ah, hell, I'll just come out and say it. Effective immediately, Maryland State Police's Criminal Investigation Bureau will take the lead on the Fitchett and Fox homicides and the disappearance of Wallace Bonnet. Senior investigators from our office will provide support as needed."

He was watching her, waiting for her to explode.

"Did James Bonnet complain?" she asked.

"I think this was the governor's idea. He's up for reelection and he's got wealthy donors with second homes around here to satisfy. The feeling seems to be this is too big for our office to handle on our own."

"Does Weller know? That he's in charge again?" She pushed away the wave of anger that threatened her superficial calm.

"His commander does, which means he does." Donahue sat back, his eyes on his lieutenant. "Meet with Weller as soon as possible. Make sure everyone is up to date. Share everything. And Tate? Keep your cool. You don't think I can see how hopping mad you are? I would be, too. Nothing to be done about it. Remember, you were the one who figured out what these killings were really about. Push comes to shove, I have your back."

"Appreciate it, Sheriff."

* * *

Two days later, she was staring out the window of Ted's Bulletin, a popular all-day breakfast place on Capitol Hill. The

Sunday before Thanksgiving was less crowded than usual but still busy.

"I wish you could take a couple of days off, come with me to Colorado over Thanksgiving," Terry said between bites of his burrito. "Mountains, fresh air. You'd like my mother. Besides, I'm planning a field trip that might interest you."

Sam kept her head to the street. She stirred her fruit and granola without looking at it.

"Hey, Tate, are you even listening to me?" Terry reached over and took her hand. "What's going on? You had plenty to say in your sleep, none of it especially comforting."

She looked at him, allowing herself to swim for a brief instant in the warm glow of his amber eyes. "What did I say?"

"Nothing out of the ordinary, if ordinary includes shouting 'save her!' or 'no!' or some such thing. I suppose it beats hearing you whisper the name of a secret lover." He peered at her. "Aw, come on. Nothing? Not even the smallest smile?"

She pushed up one corner of her mouth, though it cost her. "I'm sorry, Terry. You ought to kick me out of bed."

"Not gonna happen."

"I haven't been very good company this weekend." She pushed her parfait away, took a swig of coffee.

"Sam, I've said this before, and I'll say it again. You need to talk with someone. In fact, I have this for you." He withdrew his hand to reach for his wallet, pulled out a card, and pushed it across the table. "Joanna Putnam. She's got an opening the day after Thanksgiving. Go see her. Please."

She felt herself go cold. She crossed her arms and leaned away. "Did you also take it upon yourself to make an appointment for me?" she asked coldly.

Terry took a bite of his food and followed it with a sip of coffee. Deliberate movements designed to project an aura of calm authority, she supposed. They only infuriated her, as did the way he looked at her.

"You're under a lot of stress, Sam. You're not sleeping. Your mother spoke for the first time in, what, twenty-six years, only to issue some sort of warning we can't ask her about. You've been physically injured. I probably shouldn't ask you if you've had that looked at."

"You probably shouldn't," Sam retorted, although in fact she'd gone to an urgent care facility two days earlier and been told the wound was healing "as well as could be expected."

"You're three months on a new job," Terry continued, "with a department that sees maybe four homicides in a year and you're already dealing with half that many."

"I might be a murder magnet. Wherever I go, dead people follow."

"Sam, all I'm doing—"

"All you're doing is profiling me. Or infantilizing me. Either way, I don't appreciate it."

Terry smacked the table with his fist, hard enough to make the silverware jump. The clatter was lost in the noise of the place, but Sam flinched.

"Would you stop being so damned obstinate, Sam? I'm trying to help."

"Did you ever consider that I don't need long-distance help?" *Oh, shit*, she thought. *Now I've said it.*

Terry sat back as if she'd slapped him. "I thought we were doing okay," he said. "We don't get to see each other as often as we'd like, but given our careers, that was to be expected."

"No, you're doing okay, Terry. You're on a rewarding career track. I'm stuck in the mud, and you know it."

"Come on, Sam."

"You're looking at a pot of gold at the end of that rainbow. I'm stuck under a glass ceiling in a job that should have been a walk in the park, except this case has me grasping at straws. I'm between a rock and a hard place, my goddamned partner can't see the forest for the trees, and what if this is the tip of the iceberg?"

She realized Terry had clapped a hand over his mouth to muffle a snort that still managed to escape.

"Are you really laughing at me?"

"I'm waiting for you to run out of clichés."

She pressed her lips together to keep from smiling. "Okay, you got me. What I'm trying to say is that I'm in a frustrating situation. It's not that I'm incapable of handling change. If you don't believe that, if you don't believe in me, well, I'm not sure how to respond."

"I do, Sam," Terry protested. "I know these last few months have been difficult for you. For both of us, but especially for you. And I know how capable you are, even if the people you're working for haven't yet caught on."

He ran his hand through his hair. "On top of all this, someone is poking his or her nose into your past. We don't know who and we don't know why after all this time. I'm kicking myself for not being able to figure it out."

Sam reached across the table and put a hand to his face. "I know you are, Terry. I want to help." She picked up the card. "Maybe this Dr. Putnam can clear out the cobwebs, break loose that chunk of memory that stays hidden. At the very least, she might be able to keep me from going crazier."

Terry grabbed her hand. His amber eyes lit up. "I love you, Sam Tate," he said. "Got it?"

She swallowed. "Got it," she replied.

Chapter 22

Just before the night bled into a wakeful predawn, Sam found herself recollecting life before the madman shot up her brother's wedding. Mostly pleasant memories: the start of the baseball season (her Queens neighborhood was solidly pro-Mets), the Columbus Day Parade, which she generally watched from an enviable perch on her father's shoulders. Holiday celebrations.

Thanksgiving dinner at her Aunt Rosa's house was always a raucous affair. There was no table set aside for the children. "If they can feed themselves, they can sit with the adults," her uncle Jimmy said on more than one occasion. A dozen people or more would gather at a long table that filled the dining room of Jimmy and Rosa's modest house, laughing, shouting, squabbling. Even the discussions sounded like arguments.

The meal made no concessions to the holiday. Rosa never bothered with a turkey. "Who wants a bird that doesn't taste?" she'd ask rhetorically. They'd sit down to a big Italian feast with pasta and clam sauce, eggplant parmesan, and always a fresh ham from Rosa's favorite butcher. Dessert was panna cotta and cannoli from Joe's Bakery.

Every year her mom would suggest maybe they go out, just the four of them. Or visit Gillian and Kevin in Delaware. She'd even offer to host a more traditional meal at their house. Every year her father would wave her off. "Rosa likes to do it, Colleen," he'd say. "Besides, it's more fun when the whole family is together," apparently referring to his side, not hers.

How could Colleen object? His family was right there, same neighborhood, just a couple of New Jersey relatives who always made the trip. Whereas all she had to bring to the table, so to speak, was a brother in California whom she hardly ever saw, a childless sister in Delaware, and a couple of disreputable cousins up in Boston.

Decades later, Colleen's daughter spent the early part of Thanksgiving eating turkey off paper plates with her mother and the residents of Silver Manor and the afternoon at her computer with a bowl of nuts and a glass of bourbon close at hand. Lucy had invited her to the Donahue gathering. Sam couldn't imagine crashing a family ritual. She especially didn't want to think about sitting at her boss's table while two homicides remained unsolved.

She spoke with Terry that night, enjoyed a brief but warm conversation with his mother, and fell into a dreamless sleep.

The following day, she knocked on the door of a tasteful Georgetown townhouse that housed the office and living quarters of Dr. Joanna Putnam.

"Lieutenant Tate. Dr. Joanna Putnam. Nice to meet you."

The woman who answered the door offered a firm handshake and a bright white smile. She was petite, with skin that owed either to impeccable genes or a superb foundation. Her crisp white blouse, tailored jacket, and creased black pants suggested an eye for quality clothing. She'd pulled her shiny hair, dark with caramel highlights, back in a bun.

Sam was acquainted with the stereotype of the rumpled therapist in an oversized cardigan and ill-fitting eyeglasses. Her experienced doctors had always looked more like corporate movers and shakers than healers. She didn't mind. Those trim and tidy people projected experience, stability, and understated confidence.

"Thank you for seeing me during the holidays, Dr. Putnam," Sam said. "And please, call me Sam."

"No trouble at all," replied the doctor. Sam noticed she didn't propose they both use first names. Fine by Sam.

They settled into matching leather chairs, each with a side table. No couch. Sam liked that.

"First of all," Putnam began, "our discussions are confidential. Per your instructions, we aren't billing these sessions through your insurance. In fact, they'll be complimentary." She put up a hand against Sam's protest. "I'm good with the arrangement. Terry indicated I might be helping on a cold case. I'm glad to do so."

"What else did he tell you?" Sam asked. *How well do you know him?* she wondered.

"I've been happily married for fifteen years," Putnam said as if reading her mind. "I was friends with Terry's late wife. The four of us were close. The three of us still are." Another smile, absolutely genuine and absolutely gorgeous.

"As far as what he told me, Sam, he presented more an overview. You've had an interesting life. A stint as a country singer, an army tour, several years as a detective in Nashville, then a few more as a county sheriff in north-central Tennessee, which is where you met him. You solved a long-running serial murder together. So, you two were partners and now you're more."

Sam blushed. "You could say that."

Putnam smiled. "I gather your life was upended when your mother lost her caretaker," she continued. "Now you're the new lieutenant in a department over on the Eastern Shore and you've landed two homicides in your first three months that are anything but straightforward."

"That's putting it mildly."

"A lot of changes. How are you handling them?"

Sam squirmed. "New situations always take getting used to," she replied. "As for complicated homicides, I've experienced my share of them."

"And your mother?"

"I suppose Terry told you she was the victim of a shooting that scrambled her mind."

"Yes."

"She doesn't know who I am. That's hard. It's been years. You'd think I'd be used to it."

"I'm not sure that's something you get used to. When did this shooting take place?"

"The Queens incident?"

Putnam cocked her head sideways, like an inquisitive bird. "Is that what you call it?"

"Well, I could call it 'the wedding massacre that decimated my family when I was nine, traumatized me, sent me into therapy, and then sent me running', but that's a little awkward."

"Indeed."

"You already know about it, Dr. Putnam. Either that or you don't shock easily."

"Both are true. And no, Terry didn't betray any confidences. I did some research." A slight upturn of her beautiful mouth.

"I suppose you want to know if that trauma continues to inform my life?"

"You tell me."

"Everything informs my life. That doesn't mean I'm suffering from the loss any more than anyone else would. But something about that day bothers me. I mean beyond the trauma. I missed something. A clue, something I registered but can't recall that would explain, well, everything."

Putnam folded her arms. She looked either amused or irritated, Sam couldn't tell.

"Hold on. You were a child and you were being shot at and people you knew and loved were falling down dead and injured around you. And you're disturbed that you might have missed something? Don't you think that's particularly unfair to the younger version of you?"

"No. I was always good at recall. Why is this any different?"

Putnam reached for a pen and paper. "Do you have nightmares or disturbing visions?"

Often, Sam thought. "Sometimes," she replied.

"Drugs or alcohol abuse?"

Sam hesitated a beat. "I like to drink. Like so many other cops, I'd guess."

"No thoughts of suicide?"

"No!" Sam answered a little too forcefully.

"Okay." Putnam set her pad aside, looked up. "Have you ever been treated for PTSD?"

Sam clenched her hands. She took a breath in and released it as slowly as possible. "We're getting off-track," she said.

"This line of questioning bothers you." Putnam made it a statement.

"I don't think that's my problem."

"Why? Because you can hold a job? Have a relationship? Because you survived the shooting that took your family? Because you served in Afghanistan, lost your fiancé in a car crash, work in one of the most stressful professions in the world, and still manage to get up in the morning? Because it isn't a good look on you?"

Sam flushed. She felt under attack.

Putnam sat forward. "Sam, I'm not saying you have post-traumatic stress disorder. I'm extremely careful about diagnosing something like that, much less treating it. At the same time, you're here because something continues to bother you. Something above and beyond the stresses of your job. Something you're smart enough not to ignore or bury with work or pills or alcohol." She looked pointedly at Sam.

"I'm not—"

"I don't think you're a danger to yourself or anyone else. Nor do I think your issues will tie you up for the rest of your life. But your past is eating at you."

Sam wanted to jump up and leave. She folded her arms across her chest, then realized she looked defensive. *Slow breaths*, she reminded herself and folded her hands in her lap.

"Did Terry mention that someone may be after me now—today—for some reason related to the wedding incident?" she asked. "Because what's eating at me right now is that I might be in danger. Worse, my mom might be in danger."

"He did."

Her gentle tone cut Sam's anger and angst in half almost immediately. "Doctor Putnam," she continued. "No question, I have issues. No doubt a trained psychologist like you can help. I have a problem that worries me even more than the crazy case I caught at work. Which, by the way, involves two homicides complete with pirates, shipwrecks, maybe a Mexican cartel, possibly the Russian mob, and a priceless treasure people are literally dying to possess."

She caught Putnam's surprised look and laughed.

"My point is, I have plenty to stress about already. Which is why I need to get at this wedding memory."

"Ok. Tell me what you think you remember."

Sam took a breath. "There was one guest in particular. A man wearing a brown suit. I mentioned him during my closed-door testimony but only in passing. I didn't think about him again until years after the incident. Now he routinely shows up in my nightmares. I still can't see his face. I don't know his significance, only that identifying him is crucial." Sam tapped her forehead. "I've tried to access what I recorded."

"Recorded?" Putnam sat straighter.

"Recorded in my head. That's how my mind has always worked, even as a little kid. I have a high rate of retention, even if I can't always sort my recollections into neat piles. What did I see that day? What am I struggling to remember? How can I achieve any kind of understanding about myself if I'm struggling with something like that?"

"I think we're both capable of multi-tasking, Sam," Putnam said quietly. "But we can start by addressing what's disturbing you about that incident."

"Can you perform hypnotherapy to extract suppressed memories? My shrink back in Nashville proposed something like that. I didn't want to at the time."

"Jayne Sommers." Putnam nodded. "The psychiatrist with MNPD who briefly treated you before her murder. When you gave me her name the other day, I went looking for notes. I couldn't find any."

"She wouldn't have kept mine on file within the Nashville police force. And no one ever found anything after she was murdered. Terry and I checked, using separate sources. No laptop, nothing on the cloud. It's as if she never saw me." Sam shivered.

"Never mind. Dr. Sommers offered to engage in a kind of recovered memory process?"

"Yes."

"And you declined. Not a bad decision." She looked at Sam with her dark eyes and steepled her hands.

"Sam, the theory that repressed memories can be recovered through hypnosis or some other guided process is extremely controversial, almost out of date. Most present-day psychiatrists hold serious reservations or dismiss the notion altogether. Extracted memories can be true or false, but there's no way to know which."

Sam' shoulders sagged. "What can we do?"

"We may not find it helpful to probe the unconscious, but who's to say you can't pull what you need from your conscious mind? Sam, you just said you've always had the ability to take mental notes of what you were seeing. You probably remember a lot about the day. Have you ever talked about it in great detail? I mean recently, as an adult. With Terry or with Dr. Sommers, perhaps?"

"No. Terry read the reports; I think that was enough for him. Sommers tried to take me through it, but I resisted." She stopped to collect her thoughts. "I always felt a little reluctant to open up to her."

"Something told you not to."

"Maybe. Sixth sense or gut instinct. What if I were protecting information I already had?"

"It's possible. But in order to find out, we'll have to take you through the day in as much detail as you can recall. If you'd like, I can retrieve the notes from the court-appointed psychologist who interviewed you at the time to help jog your memory."

Sam shook her head. "I don't need you to. I can do this."

"Start talking, then."

"Do you want to write anything down?"

"I want to listen."

Sam took herself back to the child she was, a nine-year-old named Sophia wearing a pink dress and grown-up shoes. She recalled the smell of perfume, the blue of the sky, the pride in the eyes of her parents, the spark that passed between them she hoped might end their squabbling. She again felt the thrill of being included in the wedding party as "maiden of honor."

She watched her parents head down the aisle, followed by a succession of groomsmen and bridesmaids. Then it was her turn. She moved slowly, head up, looking neither to the right nor the left but only at her brother Stefan and her handsome cousin Johnny, both of whom seemed to guide her to the platform.

"You didn't notice the man in the brown suit as you walked down the aisle?" Dr. Putnam asked.

Sam considered the question. "Not until I reached the dais. But I think maybe—" she broke off. "My parents were smiling when they started down the aisle. Then my mother stumbled. I remember that because my father caught her. She'd glanced to her right, I think, and then she looked scared, as if she'd seen a ghost."

"Do you have any idea what she saw? Or maybe who she saw?"

"I hadn't thought about it until just now. Anyway, we were all on the dais when Arthur Randolph started yelling about losing the love of his life and how if he couldn't have her, no one could. Everyone else started screaming things like 'he's got a gun' and my parents stood up. I told all that to the people who interviewed me. I may have mentioned a man in a brown suit, but it was more like a throwaway detail, I guess. I 'm not sure."

She closed her eyes and opened them again. "The 'ghost' my mother saw was Brown Suit. That's why I remember him. I also remember that he stood up and pointed his gun at us, not Randolph." She put her hands to her forehead. "How did I not remember all this until now?"

"You held onto it. You simply didn't allow it to surface."

"Two shooters," Sam said. She jumped up and paced the room, trying to slow her pounding heart.

"It sounds that way," Putnam agreed.

"Two different agendas, though."

"What makes you say that?"

"Randolph was crazed. A lot of his shots went wild. Brown Suit was calm."

"A trained killer, perhaps," Putnam said.

"I think so."

"You must be wondering why an assassin was at your brother's wedding."

Sam stopped and stared at the therapist. "And who was he targeting?"

Chapter 23

Terry got out of the rental car and stretched. He looked around, took a moment to focus. All along the drive away from Colorado Springs, he'd been awash in nostalgia. His hometown at the base of Pikes Peak had grown so fast he barely recognized it. Colorado Springs had been touted as one of the country's most desirable places to live. Millennials and retirees alike flocked to the small city because of relatively low taxes and breathtaking scenery (minus Denver's air pollution).

What mattered to Terry was that his mother, who he'd stopped to visit, appeared to be thriving. She'd recently relinquished her position as the junior high school principal and found a compatible companion named Neil with whom to share morning hikes and who knows what else? Terry didn't want to think about that. He was pleased for her and she for his professional success. He told her about Sam. Ever reserved, she just smiled and mentioned the joys of having a partner.

He wished he could have brought Sam, but she was slammed. The latest death in her small community muddied the waters. Charles Fox's tie to Arley Fitchett provided grounds for suspicion. Walter Bonnet's disappearance was disturbing. At least Weller was coming around, however reluctantly.

The idea that homicides get solved within seventy-two hours or drag on for months or years was more than an old wives' tale. Trails ran cold, leads dried up. Terry had chased the Wedding Crasher for six long years, all the while trying to reassure his bosses he was up to the task. He knew Sam was going through some of the same experiences.

He drove the three hundred miles to Telluride along familiar roads. He and his father had stayed overnight twice before the older man's death. In high school, Terry managed to snag an invite to the "winter home" of a wealthy pal three years running. These outings were supposed to be chaperoned; at least that's what he told his mother. He smiled at the recollection.

Long a top-notch ski resort, the town retained an unspoiled, almost fairy tale quality, helped by its National Historic Preservation designation. The locals prided themselves on the town's authenticity. No chain stores and no stop lights. Plenty of money, though, along with a healthy respect for privacy. All of which made it an ideal residence for someone like Jonathan Sells, the man Terry was on his way to see.

Main Street was crowded with tourists and ski bums willing to risk unpredictable weather to get in ahead of the holiday crowds. At the other end, he took a series of turns that had the little Toyota puffing from exertion. At last he came up on a small sign that said simply "Sells" and a small number. Exceptionally subtle, it would be an effective way to cut down on visitors.

Per his instructions, Terry left the car in a small turn-off and headed up a winding path. After perhaps forty yards, he came upon a flight of steps cut into a hill. He climbed a dozen carved steps to a slate path. That in turn led to an ornate gate almost hidden behind a mix of pines and aspens.

He pushed through to a garden and a second pathway that ended at a one-of-a-kind house that looked like a cross between a fairy tale cottage and an upscale mountain resort. He heard water, maybe a brook. When he knocked on the simple front door, the peaceful burbling was replaced by a lively chorus of woofs and yaps.

The woman who answered was slender, with a plain open face that had spent time outdoors. She'd pulled her faded blond hair back with a rubber band. Surrounding her were four dogs: a black lab, a golden retriever, and two smaller canines of indeterminate origin, all barking in a loud but friendly manner.

"Jack! Sadie! Tieg! Lola! All of you, sit!" The dogs quieted and sat, except for the smallest, a terrier mix who barked anxiously, eyes on his mistress, until she picked him up.

"It's okay, Tieg," she cooed. "It's all good. Sorry about that," she added, her grin wry and knowing.

"It's fine. Are you Mrs. Sells?"

"Hogan. I kept my name. You can call me Kate. And you're Agent Sloan."

"Special Agent Terry Sloan. You can call me Terry. Thanks for taking my call."

"John's in his studio."

"His studio?"

"He's an inventor. Fun things that entertain children. Important things that keep airplanes flying. Things that pay for all this." Her smile lit her face. "He's expecting you. Follow me."

She led him out of the modest hallway into an enormous living area with beamed ceilings that stretched thirty feet up in parts. At one end, a circular staircase wound out of sight. Soaring windows looked out onto a spectacular vista of jagged snow-capped peaks. The area beyond the spacious back deck was relatively compact and ingeniously designed. Small ponds bisected multi-tiered patios, all connected by imaginatively designed foot bridges. The pool was flanked by a hot tub and an open fireplace.

A waterfall tumbled next to a secondary building. "My drawing studio," Kate explained.

"It's all magnificent," Terry told her, stopping to look at the view.

"We've been fortunate," she replied.

Their journey continued through a small book-lined den with a huge window and a galley kitchen to a room that looked like a tinkerer's idea of a perfect workspace. Tools of every imaginable size hung from the ceiling or on a pegboard. A computer with an oversized screen sat in one corner. Two well-lit tables dominated the room, each with a high stool. A man perched on one of them with his iPad Pro hopped off to greet his wife and guest.

John Sells stood perhaps five foot eight inches, much of it muscle that pushed against his flannel shirt. Broad-chested and narrow-hipped, he looked like a body-builder. His trim beard was salt and pepper, as was his full head of hair. His hazel eyes beneath bushy eyebrows were wary.

Terry took the lead, beginning with a firm handshake. "Mr. Sells. Special Agent Terry Sloan. Quite a place you've got here."

"We like it." He looked at his wife.

"I'll just leave you two," Kate said.

Her departure seemed to drain the room of light. Or maybe it was the defensiveness that radiated from Sells. Best to get to it, then.

"Thanks for seeing me, Mr. Sells," Terry said. "You're not an easy man to locate."

"It depends who's looking for me and why. John Sells has investors, a seat on a Silicon Valley Board, and a Wikipedia page. He's married with a lovely wife and two kids. He's intensely private about his personal life, but who isn't?"

"I wasn't looking for John Sells," Terry admitted. "Not at first."

Sells folded his arms across his chest. "Why are you here, Special Agent Sloan? You were enigmatic on the phone, to say the least. That's supposed to be my specialty."

"I was looking for Wyn O'Brien."

"And what would you want with Wyn?"

Terry took a breath and pushed it out. "My girlfriend, Sam Tate, knew Wyn as a child. Back when she was Sophia Russo. She changed her name, obviously."

Sells' hard expression dissolved. "Sophia Russo. I've wondered what happened to her. Wyn O'Brien also changed, obviously." He chuckled. "But wait, Sam Tate. I know that name. She was in the news just last year for cornering a notorious serial killer. Something about brides, am I right?"

"The Wedding Crasher, yes."

"And you were the FBI agent who worked with her, right? Special Agent Sloan."

"Terry's fine."

"Terry. I'm sorry I've been behaving like such a prick. Let's go sit in the den." They walked back. Sells indicated a comfortable leather chair, one of two facing that view.

"Can I get you a drink? It's early in the day; maybe you'd like coffee. I also have an assortment of craft beers and some damned fine whiskey."

"Beer's good, Mr. Sells."

"Call me John." He went into the kitchen to get Terry a beer, then poured himself a generous Scotch. "Sophia Russo became a gun-toting, criminal-catching sheriff from Tennessee named Sam Tate. I did not see that coming. You two made quite a splash. Hard to believe someone didn't connect the sheriff with the massacre survivor from Queens."

"I'm surprised, too. Fortunately, we dropped out of the news cycle pretty quickly. Anyway, Sam—Sophia—left Tennessee last summer to take a job in Maryland so she could be closer to her mom."

"Colleen. How is she?"

"The same."

"And Sophia? I mean, Sam?"

"She's good. She still has unresolved issues that, well, you understand. It's a process."

Sells nodded. "I heard she'd moved in with her aunt and uncle," he said. "Nicole went back to her family. I left, but that was always gonna happen."

"Where'd you end up?"

"Berlin, believe it or not. I spoke a little German. I got a job in the tech sector. I found a support group. I took the requisite drugs, had the requisite surgery, continued the drugs and will do that for the rest of my life. Small price to pay. Anyway, I came back, changed my name, went to work in Silicon Valley, and came up with an idea. The rest, as they say, is history."

"You didn't testify at Arthur Randolph's trial. Why was that?"

Sells took a healthy swig of his drink.

"You seem like a smart man, Terry. I could tell you I didn't want the world to see me in all my pre-transition glory. But that isn't true. After all, I was Stefan's best man. I stood on the dais with the rest of the wedding party. Everyone could see us." He stopped.

"And you could pretty much see everyone."

Sells nodded.

"Sam remembers a second person from that day who seemed off," Terry said. "I mean, apart from Randolph. A man in a brown suit who may or may not have had a gun. That last recollection is more recent; it's not in her closed-door testimony. Are you okay, John?"

The other man's breathing had become more audible. He clenched and unclenched his fists and looked around the room as if he wanted to punch something. He took another swallow of his drink. "There was a man in a brown suit," he said. "And he did have a gun. I saw it."

Terry felt like jumping out of his skin. He told himself to stay calm or at least fake it. "Is there a reason you didn't share that information with the authorities back then?" he asked.

"Why would it matter after all this time?" Sells studied his guest's face. "Have you found something out?"

"Someone may have gotten their hands on privileged testimony. I only found out because I was following up on something I learned from Randolph's mother. Randolph seemed to imply he didn't act alone."

"He was insane," Sells said flatly.

"Yes. And now he's dead."

Sells didn't reply.

"What I want to know," Terry continued, "is who would care about what a traumatized child thought she saw twenty-six years ago? Was it the man in the brown suit? What was he doing at the wedding? Working with Arthur Randolph? Working for him? The other way around? Did Brown Suit somehow convince Randolph to show up and shoot up the place as cover for whatever Brown Suit came to do? What was that, exactly?"

He stopped abruptly, suddenly aware that Sells still hadn't responded.

"You never answered my question, John. Why didn't you tell the authorities what you saw? Unless you recognized the man. And he frightened you."

Sells looked up from his drink. His face was drained of color. "I recognized him, Terry. I'd seen him more than once on the same block where Sophia and Stefan lived."

Terry almost slapped his knee. There was the connection. He hated to ask the next question. "Did you hear anything about this man belonging to a criminal organization? Maybe

Sophia's father or brother had something going on with him. Maybe the cousin did."

"You think the Russo family was tied to the mob?"

"I'm just trying to look at all the possibilities, John."

"I can guarantee you Stefan and his father had nothing to do with La Cosa Nostra. Johnny fell in with some bad people he ended up owing money to. A couple of family members settled the debt. He was going to straighten out, Terry. He planned to stay out of trouble and pay everyone back." He cleared his throat.

Terry waited, then asked, "Okay, the Russo family wasn't necessarily connected to the mob. Was Brown Suit?"

"I don't know. Someone said he went by Quinn. I can't say if that was his first or last name. That doesn't mean he was working for the Irish mob." He tried to smile.

"You're right," Terry said. "There's a lot of cross-pollination these days between the groups. He could have been working for any one of them. Or he might have been freelancing. What made you afraid of him?"

"I can't put my finger on it. He was well-dressed, notwithstanding his choice of a brown suit to a wedding." Sells tried to laugh at his joke. "He wore sunglasses, smiled a lot, nodded to the ladies. He gave off a vibe, though."

"Creepy?" Terry asked.

"Dangerous. You didn't have to be eagle-eyed to see he was always carrying some kind of a weapon under his jacket."

"Why do you think he was in the neighborhood?"

Sells was clearly uncomfortable. "People talked, you know? Gossip, innuendo, that sort of thing. My mother was as guilty as the next. She claimed her friend spoke to this Quinn, asked him if she could help him find anyone. And he answered, 'No, thank you. I've already found her.'"

"Found who?"

"He was there for Colleen, Agent Sloan. Sophia's mother." Sells looked stricken. "That was the story. No one knew how he knew her, or how well. But he knew her."

Darling Teresa,

The sailing weather has been ideal. Blue skies, brisk winds, nary a storm in sight. After weeks without seeing land, it is now a constant as we move along the coast. My pleasure may derive from my accommodation to life on a boat, or perhaps I am reassured by the sight of a sandy beach or a pine forest.

Having safely navigated the myriad barrier islands and the notorious Cape Fear, we have stopped for a fortnight in Bath, the provincial capital. While quite small by British standards, we are told that the town has grown substantially in the last few years thanks to a successful campaign against Savages hostile to the British presence. The presence of a number of powerful and wealthy plantations along the shoreline has no doubt added to its prosperity.

We were greeted by North Carolina's Governor Charles Easton, who regaled us with an amazing tale. Quite recently it seems, Blackbeard applied for the Kings Pardon, as did his fellow offender Stede Bonnet. As you may recall, that pardon was offered only to miscreants who ceased their criminal pursuits at the beginning of this year. I marvel at the pirate's sheer audacity. He behaves as though the incidents at Charles Town never took place and that forgiveness is open-ended.

Yet the Governor has waived that stipulation for reasons I am at pains to understand. Perhaps it simply costs too much to pursue these sea bandits. Or perhaps he is eager to demonstrate his political acumen to the Crown.

In any event, the infamous pirate may be settling in Bath even as his partner Bonnet has set sail. He is said to be looking at property and courting the daughter of a prominent land owner, a girl less than half his age. One of our Sailors reported seeing him strutting about the town with his chest puffed out and his mood exuberant.

Many, including the Governor, seem to think we are done with what he refers to as "the pirate problem." I do not share his confidence. True, Blackbeard might live as Edward Teach. He might now be able to secure a measure of stability, a home, a family, and a place within the community. Some men, though, find it impossible to be satisfied with what they have in hand when there remains something just beyond the horizon that is grander, more exciting, even more hazardous. I believe Blackbeard is such a man.

We are bound for the Chesapeake on the morrow, dear Teresa. Until we reach those shores, I remain,

Your William

Chapter 24

Jackie Templeton drove her Mercedes through the sleet, cursing the reduced visibility while reveling in the heated leather seats. Life is a series of tradeoffs, she mused. For instance, she really wanted the car in Rubellite Red but settled for the subtler Lunar Blue. She would have loved to drive a convertible but settled for a four-door. So much settling, but that's the way it went. Too bad. She was a red car, top down, hair blowing in the breeze kind of girl.

Right now, though, she needed to keep her profile low. Or rather, tightly managed. Her life at this point necessitated she operate like a magician or a poker player. Don't show them what's in your hand or up your sleeve. Reveal this, hide that. Be both visible and invisible. Guard your secrets.

She'd been an impetuous girl, sensitive and quick to anger. She'd needed years to learn to control her impulses, slow her reaction time. Her temper was an entity unto itself, a beast she kept locked up and fed only sparingly. When she was a child, she took a portion of the parable of the angel and the demon, each whispering in an ear, quite literally. That is, she could swear she felt burned where the demon perched. She never imagined an angel, at least not one that inspired goodness. If she heard anything at all, it was in the form of self-taught advice: *Play it cool. Never let anyone mess with your head.* That sort of thing.

She'd always attracted attention without trying; she couldn't help it. She was beautiful, certainly by the standards of the small town where she'd grown up. Better yet, she was fearless, even a little dangerous. Boys wanted her, girls wanted to be like her. She fed off their admiration and their desire.

Over the years, she'd had her share of would-be suitors as well as a few undesirables who misread her intent. She knew how to handle difficult situations. Vigilance was key. Not paranoid but attentive.

That's why she paid special mind to the car she'd picked up outside the Beltway. It was a nondescript mid-priced vehicle, dark gray. The driver, who she decided was a man, pulled a little too close behind her. She pushed the speed. The gray car did the same. When she changed lanes, he did as well.

She figured her Benz could outrun whatever he was driving, but she didn't want to risk it in case she was dealing with road rage. Maybe he'd find someone else to pick on. She slowed, just a little, to encourage him to move on. He didn't take the bait.

Oh, this is priceless, she thought. *I've got a stalker on wheels.* She decided to keep an eye out even as she let her mind attend to other matters. Multi-tasking was her specialty.

The last few days had been tremendously productive. She'd spent the previous evening at the Alexandria home of a lobbyist whose favor she had curried over the years. She was pleased to find herself in the company of a great many movers and shakers. She assumed most power players would be in Florida or the Caribbean over the holidays. Maybe that's what such people wanted others to believe. If New York was the city that never slept, D.C. was the town that never took off work.

While she'd rigorously monitored her alcohol intake, she still felt a contact high from her proximity to the power and wealth in the room. She was comfortable enough, but she wanted so much more than comfort.

After events like these, she questioned the restlessness that kept her on the move. Washington had been good to her. Everyone had an angle, and no one cared. The place ran on gossip and innuendo with very little blowback. Beneath the thin veneer of order the bureaucracy imposed, the place resembled the Wild West. No rules, not if you had the right contacts. More shadows from which to operate. The trick was to be as close to the power as possible without actually becoming a listed player.

As usual, she'd collected offers from men on leave from their families. She declined them but left open the possibility of future evenings together. Not that she intended to honor those promises. She already found her obligations divided between two men, neither of them ideal, both of them necessary.

She'd stayed at her condo in Foggy Bottom, which also doubled as a real estate office. The space had been done by a decorator and to JT's way of thinking, it fell just short of sterile. Now it was on the market for an outrageous sum of money. She wouldn't miss it all that much.

On the other hand, her store, with its small exhibit space, tugged at her heart just a little bit. She'd almost made a go of it, almost broken even. The paintings and pieces and odd bits of curios were perfectly balanced between the old and the new, the familiar and the slightly provocative, nothing too much in what was essentially a conservative town. Everything had been selected by an expert she consulted. The tourists who shopped there felt they got a chance to buy what might be found in the home of a genuine VIP. The VIPs and their representatives liked the selection and the high prices. Instead of being threatened by art they didn't understand, they felt included and appreciated.

She hated to leave it all behind. At the same time, she couldn't afford to indulge in nostalgia, not with so much on her plate. She had a lot of unfinished business to complete, starting back in St. Michaels.

She glanced into the rearview mirror, thought the headlights had moved a little closer. Who could tell, though? I-95 between Washington and Baltimore was busy even this late at night on a holiday weekend. The weather was horrible, a mix of rain and ice typical of the area. She'd lose the guy when she turned off for Annapolis. She was good at losing people.

Her thoughts turned to Wallace Bonnet. How had she lost him? They'd worked so well together. Wallace, with his multi-million-dollar home, his wealthy family, his connections in the political and art worlds, his untapped talent, and his easy charm. Wallace, who managed to be maddeningly ambivalent about his many advantages and how they might further his career.

Bonnet's nonchalance enticed and infuriated her. It caused her to make a rare miscalculation. She'd misjudged his pride, his artistic integrity, his devotion to his craft. She thought him malleable; he found her artistic inclinations wanting. Because she'd come up the hard way? Because she didn't have any fancy art degrees or even a pedigree? Because her interest was in harnessing and monetizing perception?

The truth was, Jackie Templeton didn't care about art, modern or classical. She pretended a passion she didn't feel. She had opinions on particular antiques, paintings, sculptures, or carvings, but only in terms of their relative value to prospective buyers. Her ability lay in convincing customers that the items she offered for sale were worth everything she asked for and then some.

She hadn't come out and said any of that to Bonnet. Yet he sensed it.

"I think it went well, don't you?" she'd asked him as they lay together in his bed the night of the opening. "People were properly impressed. You'll finally get the attention you deserve."

"As what?" he responded. "A woodworker or an imitator? Someone who knows how to spruce up an invaluable antique or create a pale imitation?"

"Wallace, dear heart, you're not being fair to yourself or to me." She tried to sound as if she were genuinely wounded. "You're a superstar. I'm not trying to present you as anything else." She reached for him, but he batted her hand away.

He jumped out of bed and started to dress. "You're playing a game, JT. With other people. With their money. With my reputation. With me, damn it! I want it stopped."

He left, slamming the door for good measure.

Dear Wallace. So naïve, so inflexible. If he only knew the half of it. He would soon enough.

In one respect, Wallace was wrong. She wasn't playing, she was planning. She had an opportunity to make a great deal of money, some of it from his own family. Her project might have moved along more smoothly were it not for Arley Fitchett's hopeless quest. Or Charles Fox and his hunger for recognition. Both of them trafficking in fantasy without understanding either its power or its limits.

She turned onto US-50 east, headed towards Annapolis. Not too many other vehicles followed. The gray car was one of them.

Was it an official vehicle, she wondered, law enforcement or some government agency? Weren't those always black? She couldn't make out a license plate, not at night. Her heart clenched for an instant. She'd moved around a great deal in her early years, eager for money and the things it might buy: freedom, power, respect. She was able to rely on her assets, her looks, her wit, her charisma, and her instinct for what people needed to see, to hear, and to believe.

Not all of her activities had been absolutely aboveboard, though she'd taken a great deal of care along the way not to raise any alarms. True, the situation in Chappaqua almost tripped her up. She'd had to leave rather quickly. Change her name again, take up a second occupation as a real estate agent.

At least her departure allowed for a serendipitous event. Her new job at an antique store just outside Philadelphia put her in contact with Henry Templeton, a much older and recently widowed investor. When he proposed marriage, she accepted without reservation. They enjoyed a peaceful couple of years. When he died unexpectedly, his substantial riches shielded her from the world's capriciousness and her own erratic urges.

Even after she discovered some unpleasant truths about her departed husband and his apparent fortune, she was still able to keep up appearances. Washington, D.C. provided her with cover. She began to thrive. Then she strayed across the line, the victim of both immediate necessity and ongoing compulsion.

She shook her head. Self-doubt would never do. She didn't want to feel stressed; stress was bad for her.

She half-hoped the gray car's end point was the state capital. But when she left Annapolis and moved onto the Bay Bridge, he was still there. Or they. At least she thought so. The sleet was changing into fat, sticky snowflakes and the road, ever more treacherous, demanded her concentration. By the time she exited the bridge and turned south, she couldn't have described the color of any of the few remaining cars traveling in her direction.

She took 322 around Easton and turned onto St. Michaels Road. The byway passed through Royal Oaks, an unincorporated community at the edge of Miles River. Housing generally ranged from $175,000 for a tiny bungalow to four million for a grand mansion on the water. Construction was underway on a promising residential project. A high-end gated community, no homes for under $1.7 million. Water views for all. Private security. Access to a golf course, tennis courts, private beach, fitness center, indoor and outdoor pools, spa, snack shack, even a top-notch restaurant. All anchored by a lodge with meeting rooms and a library.

After a small kerfuffle involving the historical society, the project was back on schedule and slated for completion by next summer. Pre-sales were reported to be robust.

JT had ponied up a sizable investment. Given the demand, she figured to collect a decent return. Unfortunately, she'd have to miss the grand opening.

She smiled to herself. With what she stood to make on that and her latest venture, she could throw her own opening to introduce a new and improved JT 3.0.

She caught a glimpse of headlights behind her, slicing through the heavy fog. No way of knowing if it was the same car that had trailed her for at least eighty miles through this godforsaken night. The thought didn't so much frighten her as enrage her.

"Don't mess with me!" she yelled at her rear-view mirror. She was tempted to slam on the brakes. Or make a U-turn and maneuver the car onto two wheels like some sort of stunt driver. She decided to pull off the road and wait.

The vehicle drove past her, clearly headed to St. Michaels. She let out her breath on a giggle. The car on her tail was just another weekender heading to the countryside.

She shook her fist at the receding tail lights. Feeling triumphant but also cautious, she waited five minutes, then started the engine. The big car purred with approval. JT felt repurposed, reenergized, refocused. Change was in the wind. She had a plan.

Chapter 25

The scene hit Sam like a sucker punch to the stomach. The flashing lights of the emergency vehicles, half smothered by fog. The disembodied voices, some from the competing crackle of radios. The upended car with the crumpled fender and a body strapped in the driver's seat.

One year ago, almost to the day, then-Sheriff Sam Tate came upon a setting that nearly duplicated the one she now faced. The driver, Deputy Tara French, had been a rising young star in the Pickett County Sheriff's Department. Her death was a murder made to look like an accident.

This is not that, Sam reminded herself.

It was perhaps worse. The crashed vehicle, or what was left of it, burned ferociously, sending flames skyward. In the pitch black, the hastily assembled LED lights created a bright white circle beyond which nothing could be seen. Sam knew this to be a construction site, uninhabited but likely to contain enough flammable material to feed an unruly firestorm.

Four firetrucks encircled the blazing wreck, which lay against a concrete slab that jutted randomly out of the ground. It was as if an angry child had thrown a toy against the wall. The back end of the car had been obliterated. Sam could make out a body, burned beyond recognition and long past rescue. The horrific image was likely to be scorched onto the memories of even the most hardened responders.

Jim Phillips materialized out of the gloomy soup, a white-coated creature with a black nose. He was wearing hazard gear and carrying an extra gas mask.

"Morning, Lieutenant. You'll need to put this on. We're not just dealing with a car fire. There's been a propane gas explosion."

"I heard the blast back at my house," Sam said. "Sounded like a bomb went off." *Or cannon fire,* she thought. She couldn't very well tell the chief she'd been tossed from a dream in which she and her family were under attack by a black-bearded man in a brown suit.

She pulled on the bulky mask, took a second to get used to it, then asked, "Did the car run into a tank and cause it to blow?"

"More like a single canister and no, the car didn't rupture the container. They're built for safety. You don't bump them or drop them or even shoot at them and *kaboom!* Could be the driver pulled off the road, lit a cigarette, dropped a match, and started an interior fire. Couldn't get out of the car. Four or five minutes later, we had ourselves a BLEVE. Hadn't seen one of those in a while."

A BLEVE, or boiling liquid expanding vapor explosion, occurred when the pressure in a propane container exceeded the ability of its relief valve to vent to the outside. Such an explosion was highly dangerous and extremely rare.

"Where'd the canister come from?" Sam asked.

Philips shrugged. "Beats me. If propane is anywhere on site, it's usually secured at a safe distance from the active areas."

"How can we help?"

"Our first priority is containment. We need to prevent any escaped vapors from igniting. Otherwise we'll have not only a fireball but also a serious contamination problem. MSP will send a crash team to investigate, but there's nothing to see until daylight. It does seem ..." Phillips stopped.

"Chief?"

"We've seen an awful lot of incidents involving fire these days."

Sam made a face behind her mask. "Yeah, we have."

"I gotta get back," Phillips said. "Keep your mask on outside your car." He turned abruptly and walked toward a group of firefighters maneuvering the bulky hoses so that they could work and still stay as far away from the fire as possible.

Sam went back to her cruiser. She wasn't sure what she could do, wasn't even sure what she was doing at an accident site. She thought about texting Gordy, but what would she say? That she woke from a bad dream? Or that she had a bad feeling about this accident site that had nothing to do with the potentially toxic air?

She sent a short message, giving him the option of showing or not at this point.

"Hey, Lieutenant." Sam awoke to rapping on her window, and opened her eyes to an eerie pinkish gray light. Dawn. How long had she been dozing?

Three snouted heads hovered by the driver's side. Her fogged brain took a moment to recognize the muffled voice as belonging to Bruce Gordy. Behind him, Carol Davidson and Martin Lloyd also wore full-cover protective face masks with built-in filters. Gordy raised up a large coffee carafe. Davidson had cups, Lloyd a paper bag.

"We came prepared," Gordy said. "Open up."

The three crowded into her car and yanked off their gear. Lloyd sat in front in deference to his long legs. Gordy handed Sam a mug of steaming coffee which she swigged without thinking. A burned tongue was a small price to pay.

"Got your text just after the 9-1-1," he said. "Carol called, told me Martin Lloyd had to be there for the body, so she decided hitch a ride, see if she was needed."

"Am I?" Carol asked. "I mean, what's our role in this?"

Sam took a bite of a blueberry muffin and another hit of coffee, then summarized the information passed on by Phillips. "The three of us from the sheriff's office are here as support," she said, "because right now, it's an accident with a possible complication from toxic fumes."

"Right now?" Gordy asked.

"I find aspects of this accident peculiar. That isn't to say that things don't happen. They do. If the driver was under the influence, if he or she were texting or smoking or falling asleep at the wheel ..." She paused. "What do we know about the property developers or the builders for the site?"

"Sign at the entrance says it's FCP Builders. Stands for Full Court Press. Owned by Oliver Cummings, who used to play for the NBA's Washington Wizards."

"He was a great player back in the day," Lloyd added.

"I'll take your word for it. Let's see if we can locate the project manager, get him over here."

"Taking charge?" Gordy asked.

"Helping out," Sam replied. "The crash team is due any minute. Carol, why don't you greet them when they arrive? Which is my way of saying, stick to them like glue. See what they're seeing, make note of what they're collecting or measuring or photographing. Document anything you can without ruffling feathers. Martin, you'll obviously be on standby to get at the body. Gordy and I are headed the same direction, as it happens. Masks on, people."

They pulled on their masks and exited the car. To the east, the band of pink had morphed into an arc. Sunrise.

The firefighters had made headway with the worst of the inferno. The flames had been brought under control. A cloud of inky smoke lingered but seemed to be thinning out. At least that's what Sam wanted to believe.

"I'm going to see if I can start work," Lloyd said.

Gordy held up his phone to zoom in on the wreck. "That car is totaled," he said. "No back end to speak of. Looks like a sedan, not an SUV or a convertible. That doesn't narrow it down much." He pocketed his phone. "Wonder if we can find a wheel? If it's an upgrade, we might be able to ID the car and its owner even if we can't see the VIN. Oh, look, the cavalry."

The MSP crash team arrived, all lights and sirens and troopers in full hazmat suits. They jumped from their vehicles and immediately swarmed the scene, carrying infrared lasers and electronic tool kits. The collected data would be used to digitally recreate the accident from every possible angle. It could take days or even weeks.

Sam's gut told her they didn't have that much time.

"Lieutenant?" Gordy asked.

"Go look for that wheel."

She was jarred by the sound of smooth music from her phone.

"Where are you?" Donahue barked.

"Sylvan Crest, the new development over in Royal Oaks."

"Is Detective Gordy with you?"

"He is."

"Did the crash team arrive?"

"Yes, sir." Couldn't she give more than a two-word answer? "Detective Gordy is trying to trace the car through a wheel that came off. The body is pretty charred, but maybe they can find useable DNA."

"God, I hope it's not somebody's kid," he said. After a beat, he asked, "Are we looking at a widespread toxic air alert and are you all protected?"

"We are. As for an alert, it might not come to that. The amount of propane released seems relatively small and likely to disperse. We've been advised to exercise caution."

"Good. I appreciate your handling this, Tate. I don't know that your presence will be required much longer. Unless you have reason to suspect this wasn't an unfortunate accident. Do you?"

She considered her answer. "I don't have enough information, sir. It's probably exactly what it appears to be."

"Make sure I'm in the loop."

"I'll do that, sir." She disconnected just as Carol popped into view with another masked figure.

"Look who's here," she said. Behind her, Tyler Caine waved a hand in greeting.

"Morning, Mr. Caine," Sam said. "Didn't expect to see you at an accident scene."

"I've been known to work with the crash team," Caine replied. "Especially when the circumstances are a little unusual." His easy smile was just visible behind his face mask.

Especially when a certain detective sergeant asks you to show up, Sam thought. "That fairly describes the scene here," she said.

"So, a car, a loose canister of flammable gas, and a concrete slab. The beginning of a bad joke. Any thoughts, Lieutenant?"

"Impressions that aren't necessarily based on science," Sam surprised herself by saying.

Caine's eyes twinkled behind his glasses. "Ah, but based on experience. Maybe CSI Davidson and I can work together, to find something to add weight to some of those impressions." He looked back and forth between Carol and Sam.

"That will be all kinds of helpful," Sam said. "May I ask you for another favor?"

"Why not?" He sounded amused.

"Can you get this to the DNA lab the crash team will be using? My DNA and fingerprints are also on it."

She reached into her jacket for her wallet and pulled out a matte dove-gray card, taking care to hold it at the corner. She dropped into the evidence bag Tyler produced.

He glanced at it and gave an almost imperceptible nod. "They should be able to make a match off a business card. Ready CSI Davidson?"

"Lead the way," Carol replied. She sounded almost cheerful.

Sam went back to find Lloyd half lying inside the burned-out car. He must have been uncomfortable, yet he worked with deliberation, moving slowly, taking his time. He'd abandoned his gas mask for a simpler blue version like doctors wore.

An hour passed. Sam removed her mask but kept her scarf over her mouth. Lloyd finished inside the car and folded his frame back out through the driver's side door. He walked around snapping pictures of the body from every angle. Sam kept still until he'd completed his work. She was used to waiting at crime scenes.

Gordy came up to her as she stood, arms folded, scarf pulled up, and Ray Bans on. She realized she looked like a bandit.

Gordy didn't seem to mind. He pulled off his own hardware, pulled out a disposable mask and slipped it on.

"Be prepared," he said with a shrug.

"Any news?"

"We found the wheel. It's an upgrade for a late model Mercedes E-class 4-door sedan."

Sam grimaced. "How long will it take to connect the wheel to a car and, more importantly, an owner?"

"Each tire has a unique serial number that's entered into a database when it's purchased. We just have to get to the right dealership."

"Text Shana," Sam told him. "I want her to access purchase records at Mercedes dealerships between D.C. and Annapolis. I don't care how many back doors she has to use or rules she has to break. I want to know who owned that car before anyone else does."

Lloyd finally finished and walked over, shaking his head. "Can't do much onsite. A body this badly burned needs to be in a lab. Better equipment, a radiologist familiar with post-mortem computed tomography. That'll help with both DNA sampling and cause of death."

"Can you use the teeth?" Sam asked.

"That's the odd thing. The teeth are all smashed in."

"Smashed during the explosion?" Gordy asked.

Lloyd shook his head. "There's no obvious injury to the cranium or the bridge of the nose. The damage to her mouth is so precise as to suggest a deliberate and well-aimed blow, as if someone took a hammer to the mouth. Or a baseball bat."

Sam and Gordy exchanged looks.

"One more thing, Lieutenant. I found a hair. Only partially burnt. That's to be expected. You can still see the color." He held up a small evidence bag.

A single hair, blackened at one end. Farther up the shaft, auburn.

Sam put her face as close to the bag as she could. "It looks—" She began again. "Is there any way to tell if—?"

"Lieutenant! Up here." Carol was waving from up the embankment.

"Excuse me," Sam said and remembered to add. "Nice work." She trotted up the hillock, pulling her scarf down. Gordy right behind, his mask around his neck.

Her CSI fast-walked over without her mask. "Did you hear the fire marshal issued an all-clear on the air quality? That's not what I want to talk to you about. Follow me."

She led them to a set of tire tracks and squatted just outside the taped barrier. Sam noticed the crash team watching them. Tyler Caine stood slightly apart. This was Carol's moment.

"What are we looking at?" Sam asked.

"Do you see how the dirt builds up at the edge of these tire marks? The car pulled off and stopped."

"The driver stopped to have a cigarette," Gordy suggested.

She looked at her brother as if he'd grown a second head. "At four in the morning? Never mind." She eased down the incline, pointing at the ground. "The car moved again, but it didn't get far before it exploded and flew into the concrete slab. But this is what I really need you to see." She climbed back to the edge of the road and crouched next to Sam.

"A footprint on what would have been the driver's side," Sam guessed. "The victim got out to smoke. Then got back in with a lit cigarette."

"That's what I thought. Until I saw this." Carol walked in a wide circle, pointing at the ground and stopped to the right of the tracks. "Why would the driver walk around to the passenger side? And then away?"

"There was a second person." Sam stood abruptly and called out, "Listen up, everyone." Her voice carried. "My name is Lieutenant Sam Tate, Talbot County Sheriff's Department. As of this moment this a crime scene. Please treat accordingly."

"And just like that," Sam heard Gordy say to his sister, "we're back in the game."

"Maybe," she replied. "But whose team are we playing for?"

Chapter 26

Sam called a half dozen Talbot County deputies back from vacation. She put four with Gordy to help with a grid search and assigned the others to traffic duty. Over a six- hour period, they scoured the Sylvan Crest site. "Wear gloves, but don't pick up anything until you've called over CSI Davidson or Detective Gordy," she instructed them.

"What are we looking for?" one of them asked.

"Cell phones, wallets, pieces of clothing." *Pieces of eight,* she thought.

The crash team leader, a hawk-faced man by the name of Flint, seemed only too glad to share information with the lieutenant. "Holiday weekends are extra busy," he explained to Sam. "Everything's a priority. We're stretched thin and expect to be even more so by end of day."

"I understand," Sam replied. "Look, I know you'll want to get into the labs to do your modeling. If possible, though, could you make a preliminary assessment about where the canister was in relationship to the car when it exploded?"

"You want to know if the canister was adjacent to the car or directly under it when it exploded."

"Or in it."

Flint's dark eyes glittered. "We'll do our best."

The body had been removed and sent to Baltimore under Martin Lloyd's supervision. An autopsy was scheduled for 10am Tuesday morning. Sam wished it could have been even sooner. She knew someone, probably Donahue, had pulled strings to get it that fast. He intimated as much when she reported to him.

"Homicides aren't a regular occurrence around here, Tate, even with the increase in drug and sex trafficking. We've had three in one month. Can you tell me if they're all related?"

"As soon as we ID the car and the driver, we'll have a better idea."

"If they are, you'll bring in Weller."

"Yes, sir. Oops, gotta go."

A maroon BMW screeched to a stop by the road. A barrel-chested man with dark blond hair, light eyes, and thin lips catapulted from the car and called out, "Who's in charge here?" He did a credible job of ignoring the two deputies who advanced on him.

"Let him through," Sam ordered. She walked over, hand outstretched. "I'm Lieutenant Sam Tate, Criminal Commander of Talbot County Sheriff's Department. And you are?"

"Alexei Volkov, project manager for FCP Builders. I got a text at some godawful hour this morning. Luckily, I wasn't far away. Why is a criminal commander on site? What's the crime? I was told this was an accident."

"It appears a car was set on fire and made to explode using a propane canister."

"What? Was anyone hurt?"

"The driver of the car was killed," Sam said.

"Show me where it happened." Volkov remembered to add, "Please."

Sam walked him to the wreckage. "I can't get you closer. We've cordoned off the entire area. But you can see roughly where the car exploded."

"Has anyone gone down to the site itself? Was anything taken or destroyed?"

"We're going over it now. As far as we can tell, nothing at the main building site was damaged."

Volkov exhaled audibly. "I thought it might be a nut job associated with the historical society."

"The Easton Historical Society tried to secure an injunction to stop construction last summer," Gordy explained. "The project is at the site of an old plantation."

"So what?" Volkov interjected. "It's not like it's a Native American burial ground. I'd think people would be happy we're covering up some slave owner's house. Besides which, the judge ruled in our favor. Even granted us a restraining order." He started down the embankment. "I just need to make sure everything's accounted for."

"Hold on, Mr. Volkov. Before I have one of my deputies take you through the site, would you check to see if you're missing any propane canisters?"

"You can't believe we're responsible for—never mind." Volkov strode over to the wire cage and unlocked the padlock. He tested the bindings, counted the containers, replaced the lock, and marched back.

"None of ours are missing," he reported. "I don't know what happened here, Lieutenant, but it doesn't seem to involve us. Now if you'll allow me to check my site, I can make my report, get back to my family, and enjoy what's left of my vacation." He looked from Sam to Gordy. "Wait, we can get back to work tomorrow, can't we?"

"I doubt it, Mr. Volkov. This is a crime scene. After you're escorted through the site, you can contact someone from your company. They in turn can connect with their employers, their lawyers, or their insurance agents. They can also call me. Here's my card. Please know I'm truly sorry for the inconvenience."

Volkov looked ready to erupt. He managed to control his temper, though it was clearly an effort. "Let's make it quick, Detective. I have a lot of calls to make."

Half an hour later, her phone rang. "What are you up to on this lazy Sunday?" Terry asked. He sounded rested and rejuvenated, as if he'd had his battery recharged.

"Terry! Where are you?"

"Denver, about to board a plane. I've got a lot to tell you."

"Oh, Terry, can it wait? I just got slammed with another homicide."

"Another homicide? Whoa. Fill me in."

She summarized her activities over the last few hours as best she could.

"Could this be related to Bird in Hand?" It was as if he'd thrown cold water on her. The reality was he'd said out loud what she'd been thinking for the past few hours.

"The car is a Mercedes like the one Jackie Templeton drove." There, she'd said it aloud.

"Lots of people in St. Michaels drive luxury cars, Sam."

"I've sent her three texts. I texted her two assistants as well. Only one of them, Evan Carr, got back to me, and he is clueless as to his boss's whereabouts."

"If the vic is JT, it's reasonable to assume her death is tied in with your other two homicides. You'll have to call Weller. We both know you don't want to."

Sam laughed despite herself. "I might enjoy dumping this on him."

"Never. Hey, here's a thought. Three murders by one perpetrator gets into serial killer territory. That's our specialty."

Sam snorted. "You think the Maryland State Police is going to invite the FBI to help with the investigation? You've been breathing too much thin air."

"Okay, we're not popular with the locals. I thought we could help."

"It would help if I could see you."

"We'll make that happen, Sam, I promise. We have a lot of catching up to do. Did you see Dr. Putnam?"

She slapped her head. "I literally forgot. I did, and there were some things that she thought represented some kind of breakthrough. Damn, I wish I had time to get into it."

"That makes two of us. Look, I'm going to try and come over there in the next few days. Let me catch up, and I'll make my way to you."

The relief that washed over her almost embarrassed her. "That would be great."

"They've announced my flight. I'll call you later. Go catch the bad guys."

"Terry, wait—" But he was gone.

* * *

Not half an hour later, Shana called with information on the car. A dark blue Mercedes with custom wheels had been sold by an Annapolis dealer nine months earlier to Jackie Templeton.

"You're not surprised," Gordy observed when she told him. "The business card you handed Tyler Caine. Was it JT's?"

"It was. I wanted to be sure the lab had a sample. Damn, Jackie Templeton."

Sam took no pleasure from the accuracy of her gut instinct. It meant she had three bodies most likely tied together. The unanswered question: Was Wallace Bonnet responsible for all three deaths? She couldn't square the crimes with the man she met.

Sam assumed the Maryland State Police would also be able to trace the car. They might take longer—Shana tended to work in the margins—but they would make the ID soon enough. Which meant Weller would know.

She continued to hold off contacting him. She reasoned there wasn't much he could do anyway. She was just being considerate, she told herself.

She called off the search at four, just as the light began to fail. She had the area cordoned off. She spoke with Flint as well as her own people and went over what had been accomplished and what they might expect to do. "You'll have help," she promised. She posted two deputies to watch the site overnight.

Then she called Weller.

"The killer seems to have a thing for extravagant murders," he said. "Nothing subtle or straightforward about the MO. Fitchett was strangled and his hands burned, which wasn't exactly necessary. Fox was smacked over the head and set on fire. Ms. Templeton seems to have been treated to fire and an explosion."

"If you want to meet now, I can give you my notes."

"Go home, Tate. You sound beat. How about I meet you at your office in Easton tomorrow morning? 8am? I'll bring Pollack and Caine. You can walk me through what you've got, then walk me around the site. I'm sure you have other ideas as well."

"Okay."

"Sam?" Weller cleared his throat. "We'll nail the bastard."

"We'd better."

She stopped in St. Michaels for takeout Chinese and drove home cloaked in a miasma of exhaustion, anger, and fear. Not for herself but for the victims someone was willing to put down. Why? To find an old carving? To keep it hidden? Or was there another motive entirely?

Her cottage glowed like a lantern in the dark. Had she left all those lights on twelve hours earlier? No, something was off. She reached into the cruiser's glove compartment and slid out her revolver. She wasn't sure if she felt frightened at the idea of an intruder or irritated that she had to deal with yet another unwanted visitor.

The odor hit her as she crept up to the porch and brought her up short. Not repulsive but enticing. Not unusual but familiar, a smell that brought back happy memories. The smell of pasta sauce.

She threw open the door, gun raised. She noticed the travel bag first, tucked under the side table at the entrance. Then she took in the back of a familiar figure at the stove who turned around and widened his amber eyes in mock fear.

"Whoa! Don't shoot the cook, please. At least not until you've had dinner."

"Terry!" Sam managed to flip on the safety and set the weapon down before she flung herself at Terry. He let go of the spoon he was using as she buried her face in his chest. He hugged her to him. They stood that way for several blissful seconds.

"Hungry?" he asked when they'd broken apart. "I've got the wine open. Bread and olive oil are already on the table. The pasta won't take long. Sorry I couldn't get fresh greens, but canned goods have come a long way."

Sam poured herself a generous glass of wine. "Where did you get all this? How did you get here? Is that basil I smell?"

"Hold on, Lieutenant. I promise to answer all your questions. After I got off the phone with you, I changed my flight so I'd come into Baltimore instead of D.C. I raced through an overpriced food boutique in the airport, barely made it. Flashed my badge and carried the extra bag on for free. I'm shameless that way. As for getting here, Uber from

BWI airport. I'd like to take credit for making the sauce from scratch, but I just warmed it up. Are we good?"

"Are you kidding? I'm falling in love with you all over again."

They sat down to a dinner of tagliatelle with artichokes and a tomato basil sauce accompanied by two bottles of wine and a plate of chocolate bon-bons. Sam felt some of the tension slip away.

"You are a miracle worker," she said as Terry cleared away the plates.

"So I've been told. What's on tap for you tomorrow?"

"Detective work. We try to trace JT's movements from the time she left St. Michaels on Wednesday night to the time she apparently returned. Once we secure our warrants, we'll poke around both physically and digitally. The autopsy is Tuesday," she added.

"Anything new on Wallace Bonnet?"

"He's a ghost. I just can't see him for the murders, Terry. Maybe because they were so brutal."

"Any other ideas?"

"Not right now. Why don't you tell me what happened on this so-called field trip you took?"

He filled his glass and hers and told her what he'd heard from the former Wyn O'Brien. He held her hand as she shared with him the breakthrough she'd had with Dr. Putnam.

"I still can't get this through my head, Terry. Did my mother have an affair with the man in the brown suit?"

"Don't go there, Sam. Let's start with the idea that she was acquainted with him, maybe had information on him no one else did. He might have been a dangerous man who frightened her. I can't figure out why he showed up at her son's wedding, though."

"Is he still in Queens?"

"Sells didn't seem to know."

Sam put a hand to her head. "Terry, this is a lot to digest and I've had a long day. Can we go to bed?"

"Absolutely. Get ready. I'll clean up and join you."

He finished up in the kitchen and went to find Sam. She lay on her back, fully dressed except for her shoes and so still he actually checked for a pulse. Gently, he changed her into her favorite sleepshirt, a flannel number that made her look young and almost vulnerable. Then he undressed and slipped into bed beside her.

"Love you, Sam Tate," he whispered and thought he saw her smile in the dark.

Dear Teresa,

We lingered in Bath a few days longer than expected. Captain Digg was at first disinclined to travel owing to rumors that our elusive pirate, after only a week, has taken his ship northward through the Chesapeake Bay. The purpose of this new direction is unclear, although some have suggested Blackbeard finds the many uncharted tributaries, coves, and backwaters to be ideal hiding places while he oversees repairs to his largest fighting ship, the Queen Anne.

As to how he might finance his repairs, the pirate is said to have hired himself out to a wealthy tradesman residing in the Episcopal parish known as St. Michael Archangel in order to provide protection for shipments of tobacco. I would imagine even the loyalty of a thief can be purchased for the right price.

Captain Digg argued that Blackbeard's mere presence in the area rendered travel precarious. He recommended that we wait until we had a notion of what our nemesis planned to do.

I could not in all good conscience support this line of thinking. Captain Digg's excessive caution would have forced us to spend the summer months confined to this sweltering insect-infested outpost even as we delayed our arrival and return. I could not imagine a scheme less worthy of consideration and I did not hesitate to say so.

I offered a counter view, namely, that if even a portion of the rumors were true, Blackbeard would pose no threat to us. If he is indeed without adequate funds, it would surely behoove him to honor the terms of his contract. Further, he would wish to spend time on repairs to his vessel, in service to God only knows what mayhem he intends to commit this autumn. I expected that our modest ship with its modest cargo would arouse little interest on his part. We might thus slip past him and make our way safely to Annapolis.

The captain having been persuaded of my logic and the crew being anxious to depart, we left the next day. This morning, we entered the mouth of the Chesapeake Bay just below the Sea of Virginia. The winds are behind us and the sky is a glorious azure. We are promised to make excellent time. I am looking forward to civilization and dry land in equal measure.

And then, home!

With all my heart,

William

Chapter 27

Sam awoke from a dreamless sleep to find a dent in the bed, still warm. She rolled over and breathed in for all she was worth, trying to hold onto the scent of her lover. In the kitchen, she found fresh coffee and a note that said, "Try not to worry. Whatever's going on, you'll get to the bottom of it."

She'd suggested an early meeting for the core group, Weller's three and her four. McCready brought donuts, one of which she eagerly devoured with a third cup of coffee.

For the first time, she noted a sense of cooperation born of urgency. There was no time for posturing or political infighting. Three people had died violently, probably at the hand of someone who was obsessed, ruthless, or both. Everyone in the room was committed to figuring out why and to stop more deaths.

The problem was, they were working with incomplete information. Weller had long since conceded that drugs didn't factor into the death of Charles Fox. Both the appraiser and JT had shown an interest in Bird in Hand, although possibly for different reasons.

"I'm still not sure about motive," Sarah Pollack said. "I get why the bird mattered to someone like Arley Fitchett. It was his Holy Grail. He lived to hunt it down. Charles Fox? Maybe prestige, maybe money. The letters all by themselves would be attractive to some museum or private collector. But how do those two connect with Templeton or Bonnet, for that matter? What's this old carving worth in today's market?"

"A sapphire eye would add value," Gordy suggested. "I got the impression that Jackie Templeton didn't believe in the existence of the original, but maybe she was playing us. Maybe she really was trying to get her hands on it. The only person who wouldn't want it found would be Bonnet. Because he'd look like nothing more than someone who carves imitations of the real thing."

"Is Wallace Bonnet still our prime suspect?" McCready asked.

"Until we come up with a better candidate," Weller said. "Lieutenant, thoughts?"

Sam hadn't spoken during the meeting. Fatigue, yes, but something else kept her from contributing. Something that nagged her.

"Didn't MSP upgrade the APB on Bonnet?" she asked.

"Over the father's vigorous objections," Weller replied. "He was on a popular D.C. talk show this morning to complain that law enforcement was targeting his son without proof. He demanded to know why we believed Junior was a killer and not a victim."

"What if he is a victim?" Carol Davidson asked.

The room fell silent.

Sam cleared her throat. "Seems to me plenty of agencies are looking for Wallace Bonnet. Last I checked, his name was on an Interpol list. If he's findable, he will be found." She swallowed. "Right now, we need to determine what happened to Jackie Templeton. We've identified the car as hers, and once we've established that the victim is—" She stopped to grab the image that skittered across her mind and made a note on the pad she kept with her.

"Lieutenant?" Weller prompted.

"Sorry. We need to know who else was in the car. So far, no one's been able to lift prints or DNA from the passenger side."

"If we figure that out, won't we know who the killer is?" McCready asked.

"It might narrow things down," Sam conceded. "But before we go down that rabbit hole, let's trace Jackie

Templeton's whereabouts over the previous four days. What did she do, who did she see? Gordy, you've got solid contacts inside the D.C. police department. Let's have you head over there with Detective Pollack."

She swiveled in her chair. "Detective Sergeant Weller and I need to walk the site with Carol and go through JT's places in St. Michaels. Tyler, any information you can get in the way of lab reports will be helpful. Pat, I need you to secure warrants for phone and bank records for Ms. Templeton's personal and business accounts going back at least six months. Maybe your helpful judge here can give us a leg up in D.C."

She stopped, aware she'd been issuing commands as if she still ran the investigation. She'd overstepped and everyone in the room knew it. To her surprise, Weller nodded.

"Sounds like a plan," he said.

Sam walked out with Weller into a weak morning sun doing its best to chase off the lingering mist. The temperature had climbed to the mid-forties, and the breeze was relatively calm. A perfect day to bag evidence and find a killer.

At the Sylvan Crest site, several troopers from the crash team were back to photograph the still-smoldering car and take more measurements. Per Sam's instructions, two new Talbot County deputies had replaced the pair of over-nighters.

Weller caught site of Josh Abrams and waved over the arson investigator. Abrams responded with his own hand in the air. More gesticulating followed, accompanied no doubt by instructions to his team members, before he loped over to join the new group.

"Morning, folks. Seems your killer likes to send his victims out in a blaze of glory," he quipped. He looked chagrined when neither of them smiled. "Sorry. Arson humor is second nature."

"Anything to tell us?" Weller asked.

"I just got here this morning. Not sure how much you already knew, but the crash team found a scrap from the propane cylinder that doesn't match the brand stored here.

"So, something brought in," Weller said.

"Right. We're also thinking the canister was inside the car, either in the back seat or the trunk. I'm going with the trunk, given the pattern of the damage to the back of the car. Absolutely unnecessary if the goal was to murder the person in the vehicle. And if the point was to destroy evidence, it's poorly conceived. You might say it was overkill." He grimaced. "Ah, damn. Force of habit. Anyway, I reviewed the forensic investigator's preliminary report. He's a pretty thorough guy, isn't he?"

"Yes, he is," Carol responded with a small smile.

"It's pretty stunning the body didn't end up in little pieces. Guess that will give the ME something to work with in determining cause of death and time of death." He shook his head. "So many ways to kill someone. Why go for the dramatic gesture?"

"Statement killing," Weller said. "Someone with a thing for burning people."

Sam felt the familiar sensation of an unformed idea fighting to rise to the surface. She told herself it would come if she didn't force it. Who'd taught her that? Terry, of course. The man had the instincts and the temperament to be a professional profiler.

"Why do you think the murder happened here?" she asked aloud.

"Convenience," Weller said. "Templeton lived just up the road. The killer might think we'd be misled by the propane canisters on site."

"Could be a different kind of statement," Carol said. "Someone who objected to the project."

Sam folded her arms across her chest. "We need to find out if JT had any dealings with these developers." She looked down the embankment, then looked back at Abrams. "Could the killer have meant for the car to roll down the hill and explode on the site itself?" she asked. "Maybe he didn't see the concrete barrier."

"Why not just park the car down there and light it up?"

"Easier to get away from up here," Carol noted. "Especially if he had a ride or a second car parked somewhere else."

"You do realize you've just come up with another possible motive for this death that has nothing to do with the treasure hunt," Weller said to Sam.

"I know. But we need to consider the possibility." She texted a quick set of instructions to Shana Pierce and sent a text to McCready to remind him to push for the warrants.

McCready responded promptly. "I already have what you need. Where should I fax it?"

"To JT's. We'll be there in half an hour."

Chapter 28

Evan Carr was waiting for them at the door of JT Galleries, phone in hand. He was slight, his posture already in decline, his shoulders rolled forward. Too much screen time and too many years trying to grow under the weight of a backpack, Sam decided. Dark brown hair had been combed straight back, emphasizing a high forehead and warm brown eyes, round and filled with concern. He looked both young and vulnerable.

"Come in, please. Do you want any coffee or tea?"

"We're fine, Mr. Carr," Weller answered before Sam could accept.

"Call me Evan, please. Did you want to sit down?" He gestured at a small bench at the far corner of the foyer.

"Thank you, no," Sam answered.

"I figure you want to talk with JT. The thing is, she's not in."

"Were you expecting her?"

Evan frowned. "Honestly, I was. She likes to be back in St. Michaels Sunday night so she can get a jump on the paperwork. At least that's how her schedule has worked for the last eight weeks."

"What kind of paperwork?" Sam asked.

"What? Oh, things like inventory, sales. We sold a couple of pieces after the opening. She's commissioned some new work. And she's not completely up to date on insurance. I didn't think that was a good thing, but she said not to worry. In fact, that was something she was going to handle today."

"Insurance on the paintings or the building?" Weller asked

"I can't say. She's really professional, so maybe it was just one item she hadn't insured, or maybe she wanted to update the policy."

Weller nodded. "Bird in Hand."

"Yeah, maybe. Probably." His eyes darted between Sam and Weller, then went down to his phone and back up again.

"You seem anxious, Evan," Sam observed. "Are you waiting to hear from someone?"

"Amy. She was supposed to be in at 9:30. Which was, like, an hour and a half ago. She's never late. And JT, Ms. Templeton, isn't answering her texts, which is weird."

"How long have you worked for JT?" Weller asked. He used a gentle tone Sam hadn't heard before.

"Since the beginning of October, plus four weeks last winter as an intern at her D.C. shop. You could say my parents provided an in. They dropped a fair amount of cash in her store. I'm an art major, though, and when she invited me to work here for money, not that it pays much, I said yes, absolutely. I help with inventory, some event planning. I guess you'd say my job is evolving."

Eyes down again. He shook his head, put his phone in his pocket, cleared his throat. "Please tell me what's going on."

Sam told him about finding the blue Mercedes and tracing it back to JT. She tiptoed around the details, but Evan was ahead of them.

"I heard it on the news. Nothing about who the car belonged to, just that the driver was charred." He swallowed. "Was it JT?"

"We're waiting for DNA results," Weller said.

"Jesus." The young man put a hand to his head. When he looked up, his face was pale and wet. "Sorry, it's just kind of a shock."

"Of course," Sam said. "Do you need a moment?"

"I'm okay." He squared his shoulders.

"Does JT have family, perhaps a close relative or a friend we can contact?"

"I don't know anything about her family or her friends, only that she had plenty of those. She's a widow, married a guy a lot older and inherited a lot of money when he died. Maybe he had a family?" Carr sounded doubtful.

"We can look into all of that," Weller cut in. "What about clients? Who bought her stuff?"

"She had returning customers who came through her Georgetown store. Then there were all her high-end real estate clients. People from all over the world. There's a list we used to invite people to the opening here. I think it's in her office. Amy would know. She's more the client side." He looked as if he might burst into tears.

Sam put a light hand on his arm. "Maybe we can head upstairs, take a quick look around. Would that be okay?"

"Sure. Do you mind?" He held up his phone. "I want to send Amy another text."

"Of course." While the assistant typed into his phone, Sam glanced over at Weller. He bobbed his head. "What's Amy's last name?" she asked.

"Reed." Evan answered without looking up.

"And where does she live?"

"Annapolis." He stuck his phone in his pocket. "She loves it, likes the reverse commute. She moved there after graduating from MICA."

"Maryland Institute College of Art," Weller added helpfully. "It's in Baltimore. Good school."

"Did she spend the holiday in Annapolis, Evan?" Sam asked.

"I think so. Her parents live in Raleigh. She says it's a hassle to fly on Thanksgiving. She has plans to go at Christmas. Also, she likes to be on call for JT."

Sam nodded to herself. "You expected her back this morning."

"I already told you that." Evan's voice edged up a notch. "Why are you asking about Amy?"

"We ask a lot of questions, Evan. Comes with the job. Let's head upstairs."

Upstairs consisted of two rooms. The smaller area had been cleverly arranged to maximize space and accommodate two desks and chairs. A contented ficus plant lounged in one corner. The desks were neat, each with a set of stacking trays. Bookshelves hung against the wall.

The assistants had personalized their spaces. Evan Carr had an iPad, a laptop, a beer mug, and a scrolling digital picture frame with images of smiling people enveloping each other in bear hugs.

Amy Reed's photographs were displayed in simple frames. A family of redheads. A shot of a group of girls laughing. An image of her with JT at a dressy function. A coffee cup with the words "Art Fuel" sat alone to one side. Her tray held a single folder marked "opening" and a handwritten reminder pinned to the front to "send personal notes from JT." No laptop.

JT's office was stylish and orderly. A comfortable chair, a small bookshelf, an evocative painting of the Chesapeake whose colors suggested dawn. The fax machine in the corner held several freshly printed pieces of paper.

Weller crossed over and picked them up. "Our warrants have come through," he said, scanning the material. "Business, which includes downstairs and upstairs. Home, which means her place across the street."

Sam was examining the elegant old desk that sat to the back of the space. High quality antique with a smooth surface, glass over wood. A little heavy for the room. Nothing personal, no photos, mementos, or artwork, just an engraved gold lighter. Not even a plant. Six workable drawers with brass handles and ornate facings down the side matched the panel across the top. The bottom drawer had a keyhole.

"JT has the only key. But, well, she's not here."

Sam gave a reassuring smile. "It's okay, Evan. We've got permission."

"I meant, I'm not sure how you'll get in."

"I've got that covered."

Sam took out her pocket knife and worked it into the metal keyhole. Within a minute, she'd popped the lock.

"Helpful skill set," Weller said.

Inside, she found half a dozen files. She pulled one labeled "Bird in Hand" and found an insurance form that listed the carving's monetary value at $250,000. Sam had no idea if that represented fair market value. It seemed possible. She also found a sketch, apparently by Wallace Bonnet, that closely resembled the one they'd taken from Arley's wall.

"You think there's a secret cubbyhole?" Weller asked.

"That only happens in Victorian detective novels," Sam replied.

"It's a Victorian-era desk, if that helps," Evan piped up.

Sam felt around the drawer with no expectation whatsoever she'd find a hidden switch. Even after she pushed a small metal button, she was startled when the top decorative panel popped open to reveal a narrow space.

Lying flat inside was another file marked "BIH." Sam laid the papers on the desk. Another insurance form, valuing the carving at $22 million dollars. A page printed from an internet site on rare gemstones, another on British and American antiquities, a card from an appraiser in Richmond, Virginia, and a list with four names and dollar amounts ranging from $18 to $22 million dollars next to each. The notes in the margin read "emphasize rarity, compelling backstory, true value."

Further down, someone had written a single word, heavily circled: "treasure."

"Evan, if you don't mind, I'm going to—"

She was interrupted by the sound of a siren, so close she half-expected to see a cop car crash through the opposite wall. Evan Carr looked as if he might keel over.

"It's my ring tone," Weller said. He turned away.

"Talk to me, Tyler," he told his caller. He listened for perhaps fifteen seconds, said, "Are you sure? Do they know? Tomorrow? It has to be tomorrow, Tyler. This changes everything." He disconnected and turned to Sam

"Lieutenant, can I speak to you a moment? Evan, excuse us." Weller looked at the assistant, then the door. For good measure, he inclined his head ever so slightly.

Evan took the hint. "I'll just be out here," he said.

As soon as the door clicked shut, Weller grabbed Sam by the elbow and moved her to the opposite window. He spoke in a low voice.

"That was Tyler Caine. He called in a favor, got the lab to check the DNA from the card you gave him yesterday against a sample Lloyd got from the barbecued driver. Guess what?"

"The samples don't match."

Weller looked surprised. "Way to kill the punchline, Tate. But yeah, bottom line is, our vic is not Jackie Templeton."

Chapter 29

"When did you know?" Weller asked. He twisted in the seat to watch Sam, who was driving.

They'd spent a fruitless hour tossing Jackie's top-floor condo. The pristine apartment looked like a set piece rather than a home. The place was modern but not oppressively so. The few antiques hinted at the town's storied history without indulging in kitsch. The closets and dresser drawers were filled with good-quality clothes. The refrigerator contained little. The king-sized bed looked comfortable.

"You might want to ease up on the gas, Lieutenant. The dead aren't going to get any deader." Weller's voice brought her back to the present.

"Sorry." She lifted her foot and unclenched her teeth for good measure.

"Back to the question: When did you figure out the body didn't belong to Jackie Templeton?"

"I suspected something when Lloyd showed me the hair he'd recovered." She explained about the shaft Lloyd found on site. "I asked him to pop it under a microscope before he sent it to the lab."

"Before Tyler got hold of it, you mean. But he didn't have access to the DNA sample you turned over to my guy."

"I wasn't looking for DNA, Weller. I was looking for dye."

"What?"

"Hair dye. Jackie Templeton was—maybe is—a beautiful woman, but her hair was colored. Under a microscope, a shaft of dyed hair looks smooth. Natural hair is comprised of little granules. Lloyd got back to me while you were talking with Caine." She held up her phone.

239

"Talk about serendipity," he replied. "But how'd you know Ms. Templeton colored her hair? Not from personal experience."

Sam didn't smile. "In a way, yes. My mother is a natural ginger. I can see the difference."

"You know who else seems to have her own head of red hair?"

"Amy Reed."

Weller punched a number into his phone, hit "speaker." "Since you're so tight with your fellow lab rats," he began without preamble, "can you get someone to pick up some DNA off a sample?"

"Do you have the sample?" Tyler Caine matched Weller's no-nonsense tone.

"I can drive it up to you within the hour. We're going to need this before the autopsy tomorrow."

"I assumed as much. I'll see what I can do."

"Thanks. See you soon."

Sam cut her eyes to her partner. "What'd you take from her desk?"

"The most obvious two things I could find. A mug she hadn't washed out, and a pencil she'd obviously chewed on." He held up two clear plastic bags. "Which begs the question …"

"Only one?" Sam asked. "I can think of at least three. Is the victim Amy? If not, who is it? Who was the second person in the car? What happened to JT?"

"That's four," Weller observed.

"I know."

She dropped Weller at his car behind the office. They promised to check in with each other. "We can't confirm ID or any other pertinent information about the vic until tomorrow," he told her.

"I still think it makes sense to let Gordy and Pollack in on what's happening while they're in D.C."

"What do you think? Is Jackie Templeton a person of interest or a missing person? Makes a difference."

Sam considered. "I don't know what I think. We have to wait until tomorrow's autopsy gives us a definitive ID and whatever else they can be persuaded to give us. Then we have to notify next of kin. At that point, things are likely to go public. That means your boss and my boss are going to have to hold a press conference or at least release a statement. So, we'd better pull together as much as we can about the elusive Ms. Templeton so when you step up to the microphone, you'll have a lot to report."

"Me?"

"You're the experienced Maryland State Police homicide detective leading these investigations." Sam softened the statement with a smile.

"Let's not forget one thing." Weller started his car. "You're the hotshot sheriff who tracked down a serial killer. Which is what we may be looking at, by the way." With a wave, he took off.

Pat McCready was hunched at his desk, peering at his screen and making notes on a pad. Perfect marriage of old and new technology. He gnawed alternately on his pen and on his lip. Sam felt a wave of affection coupled with pride. She stuck her hand in her pocket so she wouldn't reach out and pat his head. She cleared her throat.

"What have you got for me, Deputy?"

"Hey, Lieutenant." He turned, flashing a good-natured grin. "How was your trip to the gallery? Did you get any new leads?"

Sam and Weller had decided not to let anyone know what Tyler Caine had shared with them. The autopsy was tomorrow and while the full results might not be available, an ID would be made.

"Not much that's useful. What did you find?"

"It's what we didn't find that's interesting. I asked Shana to help me. She's good with the deep dive research."

"Before you fill me in, I need to ask her for something. Meet me in my office in five minutes or so."

She found Shana, gave her the assignment, and retreated to her office with coffee and a breakfast bar.

Exactly five minutes later, she heard a knock. The deputy and the IT specialist. The three of them had barely settled in before an eager McCready began.

"I did some checking. Jackie Templeton is a stakeholder in Sylvan Crest, just like you thought. She invested in a company that bundled investors for Full Court Press. Cost a lot to get in—we're talking seven figures—but all legal. Nothing shady about the builders, either. Well-run, well-respected firm, lands a lot of state contracts. Even so, I passed the information to Detectives Gordy and Pollack. Thought they might decide to pay FCP a visit."

"Good thinking," Sam said. "What else?"

"Both her D.C. properties are on the market for a lot of money. Some interest, according to the real estate agent handling them, but no firm offers."

"Yet she bought two properties out here. How'd she leverage that?"

McCready looked down at his notes. "She has two accounts at PNC Bank. It'll take some time to work through the official channels to see those. My mom knows the real estate agent out here who sold Ms. Templeton both St. Michaels properties. Melinda Connolly. She says JT financed the building where she has the gallery.

"The other building where JT has her condo has some sort of historic designation. She got around that by agreeing to maintain parts of the original structure, especially below ground. There's even talk it could become a tourist attraction." McCready shrugged. "And get this. She doesn't actually own that building. It was bought for cash by a company called Eastern Chesapeake Developers. Which seems to be one guy. An Egyptian diplomat named Nur Asim."

"Interesting. I wasn't sure diplomats could buy property in the United States."

"Mortgages and loans are a problem, Melinda says, but cash is not."

"Send that information to Detective Gordy, will you? He'll know what to do from there. And Pat, good job."

He beamed.

Sam turned to the young woman. "Shana, go ahead."

Shana had been trying not to squirm in her seat. She pushed her hair out of her face and sat forward, iPad in hand.

"First, the quick background on Amy Reed you asked me to do. Born Skokie, Illinois, twenty-five years ago to Terence and Eileen, both biology professors, different specialties. Amy chose a more artistic path. Accepted to MICA, graduated with honors. She's exhibited some of her work in Baltimore and sold one sculpture. She's got a Facebook page, not so active, an Instagram account, more going on there, and a couple of videos on Tik Tok. Nothing since Saturday afternoon."

"Go on."

"Jackie Templeton is kind of interesting. She's been in D.C. for five and a half years. She moved from outside Philadelphia not long after her super-wealthy and much, much older investor husband died. Well, once upon a time super-wealthy." She caught Sam's puzzled look. "Yeah, I have a separate folder on him I can air drop to you. Templeton is one of those Eastern shore names that used to matter a hundred and fifty years ago. Maybe that's why JT wanted to move back. Not too clear that all his money was made on the up and up."

"Well-connected in real life but maybe wealthy only on paper." Sam stated.

"I don't know about that. JT threw around some money when she came to D.C. She got herself noticed, including by our Mr. Asim."

"Noticed how?"

"Depends on whether you read between the lines of the gossip columns. I found a picture taken at a party last year. The two of them look pretty chummy. Then again, he's a super good-looking guy, I mean, if you like the type." A faint flush colored her pale cheeks. "She's not too shabby herself, with all that red hair. Beautiful people always look like they're flirting."

"Not a bad observation," Sam said.

Shana blushed again, then continued. "She's licensed as a real estate agent in both D.C. and Maryland. Mostly rich clients. She bought a condo in Foggy Bottom and a run-down little retail place in Georgetown that she turned into a high-end art and antique establishment. Doesn't seem to have done that well."

"How long was she married?" Sam asked.

"Six years. Here's another fun discrepancy. Her marriage license says she was thirty-three when she got married, which would make her forty-four now. Her driver's license says she's forty-six, her passport puts her at forty-eight."

Sam took a sip of cold coffee. "What's her birth certificate say?"

Shana exchanged a conspiratorial look with McCready. "That's the funny part. She doesn't seem to have one, at least not one that I can find. The marriage license identifies her as

Jackie Lincoln from Canton, Ohio. I found someone with that name and social security number who lived there maybe a dozen years ago."

"And?"

"She died at the age of ninety-four. Right around the time our Jackie met her future husband."

Chapter 30

The pirate stood on the mast at sunset, a sword in one hand, a gun in the other. He'd set his hair and beard on fire. She could smell the sulphur and taste acrid smoke. The flames and the fiery light of the dying sun made him appear as a redhead.

"Stop!" she yelled. As usual, her unconscious cries worked like an alarm clock. She almost wished she could return to her reverie, rather than face a day that would be filled with different questions and at least one nightmare come true.

Weller was up in Baltimore to "move things along," as he put it. The Office of the Chief Medical Examiner didn't appreciate being pressured, Sam knew. The attention was on being thorough and accurate. The full report might take two weeks or more even with additional pressure from the State Attorney General's office.

At least expedited DNA testing became possible when the head of MSP convinced officials that the body was connected to a killer still at large. Weller was to be one of the first to have an ID for the latest victim.

Gordy came into Sam's office to report on the D.C. trip he and Pollack had taken.

"You brought coffee," Sam said. She reached gratefully for the mug and pushed her cold cup to the side.

"I didn't bring a lot else," Gordy replied. "Pollack had a contact inside D.C. Metro that was better than mine. That got us into JT's condo. We found nothing, and I mean nothing. No files, no computing devices, no flash drives, no hidden compartments, no wall safe. The bed was stripped, the closet was empty. The security camera near JT's parking space was inconveniently on the fritz, so no time-stamped video to tell us if she stopped there over the holidays. Oh, and the realtor handling the condo sale says JT dropped off the keys sometime over the weekend, but she can't be sure which day."

"She wasn't planning to return," Sam said. "We couldn't find a laptop at her workplace or condo out here, either. Her assistant told us JT always took hers with her. Shana's trying to see what she can pull off the cloud. Did you check the store in Georgetown?"

"Already cleared out."

"I was afraid of that. What else did you learn?"

"You wanted information on the development out here, Sylvan Crest. So, we stopped by the offices of Full Court Press. We actually met the owner, Oliver Cummings. Really nice guy, very down to earth, not full of himself like you'd expect a star athlete to be." Gordy looked a little star-struck himself.

"And?"

"Right. He'd heard of JT, mainly through the society pages. He thought he'd been at a few of the same events. He didn't know the names of the Sylvan Crest project investors. I guess someone else takes care of the details. He offered to let us look at any records we needed to see. I told him we'd let him know. Nothing suggests that the project is going to be anything but successful. The properties are nearly all sold and the first house isn't even finished. The guy was friendly and cooperative. Unlike our Egyptian diplomat."

"How so?"

According to Gordy, Nur Asim was a ten-year veteran of the foreign diplomatic corps. He lived in an apartment that rented for upwards of $12,000, paid for by the Egyptian government. His family visited eight weeks a year and he went home for eight weeks.

"The guy lives eight months a year in D.C. as a bachelor," Gordy observed, "and I don't mean the monkish kind. My friend writes a society column. She says our diplomat enjoys the company of women he's not necessarily married to. Meanwhile, we were told Asim remained in town over the holidays for work. We tried to see him. No go. I thought Pollack was going to take a swing at the embassy spokesperson. I had the same kind of reaction to the concierge at his apartment complex.

Sam allowed herself a small chuckle. "That I would have liked to see."

"His royal whatever finally sent word down that he'd write a detailed report as to his whereabouts over the past few days and have it faxed to my superior. I guess that's you. He also admitted to knowing Jackie Templeton but not where she was after a dinner party Friday night."

"Friday. Well, that gives us something."

"She comes back Saturday and is killed that night?"

"Not exactly." Sam filled Gordy in on her discovery the day before and on the report from Tyler Caine.

"That makes things interesting. When's confirmation?"

"Noon. After which I'll need you and Pollack to go over to Amy's apartment in Annapolis."

"Will do." He rose to leave. "Is Jackie Templeton a suspect or a victim?"

"I'm still working on that."

Sam spent the morning looking at the rest of the information on Henry Templeton, JT's husband. He'd parlayed his inherited wealth into a series of lucrative investments that ranged from natural gas to real estate, including a block of prized homes along Philadelphia's Main Line. He also dabbled in antiquities, buying and selling pieces of great value. At one time, his net worth was estimated to be in the hundreds of millions.

Much of it was frozen just before his death, the result of several poor investments and at least two lawsuits concerning a questionable real estate venture. Templeton's clout probably forestalled criminal charges. The litigants weren't going to be happy until they exacted their pound of flesh. The lawyers were bound to make out like bandits, but no one else stood to profit.

Yet Jackie Templeton seems to have arrived in Washington relatively well-situated. Such things could be achieved in the age of digital transfers and electronic management. She might have been able to sell their two homes and keep the money shielded from an angry client or a phalanx of lawyers. Six years was a long time to walk a financial tightrope, though.

At noon, Sam received confirmation that the dead woman was indeed Amy Reed. Weller had been able to pry a few other tidbits out of the assistant to the pathologist, a specialist in autopsying burn victims.

"Fire deaths are complex," he told Sam when he called. "My contact said Reed could have died from anything from carbon monoxide poisoning to broken bones due to intense heat to shock. The explosion itself could have killed her. There is evidence she took in smoke, which means she was alive before the fire. The teeth smashing likely took place before the fire."

"Before she died."

There was a pause at the other end of the line. "Yup."

"My God."

"Not to state the obvious, but we seem to be dealing with someone who enjoys inflicting pain."

Now it was her turn to go mute. "You coming back?" she asked.

"I gotta report in. I'm going to try and get my commander to hold off on contacting the governor's office or setting up a press conference. If I can get him to agree to wait a day, we should meet this afternoon. Oh, and someone's gotta do the notification."

"I'll call Amy's parents."

Sam had made such calls in her time as a homicide detective and before that, as a squad leader in Afghanistan. They were never easy. The horrific nature of this particular death and the unanswered questions surrounding it added to the heartache.

Sam took it slowly with the shell-shocked parents, providing only the barest of details. "It'll take some time before you can bring her home," she told them. "Please know we will make every effort to move that along."

Terence Reed spoke, his voice choked. "Thank you, Lieutenant Tate. We have a number of calls to make. We'll be in tomorrow to—wait, is her apartment a crime scene?"

"We need a few days. Professor Reed. Check back with me Friday and I'll see that you get into her apartment."

"Thank you. And Lieutenant? Please catch the monster who did this."

* * *

After the call and a forgettable lunch, she went back to the digital file on Henry Templeton. There was a portrait from his younger years. He looked determined, efficient, in command. A real leader. Three articles from the *Philadelphia Inquirer* featured both Henry and his new wife. The first showed a younger Jackie (but how young?) on her wedding day, dressed in white lace and clutching a large bouquet. Her impossibly red hair was piled on top of her head. On her finger was a sapphire ring surrounded by smaller diamonds. She stood next to a man with snow-white hair and the beginning of a stoop. Henry Templeton was in his eighties when he wed Jackie, which made him nearly a half century older than his new bride.

The ring made an appearance in two other pictures of Jackie with her husband. In one, they were dressed for a formal occasion. In another, they were at a picnic for a charity event. JT always seemed to position her hand so as to show the ring to its best advantage. It worked. An accompanying article valued the finished ring at $15 million dollars.

Sam clicked on a different set of images Shana had scooped up off the internet. JT at various D.C. events. No ring in those pictures. Of course, widows and widowers often removed their wedding rings after the death of a spouse. This jewelry, though, could have accompanied a black dress or made an appearance at one of JT's many social outings. Otherwise, where did such a dazzling piece go? In a box? In a vault? In a display case?

Sam knew next to nothing about gemstones, except that their value often derived from their scarcity, their weight, and any unique features they might have such as color, cut, or distinctive markings. The stone in the ring was large, but what caught Sam's attention was the color. She was reminded of a bottomless lake or an evening sky just where it met the horizon. Or an eye.

She looked off into the middle distance, then down at her desk. She pulled out the folder she'd taken from JT's desk at the gallery and another with images of Arley's wall. She went back and forth between the two folders and her computer screen. She printed several pages off the computer, apologizing to those trees that had been sacrificed in service to her need for physical copies. She started a list and began her unconscious habit of rubbing the place between her eyes.

Suddenly her head jerked up as a snippet of a conversation rose in her mind.

She reached for the phone, praying to a deity whose existence she routinely questioned that her call would be answered. When it was, she made herself sound unconcerned, as if her question and subsequent request were routine and not key to finding a killer.

She ended the call, looked down at the list once more, and crossed everything off her list but two words. When the expected email arrived, she opened it, printed out the attached photo, laid it next to another, picked up the magnifier.

"Gotcha!" she yelled.

Her cell phone rang. Weller.

"Let's plan to meet today to strategize how we want to move forward," he said without preamble. "Your office is good. The usual suspects."

"We're going to do a lot more than strategize, Weller." Sam could barely keep her excitement in check.

"What's up, Tate? You sound energized. Don't tell me you're close to breaking the case?" He waited for her to respond. When she didn't, he whistled into the phone.

"Son of a gun. You've got something."

"I've got everything, Weller. Be here at 4pm. Bring your people and your gear."

He didn't ask her for further explanation. "You need reinforcements?"

"You got someone you trust as much as Pollack?

He thought a second. "Yes."

"That ought to do it."

Chapter 31

Wallace couldn't remember being so cold in his life. Not during the fraternity initiation that kept him outside in his underwear. Not during a ski trip during the chilliest winter on record. Not even when he and Arley Fitchett spent the summer aboard a dilapidated frigate in the North Sea. They spent the time pounded by stiff winds and frequent squalls that swept off the coast of Scotland.

At least he'd had adequate food and clothing and excellent company. None of which he could count on in this moment.

The calls and texts, including those from Sam Tate, shook him to his core. He initially assumed he was being sought in question with the so-called "theft" at JT Galleries. Not that he'd done anything wrong. He'd removed his own work because she'd violated the terms of their contract by tampering with it. Worse, her little scheme turned his artwork into a means to commit a criminal act and make him into an accomplice.

The fire at his house, which he knew had been deliberately set, panicked him. For the first time in his life, he felt truly afraid. The further discovery that Charles Fox had died—poor, deluded Fox, who'd come to believe in the Bird in Hand fable as thoroughly as did Arley Fitchett—sent him running.

He spent two nights in a cheap motel. He kept his head down and ate from the vending machines. The solution was temporary. He couldn't stay. Nor could he get far. His picture was all over the internet. Police and state troopers established blockades. He could shave his head, wear a disguise, slump, stoop, cut off his hand. It wouldn't matter. He might as well have worn a sign that read, "Wallace Bonnet: Fugitive."

Using three different burner phones, he rang up old friends, casual acquaintances, part-time and once-upon-a-time girlfriends, and former drinking buddies. He prevailed upon them to hide him or better yet, sneak him out of state, out of the country, out of sight. Even the ones who claimed to believe him wouldn't help him. The reports labeling him a person of interest, well, everyone knew what that meant. He was a suspect in two homicides.

He thought about calling Lieutenant Tate. She was technically his adversary. Yet she seemed smart, observant, unlikely to jump to conclusions. She might be attracted to him, he thought. He'd sensed something at the opening, a spark.

He dismissed the idea. Sam Tate was as dedicated to her job as he was to his craft. He admired that about her, expected no less.

He might have reached out to his father. True, they'd been estranged for a long time, due chiefly to the older man's profound disappointment with his son's life choices. Lately they had begun tentative steps to reconcile. His mother claimed it was because James had begun to see how talented his son was, that his work showed both aesthetic and remunerative potential.

Maybe. Wallace suspected his mother had a lot to do with her husband's change of heart. She exerted a great deal of influence over the man. She would have helped, would have gone to the ends of the earth for him. She had relatives in San Francisco and Vancouver. Maybe a private jet. But no. Law enforcement had thought of everything. They would have stopped the plane from taking off. Or he would have been forced down somewhere over Chicago. His mother would have been an accomplice.

He texted JT. He didn't expect she'd respond. He'd let himself into her gallery and taken his bird. She was angry about the switch. He felt justified, nonetheless. She'd defaced his original, although some would argue the sapphire was a significant upgrade from a crystal.

She had no right, though. That was the point. Besides, the one he left was almost as good.

Arley Fitchett would have figured out how to get him away. Wallace had no doubt about it. He liked the treasure hunter, he really did. Smart without being pretentious. Observant without being nosey. The kind of guy you'd have a drink with. Someone who'd have your back.

Arley would have come up with a deceptively simple plan. Hide under a tarp, ride to the Baltimore docks in the dead of night, pay dearly, but Wallace had something he could barter, didn't he? Out the next morning on a ship bound for who knows and who cares?

Yes, Arley Fitchett would have gotten him out of this mess. Then again, if Fitchett hadn't given in to his weaknesses, he'd be alive and there would be no mess.

Was it weakness to chase a dream, though? Arley thought he was close to something He'd shelled out a down payment on letters he believed provided a clue to the possible whereabouts of an old antique. He just needed funding in order to get them all in hand.

Wallace hadn't seen the correspondence, but Arley had shown him the sketch of the bird in the human hand. The drawing brought the winged creature and its perch to life with a few pen strokes. Wallace imagined the piece itself would be breathtaking. The age and originality alone would have added to its worth. The possibility that the woodworker had used a sapphire for an eye put its value into the stratosphere.

Arley hadn't revealed the supposed whereabouts of the treasure, not directly. When he joined in the protests against the planned Royal Oak development, though, Wallace put the pieces together.

"Come on, Arley," he teased his friend over shots and beers one evening. "What's your real interest in the site of an old plantation? Do you feel that strongly about historical preservation?"

"You didn't hear about the cave they found when they started digging?"

"Not a cave, Arley. More like a hole. A dirty old storage space under an old house long gone. What do you think you'd find there anyway? Hidden treasure?" Wallace snapped his fingers. "That's it! You think someone hid this carving you're looking for, this bird, down in a hole, where it lay undiscovered for three centuries."

"Not someone, Wallace. Blackbeard himself. Maybe with the help of your ancestor, maybe not."

"Pirates in the Chesapeake? Isn't that an old wives' tale?"

"There's plenty of documentation that proves pirates traveled across the bay," Arley had protested. "William Kidd entered the Chesapeake on his way down from New York. What these letters do is show that another notorious pirate, Blackbeard, was also in the area about the same time *Fortune's Fate* was on its final lap to Annapolis. Why is it so hard to believe the little ship looked like easy pickings?"

"Still sounds far-fetched."

Arley got cagey. "Maybe you're right," was all he'd said, but his light eyes were lit with a fire Wallace recognized from their time on the ship. The man thought he'd found his pot of gold at the end of the rainbow he'd been trailing a long time.

As much as Wallace wanted to believe in his friend's project, he couldn't bring himself to commit to it. Not that Arley would ask him for money. Fitchett had valued whatever connection they had too much to risk it over a financial arrangement. No, he wanted his artist friend's enthusiastic support.

Wallace did his best. He listened, he studied the maps, the letters, and the charts his friend showed him. No harm in encouraging Arley's dreams, was there?

At the same time, the sketch itself took hold of his imagination. What if he could make his own version of the storied carving? Not a recreation but a realization, loosely based on an old sketch bought at auction.

The more he thought about bringing Bird in Hand to life, the more he liked it. Arley didn't react well to the idea, however.

"What are you trying to do, Bonnet? Here I am close to the biggest find of my career and you want to what? Make a joke out of my efforts? Make money off the work I've put in? Pretty low either way."

The comments stung. Wallace had planned the carving as his own signature achievement. A chill settled between them. As Wallace's show approached, he simply became too busy, even when his former friend got in touch with him with news he deemed too exciting not to share.

Then someone killed Arley Fitchett.

The brutal murder shook Wallace. He dismissed the local gossip that tied the manner of death to drugs. Arley's indulgences were liquor, cigarettes, and treasure hunts. He was in many other ways circumspect about his life. Wallace didn't know where the man lived. Arley had also refused several invitations to dinner. His comfort zone was apparently on a bar stool or in some secret hideaway where he pored over clues to the treasure he hunted.

Nor did he talk about his past, except to mention he'd lost a baseball scholarship and dropped out of school. He seemed to take the event in stride, like he did everything else. Wallace had seen the burns on his back when they were at sea. He asked Arley about them. Fitchett only laughed and said, "You should see the other guy."

Arley's death had been staged to look like a cartel hit. Wallace knew it. Staged badly, as if the killer didn't know or didn't care that the police would eventually get to the truth.

Or staged in a way that would eventually lead to Wallace.

Had he also been set up to take the blame for the murder of Charles Fox? It seemed likely, though he wasn't sure at first. Fox had come to his house, barged right into the studio without calling or texting, to try and persuade Bonnet to finance a continued effort to find the hidden antique. "Do it for Arley," the appraiser insisted. As if he gave a damn about anyone or anything except his precious reputation.

Wallace had found it hard to put aside his antipathy for Fox, whom he knew to be a gossip and a greedy opportunist. He refused, politely at first and then with increasing heat when Fox pushed harder for a cash investment.

"I don't know what your arrangement was with Fitchett, but as far as I'm concerned, his search for a missing antique died with him. He never asked me for money, and I'm certainly under no obligation to cover his debts to you or help you continue his treasure hunt."

Fox had gone red in the face. "I did you a favor by coming here, Bonnet. I'm trying to help you. You've made a mistake, throwing your lot in with Jackie Templeton. Unless you think you've got her figured out. Maybe the two of you have teamed up in order to perpetrate some kind of deceit. That would make sense. You convinced Arley to show you the sketch so you could create your crude replica and pass it off as original."

"It's called an homage, Charles. Arley understood."

"Did he? Did your charm work on him as well as JT's has on you?" Fox was neatly shouting. "Or did he eventually see through you, poor man? Through the both of you. That would have been the death of him."

"What are you saying? Do you think I had something to do with Arley Fitchett's death?" Wallace found himself yelling back. "He was my friend. How the hell do I know you're not the one who had him killed?" He picked up a metal dowel and advanced on Fox, then threw it to the ground. "Screw this," he added. He grabbed one of his most recent carvings off the shelf and stormed out.

Without thinking, he drove straight to the gallery, let himself in, and switched out the sapphire-enhanced carving with the simpler version he'd brought with him. He wanted to send a message, make a point. She would understand, would contact him. Enough, he would tell her. Display my version as is or take my name off the exhibit.

The sirens had sent him racing back to his cottage to find firetrucks and police cars everywhere. Some instinct caused him to hang back. As the crowd gathered, he stayed at the back, head down, listening, picking up bits and pieces of news and gossip. When someone announced they'd found a dead body, he took off. Stupid, in retrospect.

Wallace had seen his next-door neighbors join the crowd of spectators watching his life's work turn to ash. He entered their home via the unlocked front door, grabbed some fruit from the kitchen, pulled a warm scarf out of the closet, and put twenty dollars on the side table before he left again.

He walked nearly nine miles to the far side of Easton and took a room at a nondescript motel on Route 50. Then came the futile round of phone calls and a fitful attempt to sleep. As a last resort, one desperate attempt at outreach.

What seemed like a good idea had turned into a very bad one.

In the days since, he'd gone from being an outlaw to a prisoner. The truth dawned on him gradually. Why did it take so long? Was it because he was afraid? Naive? Or blinded by need?

Even as he began to understand what had happened, what he was being asked to do, and what was at stake, he clung to the vague hope that he could talk his way out of his predicament. One way or another, he reckoned the truth would quite literally set him free. Or be the death of him.

Chapter 32

Sam was as jittery as a student about to make a major presentation. She gathered up her notes, set up her white board, paced the room. She probably should have filled Weller in beforehand so that they could jointly present to the rest of the team. She needed these people to get on board, which is why she had to make sure her working premise actually worked to everyone's satisfaction.

Donahue caught her in the conference room as she was setting up. "Mind if I sit in?" he asked.

"I was going to ask you to join us," she told her boss. "We're meeting at 4pm."

"Any major developments? Beyond the identity of the body in the car, I mean."

"Probably best to get everyone in the room and go over all of it."

He got the hint. "See you then."

At 4 o'clock, the full team gathered. Gordy, his sister, and McCready took their seats. Weller entered with Pollack and Caine as well as a square-shouldered man in a blazer who looked like ex-military. Wells introduced him as Detective Tim Lewinski. "He's got a particular skill set," he whispered to Sam as they filed in.

Donahue followed. When Sam indicated the head of the table, he shook his head. "Here to listen and learn," he said.

Sam looked at Weller. She was torn between following protocol and commandeering the meeting. Common sense won; she sat down, nodding to Weller.

"The situation is evolving rapidly," he began. "Guess you all heard the victim in the car was Amy Reed, Jackie Templeton's assistant." Nods all around. "Good. I'm going to ask Lieutenant Tate to take it from here. She's spent a lot of time analyzing the puzzle pieces. It seems she's reached some conclusions that will help us with this investigation. Lieutenant Tate?"

Showtime, Sam thought and popped up. "I'll move along as quickly as possible. You're going to have a lot of questions."

She started with background on JT, added what she'd learned from the detectives' D.C. visit and finished with the secret file from Jackie's office, occasionally pointing to images on the white board.

"Bottom line," she said, "JT was short of money. Her diplomat friend helped her secure the properties in St. Michaels. Her D.C. buildings were still on the market. The only tangible asset she had was a sapphire ring."

"About that ring," Gordy interjected. "Does anyone else think—"

"That it might make a nice-looking eye for a certain bird carving?" his sibling finished for him. "Yes."

"So, Jackie Templeton found a way to repurpose her ring," Weller interjected. "That would increase the price of Bonnet's version of Bird in Hand. But I'm not sure his carving adds to the value of the stone. So why bother? Unless …. Are you saying she decided to pass it off as a three-hundred-year-old antique with a rare sapphire eye? Who would fall for that?"

"It could happen," Gordy said slowly. "Start with a fake estimate for $22 million. Get a crooked broker, a crooked appraiser, and a crooked lawyer and pay them up front. A buyer's representative might be taken by the sapphire. Ship it off. By the time the bird arrives at its destination and the buyer decides to bring in an expert for another look-see, the seller is nowhere to be found."

"Right," Sam said. "Now imagine if you can pull off that hat-trick three times and never send the sapphire at all."

Sam expected the uproar that followed. It was loud enough that Betty Claiborne rapped on the door and stuck her head in.

"Sheriff, everything okay in here?"

"We're good, Betty," Donahue answered. "Settle down, people. Lieutenant, care to explain?"

"Wallace Bonnet made more than one version of Bird in Hand," Sam went on. "JT exhibited one on the gallery's opening night, complete with sapphire. Maybe some of the potential buyer representatives were there. Buyers from a carefully vetted list from her diplomat friend, Nur Asim, to include cash-rich, eccentric, or reclusive billionaires in different parts of the world. People who don't publicize their acquisitions. People who also might be too embarrassed to make their colossal miscalculation known. Yes, they'd call the authorities, but as Gordy said, JT would be long gone."

"The cost, the planning, the timing to pull this thing off would be massive," Pollack protested. "She would have had to be either nuts or desperate."

"Maybe both," Weller murmured.

"Are you saying Templeton and Bonnet were partners in an elaborate art fraud scheme?" Carol asked. "And Amy Reed, Charles Fox, and Arley Fitchett were collateral damage?"

Out of the corner of her eye, Sam saw Gordy's deliberate nod. He was catching up to her.

"Amy Reed, yes," he said. "Arley Fitchett never knew about the scam. I don't think Fox did, either. Their deaths are tied to something else." He turned to Sam. "Am I right?"

"Yes," Sam agreed. "Bonnet didn't know, either, not at first. Think about it. How would it help his reputation to create a forgery? He didn't need money, he needed acknowledgement of his talent. When I ran into him at the opening, I specifically asked him about the bird's eye. He was caught off guard, maybe even shocked. He didn't realize until he looked closely that someone had switched his crystal for a sapphire."

"So, Bonnet decides to steal back his bird, complete with a valuable gemstone, and leave JT a substitute," Weller mused. "I can see that."

Donahue threw his hands up. "I feel as if I'm playing a game of Clue and losing," he said. "Did Jackie Templeton kill her assistant?"

"Yes," Sam replied. "I think Amy knew something about JT's scheme. Maybe they had a confrontation."

"And did Templeton kill the others and burn down Bonnet's place?" Pollack asked.

"And where is he?" Carol asked.

"I think Bonnet turned to JT for help," Sam answered. "She's keeping him alive because she needs one more piece of art from him."

Silence. Then Weller spoke.

"Do you know where they are, Tate?"

"I think I do, yes."

"Hold on," McCready said. "If I'm hearing you correctly, Templeton killed at least three people, maybe more. I guess psychopaths are pretty good at hiding their nature, but I'm having trouble seeing her as a violent serial killer. These murders have been over-the-top vicious, Lieutenant. Not that I'm an experienced profiler or anything," he added.

"You bring up a valid point, Deputy," Sam said. "Jackie, aka JT, doesn't seem like the type who would resort to excess. There is someone who makes sense for these crimes, though."

"Great, another suspect," Lewinski muttered.

"Not quite." Sam laid out the final piece of her puzzle and brought everyone to their feet.

Chapter 33

Sam, Gordy, and McCready loaded the trunk with tactical gear and piled into one car, Gordy at the wheel, Sam riding shotgun. Weller, Pollack and Lewinski were just behind in their unmarked vehicle. Donahue stayed behind. "From a tactical point of view, you're covered, Tate," he said. "From a political point of view, I need to be here." Carol also agreed to stay behind, although she wasn't pleased about it.

"You're an investigator, Carol," Sam told her. "I know you can handle yourself. But I need you here because I want you to review everything I did, to make sure I didn't miss anything. Work with Shana; you couldn't ask for a better research assistant."

She tried the same tactic on McCready, to no avail. "I know a lot about where we're headed, Lieutenant," he said. "I think you're gonna need me"

"Make sure you follow orders," she replied, more sharply than she intended.

Lewinski pulled the patrol car abreast and rolled down the window. Sam did the same. Weller leaned across his driver and called out, "Are we going over to the Sylvan Crest building site?"

"No. Follow us into St. Michaels. No sirens or lights." She heard Weller yell, "What?" just as Gordy tore out of the parking lot.

Her phone rang. "What's in St. Michaels?" Weller asked.

"JT's waterfront condo. Built on the base of a heritage building that dates back to the mid-seventeenth century. According to plans, the lowest level was originally a cellar and was to be preserved. Not sure the arrangement called for it to be turned into either a prison or a crude workspace. JT, though, is nothing if not resourceful."

"You think she's there? With Bonnet?"

"I do," Sam answered.

"Okay. It's your show."

She directed Gordy to drive to a nearly deserted street two blocks from the harbor. The MSP car pulled in behind. Everyone got out. Without a word, each group began to remove the necessary equipment: body armor, tactical flashlights, com units, night sticks. Pollack pulled a beanie over her light hair. Everyone carried a Glock 22.

Lewinski lifted a Colt M14 Carbine out of the back seat. He noticed Sam watching him and shrugged. "Best to be prepared," he said.

"Twenty-first century gear to breech a seventeenth-century space," Gordy said. "This is a first."

"You think we should have included a couple of cannons, Gordy?" Pollack teased.

"#WhatWouldBlackbeardDo," McCready added. Weak laughter all around. How could it be anything but? They were going into an unknown setting, likely close quarters. Their target was a dangerous woman who didn't have a problem killing, seemed in fact to enjoy it. She probably had accomplices, not to mention a hostage.

Sam doubted McCready had ever fired a weapon except in a training situation. The others were experienced, had shot and even killed before. It didn't matter.

No one could really prepare for something like this.

* * *

"The new basement can be entered in two places." McCready indicated two points on the building plans he'd spread out on the hood of the car. "One is inside the building, reached by a utility elevator and available to whoever rents the retail space on the ground floor. There's a second entrance in the back. The sub-basement, the old part, can be accessed through the basement. The new owners, Eastern Shore, are required to turn it into some sort of a museum or visitor space as a condition of sale. Melinda, the realtor, says they'll probably make a separate entrance."

"Who lives on the upper floors?" Weller asked.

"Right now, Jackie Templeton is the only resident."

"Okay, let's see what we've got," Sam said.

They made their way towards the harbor and away from the few restaurants and bars open on a weekday in early December. As they passed a couple, the young man pulled out his phone, presumably to record the unexpected processional.

"Bad timing, buddy," Weller warned. The phone disappeared, along with the two bystanders.

The law officers approached the building from the side. They saw lights coming from the top-floor apartment Sam and Weller had gone through just yesterday. A wiry-looking man leaned against the building's front corner, smoking.

"There's a guy at the back, too," McCready said.

"How many more?" Weller asked.

Sam shrugged her answer.

"I can take care of the guy at the front, Lieutenant," Lewinski said.

"Just don't shoot him."

"Don't need to," he answered and disappeared.

Not ten seconds later, he'd disabled Smoking Man with a chokehold.

"You brought an impressive guy," Gordy said.

"I did," Weller agreed.

Lewinski joined them shortly thereafter. "Out cold and tied up for later. I also relieved him of his Barretta."

The man McCready had spied at the back seemed more attentive. He swept his large head back and forth in a series of slow arcs. "That's an AK-47," Gordy whispered.

"How do you want to play this?" Lewinski asked. He looked around. "Hey, aren't we missing someone?"

"There!" McCready said, just as a small figure darted out of the shadows, came up behind the man with the rifle, and delivered a decisive blow to the back of his head. He went down straight, like an old tree.

Sarah Pollack waved them over. By the time they crossed the street, she'd truss-tied the man and confiscated his rifle.

"Nice work, Pollack," Weller told her. She nodded.

"Okay, people," Sam said, her voice low. "We've neutralized two accomplices. I don't know who's in the sub-basement, only that, according to the plans, it's a fairly small space and we may not all fit down there. Lewinski, stay in the back to keep an eye out for any unwanted visitors who may appear. McCready, you show us where the lower level entrance is, then stay behind us."

Three concrete steps led them to a nondescript concrete basement. At the far end, an old wooden door that had seen better days stood open. From below, a faint glow and the sound of voices.

"Single file," Sam whispered. She went first, gun out, down uneven steps made of wooden planks stuck randomly into the ground. When she got to the bottom, she dropped off the last step onto a dirt floor covered with sawdust. The rest of the group crowded behind her; McCready and Lewinski stayed on the stairs.

The space they'd entered was maybe twelve by sixteen with eight-foot ceilings. Minimal furniture dominated by a large table with tools, wood remnants, and a familiar carving. What little ventilation there was came via two small holes to the upper basement. Some artificial light, thanks to two lamps and an overhead bulb.

She glimpsed Wallace Bonnet, disheveled and drawn. A heavily tattooed man with long hair held back with a rubber band pushed himself off the wall and pointed his rifle—another AK-47—at her group. But her attention was on the woman who greeted her.

"Hey there, Lieutenant. You got your posse with you? Not sure we got room for all of you, but we'll manage."

Sam recognized the voice, despite the folksy affect. The rest was unexpected but not entirely so. Faded jeans, a plain gray sweatshirt, and low-heeled boots. The long red locks had been replaced by a short, uneven cut colored a nondescript dirty blonde. The gray eyes in the plain, yet pretty face reminded Sam of a thundercloud. The nasty-looking scar over the right eye matched both the one she'd seen on JT's face and in a high school yearbook photo from thirty-two years earlier.

"Hey, Josie," Sam said. She kept her gun trained on the woman in front of her. "Nice to finally meet you."

"I doubt that very much." Josie Fitchett looked around. "Is this everyone? No, you must have left one or two upstairs after I assume you took out my men. Damn, I'm fresh out of help." She glanced over at the man with the rifle. "Trig, how good are you with that thing?"

"I'm good enough to get all three, maybe even that one hiding in the back."

"Hear that, Lieutenant Tate? You brought all that firepower for nothing. On the other hand—" Fitchett lifted up an electric torch— "I've got all the firepower I need."

"What are we doing here, Josie?" Weller asked. "You can't get out, can't make your delivery. Truth is, you've gone from victim to most wanted in one day. We can still end this without anyone else getting hurt."

"Oh, hush, Detective Sergeant Weller. You are such a bore. Not like your much smarter partner here." She tapped the wound over her right eye. "Very clever."

"She killed them all," Bonnet blurted out. "Amy Reed, Charles Fox, even Arley, her own brother."

"She knows, Wallace," Josie scolded.

"I'm a little fuzzy on motive, though." Sam tried for a low-key, conversational tone. The last thing any of them needed was hysteria.

Josie sighed. "I don't respond well to threats, Lieutenant. Amy went snooping in my office. I guess she didn't know about my little security camera. She asked if we could meet Thanksgiving weekend about a problem with the insurance." Josie laughed. "A lot of planning went into that so-called accident. A lot of physical work, frankly. It was pretty special, you must admit." She could have been describing a society event or a fireworks display.

"As for Charles Fox," she continued, "we crossed paths years ago at an antique store in Chappaqua that burned down. No one should have died, least of all his friend. Who knew he even had friends? Or that we'd run into each other down here?" She shook her head. "His approach was more in the way of blackmail. Help him cash in on whatever he believed Arley Fitchett had discovered or he'd expose me. What a fool. Catching him at Wallace's house was serendipity."

"Was the fire necessary?" Gordy asked, his voice low. "Or the bat?"

"Fire is always necessary, Detective," Josie answered with a smile. "I'm sorry about Wallace's belongings, but he really needed to be brought to heel. As for the bat, it was a gift from my father. I played baseball before my brother could walk. Power hitter. My team won the regional championship." She spoke with pride.

"Why kill Arley?" Weller asked.

She made a dismissive sound. "His plans interfered with mine."

"That's it?" Weller sounded dubious.

The gray eyes grew stormier. "What do you want, Detective Sergeant? A more dramatic explanation? Fine. Young girl, happy enough with her widowed father, is forced to make room for a new mother and the baby who becomes a spoiled little boy and then a monster who leaves her with a permanent mark on her face."

"You were burning him, you bitch!" Wallace yelled. "He fought back."

Josie ignored him. "I played ball, Arley played better. I was my father's little girl, but he was the apple of Daddy's eye. Arley knew I wanted to move to the Eastern Shore. I talked enough about it. My maternal grandfather was born near St. Michaels, did you know that? My step-brother could have ended up literally anywhere else. But no, he had to land here and draw attention to himself with his little treasure hunt. All things considered, he's lucky I only burned his hands."

Her anger evaporated as quickly as it appeared. "How about we save the psychoanalysis for another day? Here's what can happen in the here and now. I can set the handsome artist on fire and Trig can work his magic with his weapon. Or you can all step aside, and we'll be on our way." She put the torch inches from Bonnet's face.

Bonnet responded with a well-aimed elbow that hit his assailant in the solar plexus. Josie stumbled backwards. He swung his other arm around to try and reach the torch. A flame caught his sleeve and he screamed in pain and fell into Trig, who discharged his weapon.

Four shots went wild; one ricocheted off the lamp and hit Pollack in the shoulder. She fell, cursing. Gordy bent over to help and Trig went down with a bullet between the eyes, courtesy of Pat McCready. Sam barely had time to register her surprise; Josie Fitchett had regained her footing and held the torch aloft and behind her.

"I'll set the whole damned place on fire," she declared. She sounded calm, almost cheerful. "We'll all burn." She caught Sam watching the torch and pulled her arm farther back. "You can't make that shot, Lieutenant. Don't even think about it."

"Not that one," Sam replied. She aimed for the chest, center mass. "This one."

She pulled the trigger.

Chapter 34

Robby Laghari was eleven. Puberty had already begun its work, splintering his voice in unexpected ways so that it swooped and broke. The kids gave him endless grief, just as they teased him about the trace of a shadow above his lip. Their light taunts were edged in envy; Robby was tall and very good-looking. As Robby's father rightly noted, "You will be stealing their girls before they know how to use a razor."

Robby's two best friends, Damian Gatz and Charlie Tanner, didn't see his burgeoning maturity as an issue. Besides being a year older, he was stronger, taller, and more experienced in their eyes. More audacious. They counted themselves lucky to be in on his adventures, especially this one.

It was the night after Christmas. Technically not a school night, as they were on vacation. Still, they were out past their curfew, far from their neighborhood, and without the knowledge or consent of their parents. The subterranean space they planned to search was off-limits even by daylight. The high-profile shootout that occurred below ground was just three weeks behind them. Two dead, one wounded. They might even run into a deputy or trooper standing guard.

This was as daring and dangerous an expedition as they could have imagined. Not only could they get into trouble, they could get arrested or succumb to a variety of unforeseen hazards.

The showdown with the local killer was the talk of the school, eclipsing even the usual holiday-related excitement. The girls couldn't stop yakking about the female lieutenant who took down the killer, also a woman. Some of the boys thought it was hot.

Robby thought it was a stupid kind of crime. All that blood spilled, and for what? For some stupid carving that turned out to be a fake. Okay, the eye in the bird was a real sapphire, but that's only because the killer was also a scam artist. Plus, she was probably nuts.

The other two boys agreed with him. They generally believed that most adults were either gullible or greedy, sometimes both.

If neither Robby nor his friends cared about the Bird in Hand story, they were convinced other treasure might be found on the Eastern Shore. They'd grown up in Easton, buddies since birth, solidly middle class in an area that was becoming increasingly gentrified. Like so many locals, they believed pirate activity had occurred far more frequently than the history books reported. The area provided both manmade and natural places in which to stash ill-gotten booty. Ships might have tucked themselves into the many coves and tributaries.

Intrepid explorers, the boys spent summers in high boots, swatting gnats, slogging through tall marsh grasses, and wading into bogs and wetlands. Occasionally they'd hear about a cache of silver or even gold Spanish coins someone had discovered.

Damian's father, an accountant and an avid student of local history, tried to explain to his son that Spanish coins weren't proof of treasure but of commerce. "They were as common as pennies before the Revolutionary War," he said. "They're old, for sure. Could be they're worth something but not as much as what you boys are imagining."

Undeterred, they kept hunting. They heard rumors about a cave at the Sylvan Crest project in August and made plans to sneak in during the project's enforced hiatus. The expedition was a bust. Nothing there, not a single coin or a piece of pottery.

In November came the thrilling news about an actual cellar under an old building in the town of St. Michaels. There'd been talk of turning it into some sort of mini-museum, but plans were suspended when it became a crime scene.

"I'm not saying we'll find anything," Robby warned. "On the other hand, the police weren't looking for what we are. Besides, how cool would it be to see where they killed her?"

His friends needed little convincing. Bragging rights counted for a lot.

First was the matter of arranging a ride. This Charlie pulled off by promising his sixteen-year-old sister Tonya that he would trade a lift into town for his silence concerning a certain boy she frequently snuck out to see.

Transportation settled, the boys geared up with warm clothes, sturdy boots, flashlights, small shovels, even a bolt cutter Robby found in his dad's shed. Damian brought along a hard hat. It was too large and kept slipping in front of his eyes, even though it was jammed over a pair of fluffy earmuffs.

Tonya dropped them a block from the building at 11:30. She wouldn't let them out until she'd delivered a brief lecture.

"You know this is the stupidest of the stupid ideas you three have ever come up with, right? It's Christmas time. The town is quiet, but it's not completely deserted. I mean, you could get reported, arrested, even shot. There's about a million other things that could go wrong. Guess what? Mom would totally blame me." She turned around and pointed to the younger boys. "Your moms, too. I would be so grounded for the rest of my life."

"You could think about how much you missed me," Charlie teased.

"Seriously, you idiots have an hour and a half. I'll text you when I'm on the way back. You'd better be here. You got that?"

"Does that give you enough time to, you know, do what you need to do?" Damian asked with an air of faux innocence. The boys snickered.

"Get out of the car, now," Tonya fumed. "And remember, ninety minutes total. Or you can go to jail or get trapped down there and starve to death for all I care." She took off, the tires of her Sierra sliding on the icy gravel.

They boys headed to the harbor, keeping an eye out for late- night strollers or cop cars. They saw neither, just a police-issued warning sign about trespassing.

"Okay, guys, gear out," Robby ordered. He was especially proud of his PETZL Pichu helmet with the attached headlamp his parents had bought for Christmas. The smooth round dome was neon orange and made specifically for caving and climbing. Neither activity was especially common on the Eastern Shore, but Robby aspired to greater undertakings.

The other two boys wore L.L. Bean Trailblazer Headlamps, simple lights on elastic they'd attached to their bike helmets. All three had on heavy parkas, stiff gloves, and thick boots. Damian had been gifted a genuine metal detector from The Gold Digger website that came with controls for fine-tuning and a pair of headphones. Charlie brought a canteen, a handful of power bars, and a flashlight he took from his father's car.

The first problem was getting through the padlock on the door at the back of the building, which Charlie solved with the bolt cutters. They eased their way down the basement stairs and saw a second door directly opposite. This one wasn't locked. The steps going down were rougher. Robby almost fell.

"Shit!" he yelled.

"Shh," Damian warned.

"These effing steps are slippery."

"Is this a crime?" Charlie asked. "I mean, our being here?"

"Too late." Robby focused his headlamp and flipped on his flashlight.

Their combined illumination revealed a raw, unfinished space. The walls were packed dirt, the floor sawdust sprinkled over hard ground. The few pieces of furniture weren't even a little bit old, just cheap-looking. Table, a chair, a couple of lamps, and a bed frame were piled in one corner. Yellow tape lay on the ground along with folded signs with different initials on each.

"These mark the places where everyone was standing when it all went down," Robby pointed out with assurance.

The place managed to be both freezing and stifling. The close air smelled of frost and something feral. Robby couldn't imagine staying down here for an hour, much less a week or more.

"It looks like they cleaned it up," he said with a note of disappointment.

"Doesn't smell like it," Charlie said, wrinkling his nose.

Damian spotted a single lightbulb over the table and pulled at the dangling string. Nothing. "Guess they shut off the electricity, too."

The three of them circled the room. The headlamps and flashlights created bright spots and long, deep shadows. At first, they followed one another. Then, as if by prior agreement, they each took a section to search. They spent nearly an hour kicking up dirt, poking in the corners, looking under what little furniture remained. Damian's metal detector kept silent even through his headphones. The crime scene investigators hadn't left so much as a shell casing.

"This was not what I expected," Robby finally admitted. "I should have brought a coin to drop on the ground. Then we could pretend we found something."

"Don't tell my sister we came up empty," Charlie said. "She'll never let me hear the end of it." He glanced at his watch. "We should get back up. Hey, Damian, take off your damned headphones."

Damian was standing near the dirt wall at the back of the space. He put his face up to it and pushed at a bump on the rough surface that stuck out just a little.

"Guys," he called out. "Help me lift the detector against the wall."

Charlie and Robby were instantly by his side. Together they hoisted the machine so the cylindrical bottom rested against the wall like a portable vacuum cleaner. Damian fiddled with a couple of settings.

"Yes!" he cried. "There's something inside this wall. Set down the detector. I think this rock comes out. We just have to wiggle it back and forth. Be really careful, though. It could break off."

"It could bring down the whole damned wall," Charlie exclaimed, but he leaned in to help.

The boys took turns moving the rock back and forth, a painfully slow process that seemed to take forever. After ten minutes, they eased it out to reveal a hole the size and shape of an arm. Damian reached in; his fingers grazed a piece of material.

"I can't quite get it."

"Let me." Robby reached his longer limb in and got his fingers around a lumpy object he then withdrew. It was a leather sack about the size of a baseball, worn by time but still intact. "Heavy," he noted.

"Open it, Robby," Damian said.

Robby dumped the contents onto the table. A mix of silver and gold coins tumbled out, along with what looked like a very old ring with a green stone.

"Oh my God," Charlie breathed. "Are those—?"

"Spanish coins," Robby answered. "From way before the Revolutionary War. See this weird shape? That's how you know they're old." Robby picked up one and then another and held them close to his face. "Good condition. I can make out a couple of dates. This one says 1714, and here's another one that says 1717."

"Are they worth a lot?" Damian asked.

"The silver ones can go for up to a grand. But these other ones are real gold doubloons. At least I think they are. Those are worth some serious money. Same with the ring."

No one spoke for a couple of seconds. Then they all began whooping and yelling and backslapping until Robby shushed them. "We don't want to attract attention," he reminded them.

They immediately quieted.

"What do we do now, Robby?" Charlie asked.

"We need to think this through. This is a big find. Big. We can't say we found it here. This is a crime scene. They'll tag it as evidence. We'd have to share it with whoever owns the building or with the state."

"So, we pretend we found it somewhere else," Damian suggested. "How about we say we were hunting near Trippe Creek?"

"Yeah, that could work." Robby agreed. "We need an appraiser. And a lawyer. If this is worth as much as I think it is, a lot of people will claim it for themselves."

"That sucks," Charlie muttered.

"My uncle is an attorney," Robby continued. "We'll wait a few days, then talk to him first. We're going to need at least one or two adults to help us."

"Guys, we gotta get going," Charlie warned.

"Should I keep the coins for now?" Robby asked.

"What do you think, Damian?" Charlie asked. "Do we trust him?"

"Sure. We also know where he lives."

"Just don't say anything to my sister," Charlie advised.

"Meet at my house tomorrow at eleven," Robby announced. "Deal?"

The three boys shook hands. Damian carefully reinserted the rock; Robby put the precious bag in his waist belt. Then the best friends headed up through the basement and back out into the car, aware that their lives were about to get much larger.

Behind the rock, just beyond the reach of an eleven-year-old's arm, the narrow opening expanded to accommodate a copper container shaped like a cage. The tattered parchment wrapped in oilskin and tucked inside had long ago succumbed to the elements. The main occupant still rested comfortably on its novel perch, its sapphire orb twinkling in the dark.

Teresa,

I scribble in haste, for the unthinkable has happened. We have been caught unawares by Blackbeard and his men. Why he has chosen to attack us, we can but guess. Whatever his motives, he means to end us.

The ship is irreparably damaged. The ammunition they fire at us carries toxic fumes that burn the eyes and sear the lungs. Several brave Sailors have been felled already. Others have abandoned ship. I will stay to fight beside Captain Diggs. Duty compels me. I hope you will forgive my choice.

My precious bird must now find its own way, locked along with this note in its impenetrable cage until some future clever soul might return each to its rightful recipient.

You are my love,
W

Epilogue

Sam stepped across the quaint St. Michaels cobblestones with slightly more assurance. The low-heeled boots helped, and they worked well with the burgundy mid-calf dress she wore under a warm down coat. Perfect for a blustery February evening. Let the twenty-somethings show up in sleeveless sheaths in mid-winter. She was comfortable.

Well, almost. In truth, she felt odd attending a gallery opening in the same space that had been owned by the late Jackie Templeton, aka Josie Fitchett. The place had been snapped up early in the new year by a pair of entrepreneurial types out of D.C. with experience in the New York art world. They'd renovated only slightly and in record time; they'd also hired a Manhattan PR firm. The new place was renamed Eastern Shore Galleries.

The expanded atrium now included a gift shop and a small, well-lit café that looked out over the harbor. Work by local talent could be found, but the emphasis was more on regional artists than on those native to the immediate area. The owners had added a small media room on the second floor. An ambitious calendar of events promised provocative film and video works by up-and-coming artists.

The new owners were in attendance, dressed in black leather and looking impossibly chic. She was perhaps thirty, tall and model-thin with long blond hair. He was a decade older, bald, barrel-chested, a bit shorter. His round glasses gave him an owlish look. Ella Taft and Gus Doukas were apparently a couple as well as business partners.

"Quite a turnout," Terry observed, handing her a glass of chardonnay he snagged from a passing server. "Some of the usual suspects. And at least one newly arrived artiste." He nodded in the direction of Jake and Lucy Donahue. Lucy had several of her ethereal waterfowl photographs hanging on a nearby wall. She and her husband, flushed with pride, greeted well-wishers.

Sam spotted Martin Lloyd and Carol Davidson. Gordy was present as well. Sam's eyebrows shot up in surprise at his companion. Sarah Pollack, just out of physical therapy for a bullet that went into her shoulder, thankfully failing to cause any permanent damage. She looked chic in high-heeled ankle boots, a short skirt and a soft peach-hued sweater.

Will wonders never cease? Sam thought.

"Frank Weller isn't here?" Terry asked.

"Sadly, no. But the man of the hour, Pat McCready, has arrived with quite the entourage." McCready stood with friends and family, a rather large cross-generational group.

"Did you know he was such a good shot?"

"I did not. He's got the makings of a good detective. He's working toward that, under Gordy's excellent mentorship."

"And yours. Lucky for you two, Talbot County Sheriff's Department doesn't have IAB."

Both Sam and the deputy had been on leave for one week following the deaths of Jackie Templeton and her associate. A civilian oversight board, Talbot County's answer to an internal affairs bureau, determined the shootings were justified and went so far as to endorse commendations for the two officers.

Sam had spent the week in Washington, staying at Terry's, taking time for herself, and seeing Dr. Putnam. She had a number of concerns about her returning recollections from twenty-six years ago. About the death of Jackie Templeton, aka Josie Fitchett, she had none. Still, it never had been and never would be easy to take another life.

Pat McCready had entered into the supportive embrace of his extended family. He was also talking with a local psychologist, a move required by Sam as his new boss. She'd kept a sharp eye on him after he returned. He seemed to be settling into his new role, although he wasn't yet working any homicides.

"Smile," Terry said. "Your first case is officially closed. You're a hero. Well, along with McCready."

"I suppose," Sam answered. She paused. "I heard from my contact at the British Museum today."

"And?"

"They've authenticated the first two letters. Not only were they written hundreds of years ago, the author was a real person. Charles Calvert had an older cousin who he sent to Maryland in order to engage in some political smoothing of feathers. No word on what happened to the ship he was sailing on, but my contact found a printed notice that a ship called *Fortune's Favour* had never returned to England."

"What about the other letters?"

"No idea if they're real or faked. Rita, my contact, found out a Thaddeus Bell did serve as a doctor in Bermuda in the 1700s. She's looking for correspondence from him."

"Bell made it across the Atlantic," Terry said. "As did cousin William."

"That may turn out to be true, but it still doesn't prove they were joined by a wooden bird with a sapphire eye. That part of the tale is speculative at best."

"So, no Bird in Hand?"

"I guess we'll never really know."

He peered at her. "Are you disappointed?"

"Me? Why would I be disappointed? Like you said, we caught the killer."

Terry cocked his head. "Absolutely, and that should have been exciting enough. I can't help wondering, though, if you wanted to keep looking for the lost treasure with the help of a certain dashing artist."

Sam laughed. "I doubt Wallace Bonnet ever believed Bird in Hand existed. I mean, as a physical piece. He wanted to make a statement about the power of imagination."

"Well put," Terry said. "I suppose St. Michaels will have to do with one less artist now that he's decamped to Paris."

Sam wound her arm through his and smiled up at him. "We'll manage. And I'm sure he will as well."

"Away from his family, yes. Speaking of which, there's James Bonnet again. He's brought his favorite senatorial candidate, Sean Parker. Guess this is as good a place as any to hunt for donors."

Parker stood next to Bonnet and his wife, a glass of seltzer in his hand. He appeared to be without a partner. As before, he was impeccably dressed, almost dapper, a film version of a distinguished candidate. His tinted glasses disconcerted Sam; she wondered if he had problems with his eyes or the eyewear was an affectation. Again, she was seized by a sensation of familiarity.

"Whoops, we're being waved over," Terry said. "Or rather, you are."

Sam felt her stomach clench without knowing why. "You're my escort, Sloan. Escort me over there."

"Lieutenant Tate, how nice to see you." James Bonnet's voice carried enough that heads turned. "Life must be back to normal after solving a triple homicide and art scam just months into the job." In a lower voice, he added, "You saved my son's reputation. No doubt his life as well. Know that I will be forever grateful."

She found herself wondering which was more important to the senior Bonnet, the reputation or the life of his son. She shook off the thought and returned his firm handshake.

"Thanks for the praise, Mr. Bonnet," she said. "I was just doing my job."

"Well, you've certainly done the community proud. If you decide the glass ceiling is a little too low here in Talbot County, let me know. I've got favors I can call in. Although I imagine your friend here has some clout to spare at the Bureau."

"Not as much as you might think," Terry answered affably. Everyone in the little group laughed.

"Where are my manners?" Bonnet exclaimed. "Special Agent Sloan, Lieutenant Tate, this is my wife, Wendy Liu." As usual, Liu radiated understated money and taste in a simple black dress with an asymmetrical neckline. Her jewelry was limited to one impressive gold choker.

"Good evening, Lieutenant, Special Agent," she said, taking first Sam's hand, then Terry's. Her touch was cool, her voice soothing, like water flowing across rocks.

The serene moment was lost when Bonnet boomed, "And this is Sean Parker, soon to be a senator from your state. A carpetbagger, to be sure, as he originally hails from New York City. Queens, to be precise.

Parker flashed his white teeth. Sam felt Terry tense, almost imperceptibly, as he extended his hand. "Mr. Parker," he said. "Pleased to meet you. Welcome to the D.C. metro area. You're from Queens? What brought you down here?"

Parker deftly skirted the question. "I've heard good things about you, Special Agent Sloan. You're smart, intuitive, thorough, and diligent, according to sources."

"All true," Terry said. Sam watched his face, trying to pick up on any clues that might explain his reaction. She felt light-headed, as if she lacked adequate oxygen. Maybe she'd gulped her wine too quickly? She held Terry's arm with both hands, trying not to sway.

The older man turned to her. "Lieutenant Samantha Tate, the woman from Tennessee, the catcher of serial killers." He had a commanding voice, one made for inspiring speeches or issuing threats. It rumbled like a finely tuned car engine with horsepower to spare. Or a large and lethal cat. A tiger, a leopard. A panther. "I can't tell you how delightful it is to meet you at last." He reached for her hand, gave it a squeeze, and dropped it.

Sam blinked.

"I feel as if we've known each other a long time," Parker continued. He turned so that he faced slightly away from Bonnet and towards Sam. Then he lifted his glasses.

She heard Terry's sharp gasp as if from a distance. Sam's own breathing seemed to have stopped, along with everything else in the room. Chatter receded, or maybe it was drowned out by the roaring in her ears. She stared into Parker's eyes, large, wideset, an unusual shade of green caught between moss and jade. Eyes that invited comment. Eyes she knew only too well, although she'd only ever seen them when she looked in the mirror.

"A long time," Parker repeated with a sly wink.

- END –

From the Author

Thanks for reading *Bird in Hand*. I hope you'll take a minute to leave a review. That way, I can connect to even more readers who are looking for books like mine.

Since we last got together, the first Sam Tate mystery, *The Wedding Crasher*, has gone on to receive great reviews. The novel was named The Kindle Book Review's Best Mystery/Thriller of 2019. Kirkus Reviews called it "a suspenseful and intriguing story." I can't wait to get started on the next book.

About me: I'm the author of five books, all of which have earned critical praise. I've written essays published in the *New York Times*, *USA Today*, *Newsweek*, and *Humanist Magazine*, as well as three anthologies. I contributed to the interactive murder mystery musicals that make up the *Café Noir* series, published by Samuel French.

I'm a big fan of book clubs and offer print book discounts and free online visits. You can read more at nikkistern.com. While you're there, why not subscribe? You can get a heads-up on events, activities, and new work. You can also follow me on Facebook (Nikki Stern, Author), on Twitter, and on Instagram (@realnikkistern), where I post art pictures, nature photographs, and portraits of my dog.

Also By Nikki Stern:

Because I Say So

Hope in Small Doses

The Former Assassin

The Wedding Crasher

Made in the USA
Middletown, DE
14 September 2020